Legends of Trent II

Aunt Kathy,
You and ALAN ARE A Big Part
of this story, AND It wouldn't
have been any good without yous.
So MANY memories. I will Never
forget what we've been through.
Love you Always.
                    Chip.

Legends of Trent'n

C.S.W.

Copyright © 2011 by C.S.W.

Library of Congress Control Number:		2011905475
ISBN:	Hardcover	978-1-4628-5201-7
	Softcover	978-1-4628-5200-0
	Ebook	978-1-4628-5202-4

To order additional copies of this book, contact:
Xlibris Corporation
1-888-795-4274
www.Xlibris.com
Orders@Xlibris.com
96671

For Ariel and Ethan.

An explanation.

Special thanks to:

Charles and Nancy Wyckoff

Lauren Noel Stanley

Kelly Correia

Dr. James Borthwick M. D.

"Eyes away from me. Its dark at night and I can't see. Drugs took my eyes from me. I don't care if I can see drugs or not, they took my eyes away. I wish that I could see clear today, but that's just the price I pay. Drugs took my eyes away."

—Kelly Cambell

Contents

THE DOUBLE DOORS opened and the sun blasted his eyes with the brightness of the day. His blond hair turned white in the light and he looked almost angelic as he stepped out of the rehab and into the fresh air and his freedom after nearly 28 days. He put the place behind him as he walked through the parking lot to the car that would take him back home. He was finished with his treatment and he was unchanged.

Scott shivered with anticipation even in the hot sun; he knew what was soon to come. He was only fourteen years old but already he was haunted, haunted by the ghosts of his inevitable future. He was cursed with the blood of a father he had never met and scarred in his mind by the things he had seen growing up so close to the city. No amount of education or intervention could have stopped Scott from the direction his life was destined to lead. His mind was closed to reason and he had already decided that he was prepared to die to satisfy his lusts, and greed, and gluttonies. Had he inherited this addict mentality? Could it even be that his beautiful brilliant mind was defective from the beginning and he was just too blind to see it? In any case, he was hungry for the streets.

As he rode home from the facility he stared blankly at the passing scenery, the mountains and the trees. He thought this must be what it feels like for a convict when he finally gets released. And what he was going to do now that he was free.

Scott had been sent to his first rehab for smoking marijuana and for sniffing too much speed, but while inside he listened to all the other addicts tell their different stories. Regardless of whether addiction was a weakness or a disease, cocaine now had him hopelessly intrigued. Why did he have such an overpowering desire to try a drug that had caused so much pain and wreckage to everyone who talked about it? Was it possible to be hooked on something that he had never even picked up? Could a person possibly be that screwed up?

The winding road turned to highway and soon Scott found himself seeing surroundings that were familiar, the landmarks told him he was close to home. There was the Capitol building by the museum, before the dome was painted gold. Then they passed the Trenton Makes Bridge, this was before the powers that be built that stupid tunnel, back when the Thunder still had no Waterfront park to call their home. Scott could see the prison perched on Cass and Second Streets and he said a silent prayer that he'd never have to do a day inside. He didn't know the names of the most notorious inmates, but even at age fourteen, he feared the evil that he sensed emanating from the ominous brick walls. He was too young to remember nine years ago when Keith Alford 24, was sent there for killing Anne Mae Chicaleski 67, just twelve days before he killed Emma Jane Stockton 37. And it would still be many years before Ambrose Harris would be sent there to death row for the rape and murder of 24 year old artist Kristen Huggins. Or the retarded Jesse Timmindequaz would be sent there for killing 6 year old Megan Kanka sparking national outrage and the eventual birth of "Megan's Law."

It would also be many years until his first cocaine dealer and family friend would proclaim "They'll never take me there alive." And true to his word, when the sheriffs came for him, he killed himself with a chrome plated .45

As Scott was driven passed the prison, there was still no cheesy baseball mural painted on its foreboding Cass street wall, and there was no Sovereign Bank Arena, nor had the Governor yet proudly proclaimed "I am a gay American," to the shame of his family and state. Of course Scott couldn't have predicted any of this shit, because it was still 1986 and he was still a kid.

His mother drove him home to their house in Ewing Township, a suburb on the outskirts of Trenton. They pulled into the driveway of their four bedroom home, Mom hopeful that this stay at Rehab would save her beloved son from his disease and his demons. Her son; Scott filled with poisonous thoughts of relapse. Believing that maybe he was possessed by something evil.

They entered the front door, Scott holding his luggage, and the air conditioning chilled them instantly. It was kept like a refrigerator at Moms. It was a safe, comfortable, place where Scott could always go to regenerate, heal, sleep it off, and try to start over.

His mother Nancy and his adoptive father Wes were the best parents that a kid could have. They loved their children and denied themselves the things that they wanted to give to their sons. Scott's mother came from good blood. What the rich folks would call good stock, though wealthy they were not, Scott had everything he needed and most of the things that he wanted growing up.

His half brothers were a couple of years younger and they also lived with him in the house. They came from different genes and Chuck and Brian seemed content and serene. They say the apple doesn't fall far from the tree and in his brothers case that was a very good thing. Wes was the most decent man that Scott had ever met. Hardworking, loving and faithful, Scott sometimes wished he were Wes's biological son. But Scott was not the same, a fact that became more obvious every day. He had different blood pumping through his veins and unfortunately, the apple doesn't fall far from the tree.

Rumors of his biological father were dark and disturbing. Supposedly, he was blond, blue eyed and good looking. Supposedly, he was Aryan, he was very angry, and he was a drug addict. Scott had inherited his looks from his father and he could be very glad about that. He should have no problem getting girls. But something else was passed on to him in this noble blood of dad, something maybe defective, something very bad.

Scott sometimes wondered if his mother had to do it all over again, would she still have had him? He knew the answer to this question was yes though most days he wished that she hadn't. Scott could not explain his sadness.

Scott may have even turned suicidal if not for his knowing that he was alive to serve some purpose that was both pleasing to and ordained by God. And while his faith and obedience and sobriety would slip from day to day, his connection with the Almighty would never completely fade away.

Chapter 1

East Paul Avenue

THE BROKEN BEER bottle glass sparkled like hidden diamonds in the weeds as the summer sun shone and heated up the Trenton streets. Newspapers and litter blew in the breeze like an urban version of western tumbleweeds. In 1998 East Paul Avenue was tagged up and down with graffiti and the cocaine trade was thriving in the city. Outside Zookies bar, you could smell the stale garbage cooking in the sun. Crack viles, empty cigarette packs, and beer cans littered the parking lot. Young drug dealers on stolen bicycles flashed hard stares at unwanted white boys who ventured into their hood. Police cars would come slowly cruising by, fed up cops eyeballing everyone, some young brother would yell "5-0" and everyone would run. Summers in Trenton are fun.

People like to believe that back in the days before the gangs came and claimed their streets, that we all lived side by side together in peace. But that is just a fantasy with no base in reality, The place never existed, its make believe, like some old mans good old days speech. The beat downs and the drugs were here way before the bloods.

Zookies bar sat in the middle of the urban blight like a beacon for the poor, the addicted, the immoral, and the godless. On East Paul Ave, you could gage the race relations of the whole nation in this one little microcosm of Zookies shitty little bar, where the white motorcycle boys came to play with the brothers off Martin Luther King Boulevard. What you might not believe, is that for weeks there would be peace. They got together and got drunk and sold drugs in virtual harmony. That's not to say that people didn't get beat up, Trenton is tough, but at least for a while no one brought their knives and no one brought their guns.

Scott had an Uncle, Alan, brother of his father, who became his best friend and partner in crime. Alan had done hard time. His friends were bikers and dealers he had met in prison, and they considered Zookies to be their bar. Even after the neighborhood had deteriorated all through the 80's, still Alan and Ernie and other white boys came there and claimed it.

Scott loved it all, his disease and this city where it was never boring, where everyday things got riskier and every day the warning signs got ignored.

Across the street from Zook's, there was a filthy little alley. It ran off East Paul and it provided shelter for the dealers and hoodlums when the jump out boys came and raided the neighborhood. At night this alley was off limits to all but the craziest white boys. It was in this alley that a brother called Pez applied his trade. Pez's house in that dank alley was a hub for West Trenton cocaine. He and his boys would come across the way because Zookies had the alcohol and the pool table and everyone wanted to get drunk and play.

The small bar pool table was in the back of the establishment and there the drug deals could be safely made. The bathrooms were right by the table and even though there was usually a puddle of piss on the floor, still you could sneak away and do a blast of cocaine in between games.

"You suck at this, Al." Scott smiled at his Uncle as he pocketed the eight.

A brother walked in and said "I got next game." It would be the first of hundreds that Scott and Pez would play. They became friends immediately despite being of different race.

They hung out on the porch behind Pez's house night and day. Crackheads would come and cop from Pez while he and his white friend smoked bluntz and drank Boone's farm from Pez's uncle's liquor store.

One cool night in autumn when there was a full moon and a chill in the air, the two friends drank, and smoked, and sniffed as usual. What Pez didn't know was that earlier Scott had popped a bunch of Vicoden and that it was a night that would bring to life Scotts inner rage.

It was the start of many strange days, when Pezzies new white friend would slip off the reservation and walk around half crazed.

Scott went to his Uncles house, paranoid with chest pains, having seizures and flipping around like a fish out of water. He kicked off his sneakers in his convulsions, his baseball hat flew off and his long blonde hair fell over his face

Now, Uncle Alan hated the police, but he didn't know what else to do for his drugged out nephew, so he reluctantly called 911. And apparently, the EMT's felt that responding to a drug overdose was a bullshit call compared to the other more serious illnesses and emergencies that were out there. They considered picking up a wasted uninsured drug addict to be a waste of their incredible talents and irreplaceably valuable time. Their judgment and hostility drove Scott out of his mind. The fighting started in the ambulance and by the time they got to the ER @ Fuld on Brunswick Ave, Scott and the medical team sufficiently hated each other.

C.S.W.

They put him on the gurney and roughly pushed him inside. Maybe it was the drugs and alcohol, or maybe it was his nasty Idjit, but whatever was agitating him, Scott was now pissed off enough to punch one of them.

"What's the matter, sir? A little too much partying?" sarcastically and condemningly came the question from the doctor.

"Fuck you and fuck this." came Scotts answer as he tried to get up off the table.

The Drs. reply was two words, simply, "Security, restraints." And the orderly and the guards came behind the blue curtain and forcefully held him down. Scott had been placed in strait jackets and shackled before; it was one of the worst feelings he ever had to endure. It was like psychological torture. They strapped down his arms, stomach, and legs. He laid spread out in the position of the crucified and he withstood their stupid little verbal jabs and condescending comments.

They injected the intravenous line as Scott laid there wasting everybody's time.
"Hold still, sir!"

He did not consider the helplessness of his situation and something in his brain short circuited and all he wanted to do was get up off this crucifixion table and fight.

Scott did not consider himself to be a racist. He had plenty of black friends. He did however know when to fire off the "N" word for maximum effect. His anger always seemed to know when it would be the pinnacle of stupidity.

"Fuck you, niger!" Scott tried to get up, slamming himself against the restraints. He tried with all his might to snap them and was even a little surprised when it didn't happen. He managed to lift his head about 16 inches off the table, before the orderly, a black man outweighing him by at least 40 bounds, grabbed him by his neck and chopped his head down hard against the table. The brother really seemed to be enjoying himself now that it was just him and Scott alone in the room. He choked him more than was necessary and he smiled.

The demon inside Scott snapped completely homicidal. He could feel the hatred rage, and still the orderly taunted him. He could feel the blood rush to his head and O he wanted this man dead. His body temperature jumped 10 degrees hotter and gravity got heavier and pressed down on his lungs. He was like a rabid animal caged.

As soon as the orderly let go off his throat and tried to pull his hand away, Scott again lunged forward against the restraints. This time he snapped his teeth in the air as he attempted to bite the brother's fingers off.

The orderly pulled his hand away just in time. He was shocked to see that Scott was so out of his mind. "What the hell is wrong with you?!"

"Let me out of this now! I can't be tied down like this."

"No, relax."

"You think your bad, slammin' me around while I'm tied down. Take these things off me and I'll beat your ass."

"Listen, if you try to bite me again, I'm really gonna give you a shot."

Scott thrashed around in the thick leather belts as if he were possessed by a whole legion of demons, though it was probably just the one Idjit we talked about earlier. Whatever the case, the beast within him coughed up some phlegm from his chest and spit it at the poor underpaid orderly. The glob of spittum caught him more off guard than the attempted biting. It hit him on his neck, and it was thick when he put his hand up to it. He yelled in astonished disbelief, "Mother Fucker!"

Scott again tested the harnesses that held him. This time he was able to bite his teeth into his IV line and snap his head around until he ripped out the needle.

The volume of the otherwise quiet ER was amplified as Scott and the orderly started screaming at each other. More guards and nurses came in and tried to sedate him. They put a surgical mask over the monster to keep him from biting and spitting. As they held his head down and a nurse reinjected the IV so that they could hit him with something sweet to put his crazy ass asleep, Scott pretended to calm down. Perfectly, passively, and persuasively he said, "It's o.k. I'm sorry, I feel better now. I don't know what happened. Take these things off; I'll be good, I promise." All he wanted was one punch at the orderly, his nose, his jaw, his eye, it didn't matter which.

The sudden serenity didn't fool anyone and the head nurse repeated what they all kept saying. "Relax, sir, we can't do that yet."

After his plan failed the patient reverted back to profanity. He screamed at the top of his lungs. He woke up the seriously ill sleeping people, people with real emergencies. He disturbed the doctors, the janitors, the food servers, and the people at deaths door. Everybody in the emergency room. Everybody on the first floor.

Fortunately, Helene Fuld campus @ Mercer has a soundproof room in its ER and they wheeled the raving lunatic inside. Silence cut off the cursing when they got Scott inside and mercifully closed the door.

A nurse came into the room and pumped a syringe of something into his IV. She gave him a worried but not uncompassionate look as she turned and left the room. Scott planned on having sex with her after he woke up and killed the orderly who closelined him.

The nasty idjit did not want to stop fighting and cursing but eventually the drugs in Scotts arm took their toll. His eyes got heavy and rolled, and he rested against his restraints. The madman finally fell asleep.

Hours later, Scott came to consciousness. He awoke in a room he did not recognize. The florescent lights were bright above him and he was momentarily blinded. He used his right hand to shield his eyes and to brush his long blond hair out of his face. That was when he first realized that he had been released from the restraints.

Scott awoke a different person, the nasty idjit appeared to be gone and he seemed to be at peace. There wasn't even any hint of a headache. Slowly, the events of last night filtered into his memory and he laughed to himself in embarrassment. He was such a dick. He thought about trying to bite that guys fingers off and he giggled. What could he possibly have been thinking?

He knew that he should probably try to find that orderly and apologize to him, but because of his shame he preferred to seek escape over forgiveness. No one seemed to be guarding his room and he was no longer hooked up to any IVs. So Scott in his white socks got up and simply walked out of the ER and Helene Fuld Hospital without a word to anyone.

The day outside was sunny and bright, but it had rained the night before and there were puddles on the sidewalk and roads. The concrete was damp still and it wasn't long before Scotts socks were soaked through and the skin on his feet and toes pruned.

He walked the short distance down Brunswick Ave and made a left on Olden. It would be about a three mile walk to his Uncles house where his sneakers and baseball hat had been kicked off in last night's seizures. In the chaos and confusion.

Scott walked passed Stevie T's go-go bar, the unofficial divider between Ewing and Trenton. He walked in a dream. Perhaps the drugs they gave him in the hospital had been intended to keep him asleep much longer. Maybe that was why the restraints had been released. He walked all lethargic from the drugs and he made his way passed the video store, and the grocery, and the McDonalds, and the Burger King. He floated as if in a trance down the busy morning thoroughfare. All he wanted to do was to get to his Aunt Kathy's house and sleep for several days. But the busy commercial road stretched on forever before him.

Sweat wet his head and he plastered his long blond hair back off his forehead. His body burned with fever. At last he made a right off Olden Avenue with all its evil people and mercifully found a tree in front of someone's house in the suburbs. Scott stopped to rest for a minute, hoping that the homeowner would not come out and chase him off his property. In less than a minute, Scott was unconscious, lying with his back against that blessed tree. He may have laid there for five minutes or an hour, but when

Scott got up to continue his journey he felt neither refreshed nor rested. He felt dizzy, confused, and even sleepier. Like his mind was fighting sodium pentothal and the effects of anesthesia.

His trek leads him down Terrace Boulevard to his Aunt and Uncles house in Ewing. When he got there he walked in without knocking. He peeled off his soaking wet socks and dropped them in balls on their living room carpet. Then he collapsed on their couch and slept for the rest of the day. Sometime his Aunt came and brought him a pillow and a blanket.

When he woke up the next morning, he went home and he slept some more. He was not sure what was wrong with him. For two more days all he could do was sleep. On the third day he awoke and could not sleep anymore. He was sweating profusely and shivering like he was freezing though it was a comfortable 72 degrees in the room. Worse, his muscles were contracting like he was suffering from tetanus. His jaw shook uncontrollably and his teeth were chattering. He kept thinking it would get better but instead it got worse, until the curse was unbearable.

Eventually, Scott knew, he was going to have to go back to the hospital @ Fuld where he had made such a scene and then escaped without being discharged. Humbled and without any rage, he gimped into the ER again. Withered and shriveled and shaking, he came begging for their help.

When he walked in through the sliding doors, the nurses ran over to him and diagnosed the problem immediately, an allergic reaction from the drugs. They gave him a shot of Benadryl.

Scott had a bottle of Benadryl at home. He never would have thought in a million years that that was all he needed. The effect was instantaneous and sweet. His constricted muscles released and there was an overwhelming sensation of peace. Once again, he fell asleep. His dreams were even serene.

When consciousness came crashing back, his addiction was there and hungry.

Scott was discharged properly this time and then he and his idjit were back on the streets.

The double doors opened and the sun blasted his eyes with the brightness of the day. The morning air smelled fresh but he could sense the mayhem just two blocks down Brunswick, where on East Paul Ave., his friend Pez was applying his trade, slinging cocaine.

Scott got to Zookies early that day and the bar was almost completely empty when he entered. It was dark as usual inside and the music played softly. Only the bartender, Madelyn and one other customer were there. They were talking at the corner of the bar.

"What's up Scott? Where you been?"

"Long story. Seen Pezzie around?"

"He's not up yet. Why you here so early?" Maddy brought the dude another beer "This is Pete."

"What's up, Pete? I'm here cuz I can't wait to get started." Scott shook Pete's hand and started to walk out of the bar to Pez's house.

"Hey wait," Madelyn called after him, "I forgot to tell you. This is my last day working here. I got a job working at the Anchor Inn on Lalor Street. You should check it out; it's not as crazy as it is here."

"I like crazy." Scott continued towards the door.

"You comin' back?"

"Yeah."

"Bring me a line." In 1998, most of the white people who hung out at Zookies still seemed to prefer sniffing their cocaine as opposed to smoking it. I guess they felt a little more sophisticated than those unfortunate crackheads with their glass stems (called Uzis), car antennas, and Chore boy. It's always nice to have someone we consider more messed up than ourselves to look down on. Stinkin' crackheads. Anyway, Pez served them both.

So Scott went across E. Paul to his friend's house and knocked on the door.

Pez's girlfriend, a beautiful black girl named Connie answered. She gave Scott the same friendly but disapproving look she reserved for all her boyfriends hoodlum friends. "Where you been?" she asked. She leaned back over her shoulder and called into the back bedroom "Alfonse, get up, Chips here."

Nobody else called Pez Alfonse and Scott smiled.

"Where you been?" Connie asked him again.

"Roaming the earth and going back and forth in it" said Scott quoting Satan from the book of Job. (1:7 and 2;2 NIV)

The reference was lost on Connie and she just said "Uh-huh" as Pez came onto the porch wiping the sleep out of his eyes. His face brightened when he saw his friend. "My brother from another mother, what happened to you? Last time I saw you, you could barely walk."

Scott told Pez and Connie the story of his hospital visits and after the pleasantries were exchanged, Connie went back inside. Pez asked, as he always did "Do you have any money?"

"A little," Scott replied.

"Good, walk with me to the store." As they walked to the little convenience store across from Zook's on East Paul, they talked. They were stopped twice in this short distance by crackheads who bought cocaine off Pez, even though it was still relatively early in the day. Back then, the crack still came in those little plastic viles, you may or may not remember those, but the streets of Trenton were littered with them.

They went inside the store and bought a couple of Philly Bluntz. Pez would crack them open and dump out the tobacco, so he could fill the leaves up with weed. Sometimes, he would sprinkle the concoction with crack before rolling the thing back up and licking it. He would seal the thing back together with spit. This was what Scotts Uncle Alan referred to as a "treated blunt." A good treated blunt could run you $40 dollars and change. $20 for the weed, $20 for the coke, plus the cost of the blunt.

After they left the store, they walked through the alley to Brunswick where Pez's Uncle owned a liquor store. There they bought a couple of bottles of Boones Farm which they would guzzle on the back porch while they sold Pezzies cocaine all day. As they walked past the backyards of the row homes in the ghetto, dogs barked at them and the black folks watched as the neighborhood drug dealer and his white friend moved down the street with ease.

"You think you'll ever leave Trenton?" Scott asked.

"What are you talking about? I leave Trenton all the time."

"I don't mean to go to Philly or New York to cop, stupid. I mean quit the game, go somewhere and be different?"

"Listen, Chip, you know how they say 'you can take the girl out of Trenton but you can't take Trenton out of the girl?' Yeah. Well that goes for me and my boys too. When we go to jail, we're still in Trenton. Everywhere we go, we take the streets with us."

"That's kinda sad, bro."

"It is what it is. But since we're getting all philosophical on a Friday, (it was Sunday) let me ask you a question. Why does a white boy, such as you, who doesn't even live in the city, come down here every day to hang out with us brothers? You should be out impregnating some college girl, playing golf, and wearing a suit and tie. Why do you come here?"

"I'm trying to get close to Connie so I can get with her one day while you're out selling shit."

"No, man, I'm serious, why'd you start coming here?"

"Maybe I'm a cop." Pez didn't laugh. The police were generally disliked. He asked a very good question though. Why did Scott start coming here? The easy answer was drugs and excitement, but if you wanted to look deeper, into the juicy heart of the thing, the meat and potatoes as it were, there were probably a couple of reasons. Scott was obviously all screwed up in his head with his narcissism and neurosis. We could easily blame the nasty idjit and just leave it at that. Or maybe the reason he was here was because this was where the Lord had lead him. This was where he was to get his real education to the streets and human nature.

In Trenton, we don't talk a lot about God or our feelings and so as a way of changing the subject, Scott said, "I love you, Pez. I think it's time we took our relationship to the next level, if you know what I mean. I like my men black, like my coffee."

Again Pez didn't laugh. "Fuck around all you want, but listen. This place will suck you in. Maybe you're here by choice right now, but one day you'll look around and discover that there's no way out. Then you'll be a prisoner, whether you're in jail or on the streets. Maybe you think thats o.k. and it's all a big game, but I like you bro and I don't want it for you."

Scott was touched and he didn't make any more stupid jokes. "Lemme hit that blunt."

Pez passed it. They smoked and got high and were silent for a time.

They got back to Pez's porch and continued to sit in the silence, comfortable in the quiet, like friends sometimes get.

Scott lit up a cigarette. He thought about how the brothers in Trenton almost all seemed to smoke menthol cigarettes, while the white boys seemed to prefer regular cigarettes but would smoke whatever they could get their hands on. These were the important issues that Scott pondered while he was high.

It was a beautiful day in his ugly town. The sun threw harsh shadows off the brick houses.

Pez finally broke the silence. "I gotta go bro. I gotta go re-up; I'll meet you tonight at Zookies."

"Cool, I gotta go get my Uncle anyway."

"Hey, how come your Uncle never cops off me?"

"You know my people don't like your people." Scott smiled and Pez even laughed.

The truth was that Alan bought his coke off Ernie and the motorcycle boys because of some old prison loyalty thing. Actually, the bikers did have a higher quality product than what Pez offered. Scott had had both of their cocaines, and would take Ernie's every time given the choice. "I'll ask him."

"Word?" This was back when people still said "word." It could mean just about anything you wanted it to. In this case, Pez meant "Yes, get your Uncle to buy some coke off me tonight."

"Word." (I'll try.)

"Peace."

"Peace." They didn't shake hands; they made fists and hit knuckles. When their hands touched, it meant stay tough and keep your head up. There was a sharp contrast of white on black skin but really it didn't mean a god damned thing.

The two went their separate ways, Pez to the drug man and Scott to get his Uncle in Ewing. And the wasted day turned into a wasted night.

When Alan and Scott got back to Zookies they noticed that the usual crew was gone. Maddy and Pete had relocated to the bar on Lalor street and Ernie and his boys were off somewhere, presumable committing felonies.

Nevertheless, Scott and Alan and Pez shot pool and drank and got high the same as any other day. This time however there was unexpected reaction to the beer and the rum and the chemicals and Scotts idjit was pissed. What happened was this.

After Pezzie left, a hot Latino girl came into the bar and Scott wanted her at once.

Her name was Maria and she had this incredibly sexy brown skin and long dark hair that flowed down passed her shoulders. Her eyes were big eyes like cats eyes and she made Scott fall in lust when she smiled. She was friendly when Scott came over and said "Hi." She didn't move, she danced and she didn't just captivate, she totally entranced. It was like witchcraft how badly Scott wanted her ass.

He bought her drinks, told her jokes and she laughed. They played pool and Scott missed shots on purpose just so he could watch her bend over and shoot. He wanted her very badly and he wanted her very soon. If not for the crowd he might have even tried to pull her in to the filthy urine smelling bathroom. But when the end of the night came and Alan wanted to go home, and Scott tried to get Maria to come with him, all she wanted to do was give him her phone number.

Now, for a lot of guys this might have been taken as a very good sign, but Scott misinterpreted it as rejection and it served to further infuriate his drunk and drugged out mind.

Scott and his idjit stepped outside into the moonlight.

And the bad man came from the darkness.

And everyone was feeling warlike.

The brother came at him carrying a backpack and a razor knife. He was three or four inches taller than Scott and about twenty pounds heavier, give or take. In Trenton, the street people only come and start shit with those who are smaller than they are, than those they perceive to be weak. Some people think that they're tough when really they're pussies.

There was no way for Scott to know how much crack the guy had smoked that night.

He said, "Yo man, I need three dollars for . . ."

And whatever he said after that was lost on Scott because he interrupted him by saying 'Get the fuck away from me, I'm not giving you shit!"

Scott saw the guy take a step back and drop his book bag on the sidewalk, what he didn't see was the razor in his hand as he advanced. "Oh, you're gonna give some money now!"

"Fuck you,!" Scott screamed as he stepped into his assailants attack. Nothing in life gives you the sense of power that comes from a well connected punch and Scott got off three good ones. He caught the dude in his left eye with a right and followed with another right to the same eye, followed by a left to the side of the guys head. Whap! Whap! Whap! Scott was lightening quick for a white kid and he had a huge grin as he felt the angst and excitement flood him like a new drug. He felt there was no way he could lose this fight.

And the squared up to dance, to throw hands, to go toe to toe.

Scotts arm had already been sliced open, he just didn't know it.

Sometime, while he was punching the brother, the brother had cut open his right forearm with his razor knife, severing his ulna artery and tearing through his Palmaris longus muscle. His adrenaline was pumping so hard that he never even felt himself get sliced. He had put up his hands to protect his head and pick out his spots for some well placed shots. He had not been expecting to be cut.

He still had the same satanic smile on his face when he looked into his enemies eyes and saw where he was looking. Only then did he stop to look at his arm and that's when he noticed the blood.

It was pissing out of his arm in a bright red arch resembling a urine stream. It sprayed out about three feet. Scott slipped into a state of shock as he looked at the gash, the source of the gusher, It split open like a bloody vagina on his forearm and you could see all the meat and severed muscle. It stretched apart as the nerves and tendons were split apart and the cut went to the bone.

Scott forgot about the fight as he stared fascinated at the wound and he began to feel a little dizzy from the rapid loss of blood.

Uncle Alan witnessed all this and out of love, he jumped in between his nephew and the negro, before Scott could get cut again. The crackhead made a wild swipe at Alan that ripped his shirt open from his right shoulder to the left side of his belly button. Later there would be a faint scratch on Alan's chest that ran from just above his nipple to his stomach, but nothing deep enough to require stitches. Alan tackled the guy and they fought and rolled around.

Scott grabbed his right arm with his left hands and squeezed it to try and stop the blood flow, but it dripped between his fingers and splattered on the sidewalk. It mixed with the loose gravel, cigarette butts, and weeds growing in the expansion joints in the concrete.

Scott stumbled back inside the bar and when the new bartender saw his wound she screamed. Inside his head Scott heard a hum like the buzz of a tattoo gun, then he got all dizzy and he dropped out of consciousness and went crashing to the floor.

Somebody called 911.

When Scott came swirling back awake, he remembered his Uncle still outside fighting with the black guy. He pushed himself up off the floor and out of a small puddle of his own blood. His shirt was soaked in the front and even his jeans were stained red. He would never wear those clothes again.

He went back outside but it was quiet and dark and there was no sign of his beloved Uncle. Shortly after though, Alan came running back to the bar where Scott stood. "Man that guy was fast." Alan chased the guy down East Paul where he turned left on Martin Luther King Boulevard and disappeared. Even Scotts bad ass Uncle wasn't crazy enough to chase the guy into the badlands towards the Trenton Battle Monument. Not alone. Not at night.

Scott had always respected Dr. Martin Luther King as a man of equality, with a noble vision of peace, but from that night on Scott also had a dream. To find the mother fucker who cut him and enact his revenge. To show the brother the wrath of God that now lived inside him.

Shortly after, the ambulance pulled up and the EMT's loaded him up and took him the two blocks down the street to Capitol Health System @ Fuld. It would be his third trip inside of two weeks.

At the emergency room they gave him painkillers and stitched closed his arm. They told him that he would have to come back tomorrow and have surgery, so that they could reattach the nerves, veins, and tendons inside his arm.

Scotts middle, ring, and little fingers had curled into a claw and neither could he open his hand or totally make a fist. It burned like it was on fire, but Scott shed not one single tear. His anger and hate would not allow him to cry from the pain. It was all part of becoming a soldier.

He and Alan, who had come down to the hospital, left together and walked back to the bar. They stepped through the double doors and into the darkness of the night.

Scotts arm was bandaged and he held it out like a badge of honor, his sadistic initiation into the game. The hospital had given him some

Percocets to benumb him until he came back for surgery in the morning, but when he got back to Zookies, he noticed that his last beer was still on the bar. He downed his night supply of painkillers with the last few flat swallows of his beer. It was nasty swill, it tasted like backwash and it went beautifully with the narcotics.

Scott and his Uncle called it a night. It was a little comical to watch Scott try to drive his five speed Chevy S-10 pickup with only one arm. He had to steer and shift with his left hand, but the two of them safely made it home.

The next day Scott went and had his surgery and was blessed with a sweet prescription for med's. He mixed these with marijuana and other stuff he obtained illegally. For the next three days, Scott hibernated in his house and if he was awake, he was high. It was during this time that Scott felt that he had communed with God, and that God was compelling him to become a writer. He wrote his poems and stories left handed because his right hand was healing and temporarily ruined. In the coming weeks the sensation would return to his middle finger and ring, but his pinky would be permanently curled and deadened. His scar would serve as a souvenir, a reminder that there's violence.

When he rose again on the third day and went back East Paul to see his friend, everything had changed. Nobody he knew was at Zookies and the scene seemed to have dried up like a river in a drought.

He walked across the street to the alley to Pez's but two unfamiliar brothers blocked his way. "What are you doing here, white boy?"

Scott went to walk around them, but they wouldn't let him pass. "I'm going to see Pez."

The boys looked at each other and laughed. "Pez is gone. The jump out boys got him two days ago."

The police had busted Pez right after he had re-up-ed and so they caught him with a lot of cocaine. To make matters worse, Pez was on parole and because of New Jersey's three strike law, Pez would be going away for a long, long time.

Scott would never see Pezzie again. He would not however allow himself to shed any tears over the loss of his friend. Pez was tough, he could do jail. Plus your trained never to cry when you come up in Trenton.

That was the last time Scott went to Zookies or hung out on East Paul Avenue. As he turned to walk away, he heard the two new brothers call after him "And stay the fuck away."

The alley was now theirs and they took over Pezzies' business just that quick.

That was how Scott came to learn that your friends can be taken away and that you may never see them again.

And, no matter how tough you think you are there's always someone badder, or faster, or crazier. The violence never goes away.

And, the one overriding fact that will never change; nothing can stop the cocaine trade.

It's all a big game, and everyone who plays it gets played.

These were Scott's formulative lessons.

They are the lessons of Trenton.

Chapter 2

Lalor Street / Hoffman Avenue

I T WAS ANOTHER bright and sunny day although it was colder now with winter. God looked down from his heaven and he beheld the evolution of his creation, the spinning and the growing.

He hears the wind rustling the leaves on the trees and he spends some time listening. He sees the river ripples glistening.

Let's say today his attention is drawn to the Delaware River as it flows, lazy and dirty, slowly through Stockton and Lambertville. He follows it down to Washington's Crossing Park where it splits the history of Pennsylvania and New Jersey. He remembers the pain of those who suffered and died in the wars that were fought here. He remembers all the battles and all the blood that was spilt. Perhaps it hurts his heart to remember and so he continues to look downstream.

Eventually, he comes to the "Trenton Makes" bridge connecting Morrisville to Jersey.

Today the neon lights in the sign aren't all working and the M is out. So the sign reads "TRENTON _AKES (aches) THE WORLD TAKES, and that's probably a little more accurate. Maybe from there his attention is turned from the water and he decides to take a look around the city. And the river flows on alone to the ocean and Jehovah no longer takes notice.

The Lord looked around him as he made his way down route 29 and the John Fitchway. He viewed the nightclub called the Katmandu and he saw the congestion in the traffic caused by the construction of the Trenton Tunnel. Since he wasn't trying to pick up a women and he didn't own a car, neither of these things interested him very much. He might have wanted to watch a baseball game as he approached Waterfront Park, but it was late December and nobody was playing.

The Alpha and Omega made a left on Cass Street and headed up towards Center. He wasn't in the mood to look in on the prison and smell the evil and so he made a right on Lamberton Street. Even he had almost lost track of how many times the liquor store on the corner had been robbed.

He headed south until he came to the Champale Plant, which sat crumbling and deserted, shut down for the last several years. The building was still there, abandoned like so many other factories, restaurants, and structures that went under and remained like gravestones. Monuments of Trenton's yesterdays. Memorials to happier and more productive times.

The Lord left Champale, a lifeless shell, and a few feet down the road he came to Lalor street which runs east from the river and eventually bleeds into Broad. On the corner of Lalor, God spies an establishment called Ye Olde Anchor Inn and he decides to take a peek inside.

The bar is almost empty as it is only 10:30 in the morning, but there are two people inside. He knows their names as surely as he knows that they are drinking already and that one of them is high on cocaine. He listens in on their conversation, which is laced with lust and violence. It is peppered with curses and profanity. Regardless of the topic, they could be talking about the weather, local sports, or the purity of the pope or the virgin Mary, they took the Lords name in vain, casually and thoughtlessly.

Maybe even, God thought about Paul's letter to the church of the Ephesians, where he said, "Having lost all sensitivity, they have given themselves over to sensuality so as to indulge in every kind of impurity with a continual lust for more." Eph 4:19.

It became obvious that God was forgotten in this place and so the holy spirit left there dejected. No one knows where he went from there, but shortly after the Lord split, Scott pulled up at Ye Olde Anchor Inn. He climbed the front steps and he entered, missing the spirit of the Lord by about fifteen minutes.

When Scott walked in, he could tell that Maddy was agitated about something and when she saw him she came over to tell him the latest gossip. "Chip, did you hear about Little Ricky? He got busted last night. If he runs his mouth about Jay and Eric, I'll kill him myself." Madylin was dating the number two guy in a fairly successful drug ring. His name was Jason. His brother, Eric headed up the enterprise and they and their other brothers had their fingers in the cocaine trade at the Anchor Inn and a few other bars across Trenton and into Pennsy. Their business was thriving and they preached the code of silence, lest there be violence. "You never rat on your friends. Or anyone else for that matter." We say "Snitches get stitches."   .

Pete says to Maddy, "Don't worry about Little Ricky, he knows the code."

Ironically, when they finally did get busted, the brothers would all betray their precious code and their own blood. They started pointing fingers and blaming each other to the police in an effort to save their own skin. Rumor has it that they even threatened to kill one another and that they even threw a few punches in court.

Nobody knew for sure if Little Ricky had ratted them out or not.

But they would make the front page of "The Trentonian", the local newspaper with their pictures plastered under the caption "The dirty dozen." when they were arrested. Realistically, there probably wasn't twelve guys in their "gang" but sometimes stories tend to get sensationalized for the sake of circulation. In any case, Scott lost interest before they were sentenced.

Anyway, Peter sat at the bar drinking a draft and reading the paper. He was a heavy set country boy who had moved to the city from his Aunts farm in Titusville. Pete was without parents or siblings and he lived alone as a squatter in a deserted house across the street from the Anchor. Pete had several flannel shirts and he adopted a dog, that he named Jed.

Pete loved to talk about what he referred to as "squatter rights". Apparently, he believed that if you took up residence in a house that somebody moved out of and stayed there long enough than you had some kind of rights to the place. Scott did not know of any such rule or law, but he did think that it was extremely funny.

"What's up, squatter?" he said as he sat next to him at the bar.

"Not much. I'm about to go home and let Jeddie out for a few minutes." Pete slammed the rest of his beer in three quick gulps and wiped his mouth with his sleeve. "Then I'm gonna smoke a big fat spliff. Would you care to partake?"

"Amen, brother." Scott accepted.

The people who fled from the house across the street on Lalor did so because of a merciless mortgage payment and ridiculous taxes squeezing them until they bled. During the reign of Governor Florio and his evil regime the corruption in New Jersey was so rampant that it must have been funny to anyone who lived in another state. If you lived here however you were outraged at the how the government daily raped you and extorted your money in a military fashion, not unlike Nazi, Germany. The state police work for the insurance companies and enforce their insane taxation like the Gestapo. Good old Jim made himself rich with his policies and the integrity of a mafia boss. But again, I digress.

The house that Pete squatted in was in serious disrepair, though not exactly dilapidated.

It would have qualified as an "abandominium" if not for two factors. First, for some inexplicable reason, the place always had electric. Scott could not imagine his friend hillbilly Pete paying the bill, so constant power was a blessing and a mystery. Second, there was always running water. Although the water company would come out and shut it off occasionally, Pete would just go out and open the valve after they left.

Anyway, while Jeddie was taking a dump, the two dudes puffed on the doobie. The weed that they were smoking was the last bud of a very special plant that Peter had grown and that Scott had helped him to harvest. The following is the story of that plant.

Peter germinated the seeds in early March in potting soil in a plastic planter. He grew the weed on the second floor of his place on Lalor under a constant 60 watt light bulb. God really blessed the thing, it was hungry for life and strong.

While the cannabis was still a baby, Pete and Scott visited with it every day. They played chess beside it and watched it like parents. They played guitars around it and sang to it. They spoiled it with water and fertilizer, and love. Anyway, when the marijuana got to be about three inches tall, it split into a Y shape and sprouted into two separate branches. It grew perfectly symmetrical on both sides.

Pete, Scott, and the pot were all very happy together for almost three months until at last it came time for the weed to leave home. It needed to be transplanted outside if it was to really grow. And so, one faithful day in late May, the three of them loaded into Scotts car and made the journey out of Trenton and into the country of Peters Aunts farm.

It was a sad goodbye the guys said to their green little friend who was now almost three feet tall. They planted it in a compost heap where no one would find it. It would get plenty of sun and rain and the hillbilly and the hippy promised to come back and visit. Before they left Pete looked at him and said, "You're a good friend, Chip. I know I can trust you not to tell anyone about this. When it comes time to harvest, I'll hook you up."

"Amen, brother." Scott dropped Pete off at his place in Trenton. He didn't go back and steal any of the buds until sometime in September. In the history of great betrayals, Scott stealing Pete's weed probably wouldn't rank up there with traitors like Benedict Arnold or Judas Iscariot. Still, he felt guilty about violating their pact. It wasn't his finest hour.

What happened was this.

Scott and Alan were driving home from another rotten day at work and they were both tired and dirty and jonesin' for some weed. So, just as a way of making conversation, Scott sez to his Uncle, "I know where there's a gigantic reefer plant growing."

"Bullshit."

"No, I'm serious. Pete's growing it at his Aunts farm in Titusville. It's the most beautiful thing I've ever seen."

"Take me there." demanded the Uncle.

"Oh, I couldn't do that."

"You must."

"I can't."

"You will." And so Alan won the debate. That night, under the cover of darkness, they went and snatched some of the grass just before the end of the season. The plan was Scott would wait in the car with the engine running while his Uncle went down and plucked a few of the nicer buds.

The thing about Alan though, God love him, was that he was a career criminal and probably the worst kleptomaniac that Scott had ever met. When it came to stealing stuff, Alan really couldn't help himself. He could not go into a store without stealing a lighter, or candy, or cigarettes, or whatever. The sad truth was that Alan was very gifted as a thief and he had no conscience whatsoever about stealing. He once told Scott his philosophy on crime.

"A lot of people get all nervous and paranoid about shoplifting. They look all guilty before they even take anything. That's why they get in trouble. Me; I take stuff like it's mine and I never get caught. Also, people think that you have to be real sneaky to steal. That's stupid. Mostly the best time to grab stuff is when you're making eye contact with the person your stealing from." Alan looked at Scott, "Are you listening?"

"Yeah, it sounds like bullshit to me."

"Is it?"

"Yeah, I think it is."

"Did you see me just take your cigarettes and lighter?" Alan took them out of his pocket and put them back on the cars console in front of him. Scott had to admit he didn't see his Uncle pocket them even though it happened right before his eyes. Later, Alan's sickness would progress from convenience stores to big department stores. From lighters and candy to laptop computers and big screen t.v.'s. Power tools and IPods'.

Anyway, as Alan was getting out of the car to go and pick Peter's weed, Scott grabbed him by his arm. "What?" asked the Uncle.

"Don't take it all, o.k.?"

"Stop being a little bitch. You want to get high don't you?" With that Alan ran into the woods and disappeared down the hill to the compost heap. Sure enough, when he came back about ten minutes later, he had in his hands what must have been half the damn plant. He had buds stuffed in both pockets and in both hands. He jumped in the car and yelled "Go! Go! Go!"

Alan was never as happy as when he ganked something. His joy was contagious. And Scott gave in to temptation.

The two took the out of season weed back to Ewing, they dried it out and then they tried it. It was not as potent as it would later be, but still it burned mellow and sweet. Alan looked at his nephew with red and glossy eyes, for he was sufficiently high.

"You know I'm gonna tell the hillbilly you went and stole his weed."

Scott was pretty paranoid for he too was stoned. "Don't play Al; you think I want that crazy redneck coming after me?" And so they made a vow of silence. Neither of them would ever speak of smoking Pete's weed and no one ever found out about it until just now because I just told you. (If you see a crazy country boy named Pete with long dirty hair and a flannel shirt, don't say anything o.k.?)

Speaking of Pete, back at the home of the squatter, the guys had just finished smoking the last primo bud they had grown. They had saved this nugget for last and had a small ceremony before sparking it. Now the cloud of smoke in the kitchen was so dense that even Jeddie lay on the floor with a contact high. As he sat there baked, Scotts mind flash backed to the day of the harvest. He remembered the day he and Pete loaded into his car a box of giant black plastic garbage bags, some hedge shears, and a tree saw, and went out reaping.

And the marijuana flourished in the sun like the finger of God was on it. It grew into two separate bushes, one on either side of the compost heap. It looked like something out of Jack and the beanstalk. Its roots had exploded in growth as if planted in some kind of magical soil. The dudes beheld the buds in all their glory and they heard angels singing on high. The stalk was now about three and a half inches thick where it sprang up from mother earth. The Y shape where it was split in two was cracked down its center like a woman from when Uncle Alan came and raped her. The fracture didn't seem to have hurt her though; instead she seemed to have fought harder to live. It was a shame that they were here to kill her.

Peter the hillbilly noticed the split and he said to his friend, "Look, it snapped in half, I think some deer ran through it."

Scott agreed, "Yeah, it must have been the deer." He held open the garbage bags while Pete used the shears and snapped off the branches. For those of you who don't know, marijuana doesn't cut very easy, that's why they make rope out of it. Pete got the job done though. He filled two whole garbage bags with branches full of buds. It was the most beautiful thing Scott had ever seen.

C.S.W.

They left only a stump and took the stuff back to Lalor street to hang it up on a clothesline in the attic to dry. They put a sheet underneath the crop to catch any buds that fell off. In about a week they began weighing out quarter ounce baggies and selling them to people at the bar across the street. Peter gave Scott one free quarter for his troubles, for he was very stingy with his weed.

The rest sold like hot cakes and Peter had himself a nice little score.

Than about a week later, while Pete was walking Jed down towards Second street, he got jumped by some Puerto Rican kids and they busted a bottle on him and cut his hand pretty good. He went to the emergency room for stitches and pain medicine. When he came back, he didn't share. After that Scott didn't really like Pete as much anymore.

Anyway, as they sat stoned in Pete's filthy kitchen, they crushed out the final roach and popped open a beer. Scott lit a cigarette and they toasted the end of the bud.

Now Jeddies ears started twitching and he lifted his head up off the floor, he began to bark as he ran towards the door. Scott and Pete looked at each other and joyously yelled in unison, "MaGoo!" A few seconds later there came a knock at the door.

The cocaine had arrived.

Miguel was a Puerto Rican guy in his mid-to-late fifties. He had dark hair and a thick beard, both peppered with gray and he was always smiling. Because of his pleasant disposition, the denizens of Trenton called him Mr. Magoo. Magoo was a fixture at Ye Olde Anchor Inn and he sold cocaine in the men's room; Monday through Saturday, 6 pm til closing, around 2 am. He was there slinging religiously. On Friday nights, the line of people waiting to go into the bathroom to buy their coke was so long that if you needed to piss, you were better off just going outside.

Anyway before he opened for business, Magoo would stop by Pete's house across the street from the bar to cut his coke with baking soda or b12 or quinine or whatever he had. He would merchandise it to sell as $40 or $80 bags. While he was working, he always shared his product with our two heroes, which was what they were waiting for and why they were so happy he had arrived.

Today was a little different from other days however, because for first time Magoo had actually taken time off to go on vacation and he was returning from being on a cruise with his wife. He had been gone for about ten days and so the boys were especially glad to see him.

"Mr. Magoo. Welcome home." Pete opened the door and lead the guest into the kitchen.

"We missed you, brother. How was life at sea?" There were only two chairs in Pete's kitchen so Scott got up and gave his to Magoo as was the custom. Pete ran upstairs to get the scale so the jolly old Puerto Rican could start weighing.

"It was fun," Magoo smiled but the dudes could tell by his face that something was wrong.

"What's the matter?"

And this is the part that Scott understood all too well. Another sad fact of life in Trenton.

"I hated it," Miguel's smile evaporated and he came clean and admitted he had a problem. "I missed the bar and this shitty little street. The ocean was beautiful and the people were nice and friendly and I was bored and I wondered what I was missing on the streets. I love my wife but I wanted to kill her and dump her body overboard after the second day."

And this is the twisted nature of the sickness of the drug dealer and the addict alike. The dealer loves to sell the drugs as much as the junkie loves to do them. Jails and rehabs can never change the street people's mentality. Only God can. And maybe sometimes not even God.

Scott had seen this many times before. The pusher gets busted, goes to jail, gets out, gets busted again, makes bail, gets paroled, or maxes out on time. He is released to hit the streets and do the only thing he knows, the only thing that he loves; sell drugs. He had seen many dealers and friends arrested for a third time and because of the three strike law, he never saw them again.

Scott wondered how Pezzie was making out. He remembered him saying how "you take the streets with you wherever you go", and "where you're from makes you who you are", and other street wisdom. It applied to Pez in prison and much as it did to Magoo on a luxury liner in the middle of the ocean. In paradise or in captivity, dealers and junkies had their lusts to feed and there was no where that they'd rather be than playing their drug games on Trenton streets.

Trenton streets where everyone runs wild but no one's really free. No one's restrained or bound by any chains but still there's no freewill and all around is slavery. People addicted to different sins.

When the police finally busted Magoo weeks later, he wasn't smiling anymore. They jumped him on Lalor street right outside the Anchor Inn. They caught him with pockets full of money and quite a few bags of cocaine. They went and searched his home, which I believe was on Beatty Street, though I could be mistaken about that.

They found no more drugs but there was a briefcase filled with cash under his bed.

"Sixty-three-thousand-three-hundred and thirty two." Police man counted the loot of Mr. Magoo.

Scott read about the arrest of his friend on the pages of the Trentonian, but he never saw him again. Fortunately, for Scott and his customers (for he had a few of his own by now) drug dealers are a lot like weeds; pull one out and fifteen more pop up. Like a mythological monster that sprouts a new head when decapitated is the nature of the cocaine game in Trenton. Pezzie got popped and Magoo filled the spot. When they came and took Miguel away, Wabby stepped up and took his place. We'll get back to Wabby in a minute.

Anyway, after the dirty dozen and Magoo got busted the scene on Lalor street began to dry up like Zookies bar had years before. Scott stopped coming around. He left Peter and the Anchor alone and started spending more time with his Uncle.

After he hadn't shown up for about two weeks, Peter the hillbilly called him up on the phone.

"Hello."

"Chip, it's Pete. Listen, do you think you could come over?" Scott could hear that his old friend was upset.

"What's the matter?"

"Jeddies dead. He tried to cross the highway up by the Dunkin Donuts and he got hit by a truck. It mangled him real bad and they had to put him down."

Scott listened as his friend cried into the phone. His heart hurt for him because he knew that Pete had no family and few, if any, friends. Jed was his buddy. Strictly speaking, you're not supposed to show sorrow to other men, especially in Trenton, but like I said Pete had no one else.

And of course as everyone knows a man is allowed to cry when his dog dies.

Scott came over and got wasted with the mourning hillbilly one last time. He tried not to judge him as he balled his eyes out. And who was he to judge anyway. He had a family that loved him.

Be that as it may, Scott looked around the ramshackle dump that Pete the hermit squatted in and decided that this place was just too sad and hopeless and that he would never set foot here again. Sometimes people just leave and relationships fade away like hallucinations or vapors.

Today the Anchor Inn on Lalor Street sits closed down, darkened, and abandoned. Discarded like so many other buildings in town that got left behind as there inhabitants jumped ship, got out of Dodge, and took to the hills. The saying goes "Will the last person to leave New Jersey please turn out the lights."

Anyway, around this time Uncle Alan and his Aunt Kathy had pretty much switched their addiction from sniffing coke to smoking crack exclusively. No disrespect intended but truth is truth and fact is fact. We, who take cocaine, say "hard or soft" or "rock or powder."

So back in those days Uncle Alan introduced Scott to Wab, a dealer from Burlington, who brought his shit to the Mulberry section of Trenton by the Dodger bar. His bags were always blessed but you could usually only catch him in town once a night. Otherwise, to score, you had to drive all the way out to his town and that was a pain in the ass. It would be years before the police finally caught up with the wascally wabbit, but his living so far away was the reason why Scott and his nasty idjit went into the Miller Homes projects to cop late one evening after the bars had closed and the cocaine had run out.

It was hazy that night. It felt like a mist or a fog though there was none. The air was blurry around the yellow-orange street lights. It was quiet, but not peaceful, more eerie. It was 2:30 am when Scott walked down a seemingly deserted Hoffman Ave. with two of his oldest friends; Chris and Ken. They were all drunk and so their decision making abilities were severely impaired. They saw the Miller Homes projects on their right as they made their way deeper into the badlands. To their left the houses looked like the ghetto homes of the west coast or maybe even of an ugly city like Newark or Milwaukee.

Scott was not thinking about his faith, or his family, or his own mortality as he walked down the street, but he soon would be. He would soon be thinking about these things very intimately. God had taught him about the violence of men and how some of them liked nothing better than to hurt and to fight. He never forgot about that asshole with the razor knife and what it felt like to get sliced. It would be a continuation of that lesson tonight. Only, instead of a lesson on hate and rage, tonight's lesson was on fear, about the nature of mans cowardice.

The police cruiser came down Hoffman and the cops could not believe what they saw. They slowed to a stop and rolled down their window to talk to the three inebriated white boys from Ewing. They knew what was awaiting them down the street, around the corner on Oakland.

"What the fuck are you guys doing down here?! This is no joke, those guys will kill you."

They knew that they had come here to buy drugs. "Are you crazy walking around down here?

Get out of this neighborhood now! We're going around the block, if you're here when we come back, we're going arrest you for being stupid."

"O.K. officer, we're sorry." The three pretended to take the police officers advice as they turned and walked back the way they came in. The squad car drove away.

Scott turned to Chris, his drug addict friend. "You think they're really coming back?"

"Nah, they're just trying to scare us. Let's go back."

"I'm not going back there" said Ken, Scott's smartest friend. A wise and healthy fear.

"I'm going back to wait in the car." Kenny didn't use drugs and he had the sense to not want to go back into the hood that night. Later Ken would graduate from law school and he now works for the prosecutor's office in Trenton.

Chris and Scott were not as smart as Kenny and they ventured back into the hood together.

They had their respective idjits to feed.

And the brothers were on the corner partying and getting rowdy.

They called the boys over and two thugs came over, presumably to serve them.

Scott had never seen the boys before and was a little nervous until Chris said "Hey, I know this guy." Scott relaxed in the second before the black man attacked him. He did it like this, like a straight bitch, he threw no punch, he made no fist. He poked Scott in his left eye with a fingernail that must not have been cut for a couple of months. He scratched Scott's retina and blinded him on the left side for he was a pussy. His fear that he might lose a fair fight to a white.

It would be ten days before Scott would open that eye again.

And Chris saw him get attacked and he ran. He left him in the hood to die. Cowardice of another kind. Scott never doubted for a minute that if the situation was reversed, he would have stayed and fought with his friend. It wasn't even a question.

As Chris sped away safe the other brother turned on Scott and they both punched him in side of his face. Scott stumbled over the curb and tripped and fell. Blind, on his side, he yelled out for help as the beatdown began.

Are some men completely wicked? Totally without mercy and evil?

There was a pop to the side of his head and then no sound except for the thump of his heart. And even that he felt rather than heard. He twisted and screamed and he ripped the skin off his elbows and knees as he scraped them on the concrete. There was another crushing and deafening blow to his ear from one of the boy's boots that smashed his face into the pavement and fractured his skull.

Now Scott stopped screaming and he encountered the strangest, absolute peace. He could still feel them kicking his head and shots to his ribs but they seemed softer now as he began to except this as the moment of his death.

He experienced the certainty of God and a joy along with sadness. In his ambivalence he cried out to the presence, "Lord, I love you. I always have. I always assumed you wanted me to have kids and to leave the people a story. Take me now if you're ready." Scott regretted that he would die here, stupid like this.

Then he felt the presence leave him and so stopped the beating. Something chased the brothers down the street.

Scott came to and all he could hear was his heart, which thumped slowly at first but began to pick up the tempo with the return of his adrenalin and fear. He got to his feet and saw with terror that his attackers had run down the street the way he had come in. The only way out, he realized, was to run deeper into the badlands and Oakland Ave and find another way out.

There was drug activity on the street even at 2:30 am and the West Trenton bad boys saw Scott run by. They were obviously hostile and it was a blessing that Scott was still near deaf and he couldn't hear the curses he knew they were hurling at him. His head pulsed with pain as he ran through. No one cared to give chase. Perhaps they felt he had endured enough for one day or maybe they were just lazy but whatever the reason, God had once again lead him out safe.

He made it out of Trenton and into Ewing before he could run no more and he walked as his heartbeat slowed. His hearing came back as he snapped his fingers by his ears to test them. He could see from his right eye but wasn't ready to pry open the left, which was a mess. Both his eye sockets were turning black and blue, bruised purple and his face was swollen like a balloon.

Now maybe it was because he was still drunk, or maybe because he was beaten senseless, or maybe it was because he felt lucky to be alive, but as Scott took a deep breath and thought about all that was wrong with him and with all of mankind he began to laugh. It was a paroxysm of inappropriate emotion. He was hopelessly depressed and sad and he sat down with his back against a closed down gas station wall. He was beaten and he couldn't help it, he laughed hysterically. When it subsided to a few remaining chuckles he picked up the phone and called for a ride.

From there, he went, once more, back to Capitol Health Systems at Fuld. Where, while in the ER, the doctor sent him to have an MRI of his head. They had to pull him out of the machine so he could throw up, for he was fairly drunk. As he threw up the alcohol and chemicals, he felt as if he was also spewing out the violence and the hatred, expelling it from him in the puke. He finally found some relief, he thanked God he was alive, for another chance, then he fell asleep.

In time, he would heal. He would hear O.K. again, though for the next few days chunks of what looked like bloody earwax were coming out of his head from the concussion and hemorrhage. His eyes were black for weeks, but days later when he pried open his left eyelid and found that he could see, he was relieved to near ecstasy.

The psychological damage lived on and his idjit was unharmed.

Why was everyone so fucking hard?

And another lesson got learned. There are places on this planet where you are not welcome, where white boys are not allowed. There is holy and unholy ground. And memories of these that you take with you.

Pez had said "You take the streets with you" and Scott now knew what he meant.

There are places we go back to in our minds and revisit them all the time. Mental scars? Maybe, but Scott thought of his happy memories; The first time he got blown, or lost his virginity. The places where his kids would be conceived or where they would later be born. Even where he had written a particularly juicy poem or part of a story. He thought of these places as holy ground.

Contrarily, there are other sore spots on earth, like canker sores of pain that Scott could not go passed without remembering. Places that he saw or felt the violence of godless man or places where he lost his virginity to a new and stronger drug. Trenton is full of unholy ground.

The bible says "It's better to be quiet and humble than loud" and "God opposes the proud*"

So if you don't have a connection or protection in the projects, it's probably best if you just stay the hell out.

In the Miller Homes section of Trenton, they'll kick you until you bleed on the ground.

And you may cry out for help, but grace and mercy do not abound.

And evil is the nature of the Hoffman Avenue beatdown.

Chapter 3

Kelly and the Devil / Division Street

BECAUSE OF ITS location on the eastern seaboard and because of its crime, corruption, and stench of pollution, New Jersey is sometimes referred to as the armpit of the nation. If you look at it on a map, you may also notice that the garden state resembles the bust of a police officer wearing a hat and looking west, as if keeping watch over the whole country. This is appropriate since in a lot of ways New Jersey, with its silly seatbelt laws and war on drugs, is kind of run like a police state. With military structure and precision, they conduct daring daytime raids. They bust the bad guys and they take them away.

Anyway, New Jersey is often disrespected as a state.

The fact that George Washington once crossed into Trenton on Christmas and kicked the shit out of the British may have helped win freedom for this country, but it did not earn us a professional baseball or football team. While it is true that both the Jets and the Giants make their home in New Jerseys, East Rutherford, Meadowlands, still they both claim New York as their state.

We do have a professional ice hockey team. Maybe you've heard of them; they're called the New Jersey Devils. Clever name, huh? Well maybe not so much if you stop to consider where that name comes from.

Perhaps you know the urban legend of the New Jersey Devil. Maybe you even know more about it than me. But here's the gist of it. And I warn you, it's pretty stupid. Apparently, a long time ago, there was a woman who had a dozen and one children (I doubt it) and the thirteenth one was born deformed with horns and goats legs and a tail. (Didn't happen) Anyway, they went to slay the beast, for he was a monstrosity, but before they could put it out of its misery, it flew away; for it also had wings. (O.K. that part's probably true.)

So the devil took off and retreated to its new home somewhere in the desolate waste of the New Jersey Pine Barrens. There it lived by eating chickens that it stole from nearby farms. Occasionally, if it was lucky, it could snatch a baby.

Legend, such as it is, says he's still out there today.

And this is the well constructed fable from which the New Jersey hockey team derives their name. Again, I say, clever.

Interestingly, Scott's high school baseball and football teams were also called the Devils.

The blue devils actually. The mascot was the image of a naughty but lovable guy who was harmless and misunderstood. In years to come, God's name would be taken out of the pledge of allegiance and no prayer would be allowed at public schools. The devil would, however, remain and the students would be oblivious to his victory or to his evil. As to why he was colored blue, Scott never had a clue.

None of this silliness about Satan is true.

Here's what Scott came to know about the devil.

First of all, he does not hide out in the barrens seeking refuge in beds of pine needles and eating the heads off live chickens; he roams the streets of Trenton and your town looking for weakness to exploit, virginity to deflower and holiness and purity to corrupt. He wants everyone to go around fighting or fucking each other and giving themselves over to flesh. He wants you and your children to shoot drugs with syringes. He is the main slave trader and the kingpin of all drug dealers. He is malevolence.

The devil drives around in expensive cars and he bangs Victoria's Secret models. He has sex with the most attractive men and women in his Jacuzzi at one of his several mansions. All the money in the world belongs to him and he is empty with hate.

Satan is beautiful; the most bright shining of all the angels; chief musician, and most beloved of all created beings. But he is vanity and jealousy. The prophet Isaiah described his conceit saying "How you have fallen from heaven, O morning star, son of the dawn. You said in your heart 'I will raise my throne above the stars of God . . . and I will make myself like the most high."

He wants you to worship him but he'll settle for you worshiping yourself, anything as long as you're not worshiping God. He would rather you masturbate than pray. Such is the nature of the beast and his repudiation of God.

In the book of Luke, Jesus says "I saw Satan fall like lightening from heaven." 10:18

Lucifer is his true name. It means bearer of light, but the bible calls him the father of lies. (John 8:44) "the truth is not in him, when he lies, he speaks his native language."

He may or may not be the color blue.

But whatever color he is, he hates you.

Let us go now to the fabled home of the devil in the New Jersey Pine Barrens. Lets pay the wasteland a visit and have us a look around. We see nothing here except for miles and miles of scrub pines and dead trees, here and there, there are clearings of blackened earth where fire came and mercifully wiped away sections of the ugliness. The charred places could actually be looked upon as improvement. We see, however, no signs any beautiful fallen angels nor any tracks of a goat-man walking upright on its hind legs. The only evil we are likely to see may be found in the hearts of the men, soldiering the bases of Fort Dix or Maguire Air force base, but they are still several miles away.

Let us not let this lack of evidence convince us that Satan does not exist; he's out there, somewhere. But for now, he's nowhere to be found on this God forsaken ground.

We come to a clearing in the trees and a deserted highway that scars across the scraggly life of this desolate landscape. Route 206 breaks the nothingness and anywhere it leads has got to be better than here. Whether it's a road to redemption or a road to perdition depends, I guess, on who's traveling it and where they're going. But among its other purposes, 206 connects Trenton to the casinos of Atlantic City like an evil umbilical cord feeding greed and flesh and despair.

If we happen to be on the side of the road at 2:30 in the morning, (and we probably are because, as everyone knows, it's best to go devil hunting at night when its dark) we see a set of headlights approaching us. The posted speed limit is 55 but this guys cruising at close to 80. The music that comes blasting out of the truck as it passes is a song off Nirvanas 1993 album In Utero "Hey! Wait! I got a new complaint!" Kurt Cobain's "heart shaped box" came slicing through the silence like a razor knife through the flesh of somebody's forearm. "Forever in debt . . . ."

Perhaps at this point, the loud music jars us back to our senses and we decide to give up our quest for the world's stupidest urban legend. Perhaps even, we decide to hitch a ride with the two guys that just drove by. We listen in on their conversation as we cruise with them back to Chambersburg. Back to Alan's new home on Division Street in the heart of Trenton.

Scott turned down the music and looked at his Uncle. "I can't believe I let you talk me into this again." The 'this' that Scoot was referring to was him taking his car payment, grocery money, and weekly gas funds and wasting them on drugs and gambling. The 'again' part was referring to the fact that he had also done this last Friday night.

"You should be thanking me. You needed this. You're always so stressed out about things, Relax. Stop worrying so much about the future and enjoy the moment." Alan sparked up the second half of a treated blunt that they had smoked before going into the casino and losing their whole paychecks.

As the smell of fresh marijuana permeated the air in the cabin and coated over the odor of old pot smoke and stale cigarettes, Scott thought back to how the adventure had begun.

Friday at work had been particularly shitty. Alan and Scott both worked for a maintenance company owned by Scotts father and Alan's brother, Henry. The old man was in a rotten mood that day and in between insulting them for being druggies and threatening to beat both their asses, he tried to tell them how badly they needed Jesus. It was hard to say which was worse.

Some people never know when to shut up.

Anyway, by the time they got their checks, the two dudes had the worst case of the 'fuckit's' imaginable. They drove out to Burlington to see the Wascally Wabbit and spent a couple of hundred dollars each on cocaine. (Alan already had the weed.) Then they stopped at a liquor store and bought some rum, soda, cigarettes, and a blunt. The soldiers were ready for battle.

And they got twisted on route 206 on their way to the bad town, to the city on the Atlantic. Heading there everything was electric with excitement and anticipation of fun. Surely this time they were destined to win some money. Surely it was not ordained that they should leave here broke two weeks in a row. They would not go home empty handed again.

And they began the feeding frenzy of the greed of the beast of the disease of the machines. (Huh?) Well you know what I mean.

This is the arduous part of destiny; trying to decipher it from all the bullshit. What is God's will and what are Satan's lies. A good rule of thumb seems to be that God usually wants us to sacrifice and suffer and the devil wants us to have fun. It's deceptively simple to say that Satan wants us to party and the Lord wants us to deny ourselves of our flesh and our narcissism.

Scott and Alan must have lost this battle. They drove home broke, broken, and mentally crispy. Thoughts turned slowly over in their minds and they continued to chase that illusive perfect high.

Now it was Alan's turn to speak, "I can't believe those bastards cheated me again. Those no good mother fuckers. Just watch Chip, we'll get them next week, I personally guarantee it."

Scott laughed as he stepped harder on the gas and picked the speed up to about 85. "You know I really believe that you may be retarded. There is definitely something wrong with your mind." Neither one of them paid any attention to the set of headlights that were approaching them out of the darkness on the horizon.

It was the beginning of an unfortunate chain of events. As the dudes passed the blunt back and forth, it had begun to boat (burn unevenly) and the cherry (the fiery part) fell onto the seat and started to burn the fabric. Our hero's attention was momentarily distracted from the road as they drove and Alan tried to extinguish the nasty cherry. Sparks flew as he patted out the glowing combination of cocaine, devil weed and car seat. By the time the duo looked up, the car was passing them from the opposite direction on their left. Alan caught a glimpse of it.

"Was that a cop? I think that was a cop!"

"No way. What are the chances that the first car we've seen in twenty minutes would be a cop?"

That's when the blue and red lights went on and they saw the squad car make a u-turn in their rear view mirrors.

What happened next happened in perfect unison.

Scott looked at his Uncle and Alan looked at his nephew and at the same time they exclaimed "O shit" Then, as simultaneous as if it had been choreographed, they both rolled down their windows. If it had been a race, there would have been no clear cut winner. But the wind came blasting in and blew out the cloud of smoke.

Alan flicked the treated blunt roach out into the shrubbery on the side of the road, somewhere in the New Jersey Pine Barrens. Unfortunately the smell of pot clung to their clothes and the upholstery like an evil spirit that refused to be exorcized.

And so Scott pulled over to await the judgment of the lawman. As the cruiser pulled up behind him, the blue and red lights lit up the night and strobed on all the surrounding pines. The scene was surreal, heightened in Scotts mind by the mild hallucinatory effects of the marijuana and the crisp alertness of too much cocaine.

Wired, Alan looked over at him from the passenger seat, pearls of wisdom dripping off him, he offered this advice. "Be cool." This translates into "try to act like you're not stoned out of your gourd."

The cop approached the driver's side of the truck with his left hand on his flashlight and his right resting on the grip of his nine millimeter.

"Is there a problem officer?"

"License, registration, and proof of insurance."

Yes. Scott actually had all of these documents. Technically he hadn't paid his insurance payment for several months and his policy was probably cancelled but since he had his proof of insurance card, chances were good that the cop would not be able to check that. Maybe things would be alright after all. Scott handed over the paperwork.

"Could you step out of the car, sir?"

"Sure, is there a problem, officer?"

"Yes, sir, I smell marijuana in the vehicle."

(Damn it! Damn it all to hell!)

Scott got out of his truck and followed the cop to the back of the pick up where he was ordered to drop the tail and have a seat. Then the brilliance of the law of the barren land began to show through. "Were you smoking marijuana?" A question.

(Are you serious?) "Ahh, yes officer, yes we were. We had a little bit back at the casinos in Atlantic City."

The cop's face lit up and he beamed as if he had just cracked the case of the century. His look said "I knew it! My keen detective skills have served me well again." Before he went to get Alan out of the truck, he looked at Scott and said "Wait here."

"Yes sir, you're the boss." Scott began stroking his ego immediately for he knew that police are egotistical and stupid. He knew that cops were easy to manipulate because they are not used to thinking for themselves. They, like most Christians, just do as they are told and they believe they are doing right by simply obeying other people's orders or ideas blindly. They've learned to never question anything. Mindless followers following mindlessly.

Scott and Alan had an exceptionally strong hatred for police, but this guy was not smart enough to sense that these two men were patronizing him. Alan came around to the back of the truck and joined his nephew. There, the two antiheroes pretended to be in total admiration of the lawman and his fascinating job. They really poured it on thick, the reverence, the compliments, the respect bordering on worship. This, of course, was total bullshit but the cop ate it like it was a sandwich and Alan and Scott played him using a method very similar to the Jedi mind trick.

"You have the gun, officer, you're in charge. When I have the gun I'll be in charge."

The Sherlock Holmes in 'Cleetus' jumped to the surface and the super sleuth thought he detected a threat. "Do you have a gun, sir?" Always with the sirs.

"No, I guess that's why I've never really been in charge."

Cleetus actually laughed out loud at that and the two burn outs knew that they were basically off the hook. Once you make a guy laugh, he likes you, and once he likes you, it's harder for him to ruin your life. They were just three white boys hanging out in the barrens at night. O the comradery.

The only problem was that while Cleetus was still chuckling with his new friends, his back up had arrived. Another cruiser pulled up behind him, adding more blue and red lights to the party.

Cleetus regained his composure and went over to report to the Sergeant. "Evening, Sarg. I pulled these guys over for speeding, but then I smelled marijuana in the vehicle."

The Sarg was standing at least thirty feet from the cab of Scott's pickup, but he said "Yeah, I can smell it from here. Good work."

Now maybe you're not familiar with the racial profiling that used to go on in the garden state, but I think it's safe to say that had Scott and his Uncle been black, these good old boys would have had their hands cuffed behind their backs and at the very least arrested them. Maybe even roughed them up a little. Because of their blue eyes, blonde hair, and white skin, the yokels had no way of knowing that they were dealing with a couple of nigers from Trenton.

"Your free to go" said the Sarg "Drive safe, fellas, and have a nice night."

And just like that the two cops got back into their cars, shut off their lights and drove off. Leaving the two dudes sitting in the dark on the tail bed of Scott's truck.

A cool breeze blew down the 206 corridor, down the tunnel of trees. The light show was over and now only the full moon illuminated the night. After the adrenaline rush there was a sense of peace. They were not arrested and they were relieved. Scott said a silent prayer, thanking God for his protection and his divine intervention. For keeping him once again from being apprehended. It did not seem to be the Lords will for Scott to ever go to jail. Scott thought of the many times he could have been busted but wasn't. He reflected on God and was quiet and reverent.

Alan's thoughts went in another direction.

"Fucking Fagots! I hate cops!" He spit on the ground where the cop car had been parked a minute earlier. He started walking back to the passenger door "Come on, let's get out of this fucking wilderness."

"Amen" said Scott as he was snapped out of his prayer. He took one last look around the pines as he went back to the driver's side. Out of the corner of his eye, he thought he saw a weird goat man watching them from between the trees in the moonlight. When he looked back it was gone. It was probably only a figment of his imagination, an illusion brought on by sudden absence of swirling police lights. Maybe it was a hallucination brought on by too much drugs.

It was never really there . . . Or was it?

Anyway, the two stoners drove off towards home. They followed the posted speed limit for a few miles before the lessons learned from Cleetus and the Sergeant were forgotten and Scott resumed speeding. They finally came out of the barrens and made their way through Bordentown. Here they followed the speed limit again because, as everyone knows, Bordentown cops are the biggest pricks alive. They weren't as concerned about the Trenton police because they never really seemed to bother them. Presumably they were out fighting real crime.

And route 206 eventually bled into Broad. They made a left onto it at the Whitehorse circle and cruised down toward Division Street.

They passed four liquor stores on their way, but only one church. Indicative, of life in Trenton. If you walked down Broad Street, you were much more likely to run into a gang member or a prostitute than a righteous man or a Godly woman, and if you took that one righteous man or Godly women and put their life under a microscope you would find filth. All of man is lowly; this my God has shown me. See Romans 3:23

Anyway, they passed the Getty station where the young bloods were riding their bikes and selling drugs in the "open air" and they came to Division at last and turned right.

The row houses lined either side of the street. They were packed tightly together, except for here or there where one was torn down after bank foreclosure or a fire had caused it to become condemned and then demolished. Usually, these were crackhouses or brothels that were ripped out of the row like a rotten tooth that had to be pulled. The absence was obvious, urban blight, and an eyesore. Patches of unhealthy looking grass grew sparsely here and there on these vacant lots and the lots provided the perfect place for kids to come and get laid, wasted, or to have their after school fist fights.

People looked out of their second and third story windows like prisoners watching from their tiers. They sat inside their little cells and they watched. It was all very exciting, though helplessly hopeless, everything seemed very ugly and sad and on the verge of chaos. And where was the Lord? And where were the cops?

Alan and Scott went into the house to smoke some more pot, for it seemed to help. They sat in the living room and Alan got to twisting the shit up. Then, when Scott least expected it, there came a knock at the door and he would soon meet the girl who would change his life forever.

Alan answered the door and Kelly came inside without being invited. She was hysterically crying. Scott heard her in the hallway before he ever saw her. "Uncle A A Alan" she said "They took my money and and and they, they left me." She sounded really upset and she was hyperventilating.

Scott wondered who this girl was, why was she crying so hard, and why was she calling Alan her Uncle like she was part of the family? Scott had been with his Uncle everyday for the last couple of weeks and he had never seen nor heard of this girl.

Now, let's take a moment to investigate the phenomenon of crying, what we are taught about it in Trenton. Men, in general, are taught that it's best to build up walls against their emotion and that crying is a sign of weakness. Whatever happens, you don't cry, you build a bridge and get over it. If you get hurt, dumped, wounded, or depressed, you suck it up. We say "man up dog!" Only if someone you really loves dies are you free to cry. (Pets included I suppose, thinking back to hillbilly Peter and his display over the loss of his dog.) This is how we show we are tough and this is the mentality that has fucked us all up.

And the women in Trenton know that the men in Trenton don't know how to deal with emotions and they manipulate this knowledge to their advantage. They become actresses and their tears are their weapons.

Kelly came in crying and Scott looked into her eyes. Big, beautiful, greenish, brown eyes, wet with tears and shining. And all was lost.

The two dudes were totally out gamed. Kelly played their heartstrings like a violinist. They began to cater to her, anything to make her stop crying. If they had had any money left they probably would have handed over their wallets. They offered her the only things they had left to offer, to appease her. In this case, coffee and marijuana.

"We were about to smoke a joint, wanna smoke with us?"

The transformation was amazing. "A aa . . . O.K." And the hyperventilating stopped in two heartbeats. The crocodile tears evaporated in seconds and she totally regained her composure. It was as if the whole production had been an act designed to get the guys to get her high.

Scott smiled. She was a con artist who would use any method at her disposal to get what she wanted. She was kindred. Her brownish blonde hair flowed down to her shoulders and it was possible that Scott loved her already.

This is the story of the twisted courtship of Scott and Kelly.

Initially there was the eye contact, the flirtation, and the flattery that went along with any budding romance. The things we say and do to get into a girls pants. But some love grows faster on drugs and for them the cocaine was the fertilizer and the aphrodisiac.

Kelly was afflicted with narcissism of her own and she was insatiable. No matter how much drugs or sex Scott fed her she could not stay high or satisfied. They shared the same disease, the same demons. They were equally fallen.

The way they played the game was like this. While Scott was at work, Kelly would go to his connections and get their pills fronted. (Advanced to them on Scotts credit) She did this because she knew that Scott was addicted too and that after work he would want his Percocet, Darvocet, Fentynal, Oxycottin, morphine, whatever. (They called painkillers, pancakes) At the end of the day Scott would find her, turn her on, and pay for everything.

Kelly was also friends with Scott's cousin Alison. And the two of them would go over to Ali's mom's apartment in Morrisville to party. Come with me now to Scott's Aunt Audrey's place in Pennsylvania.

Aud lives here with her three daughters, Alison, Veronica, and Rebecca. All four of these women are blessed with beauty, blonde hair and blue eyes. They are all also cursed with the blood of "Crazy Chris" Bradley. The patriarch.

If we step into the apartment, as many men have, the first thing we notice is the smell of femininity. It is not the scent of perfume and flowers that greets us, but a more shocking aroma. It is baser, more human, and therefore much more arousing and erotic. We inhale the scent of wet towels, sweat, girl piss and yes, the ever present scent of marijuana. These are the smells of Scotts cousins and his Aunt, the females in his bloodline, his family. They are always hungry and in this place there is always a party.

Scott and Kelly spent a lot of time here at the inception of their relationship because Kelly felt comfortable here. Audrey's was a flop house for all her daughters' friends. Drug addicts were attracted to this place, and there were lesbians, go-go dancers, and nymphomaniacs.

All of naughty Audrey's daughters were born from different men. But let us save our boring misogynist moral judgment and condemnation and thus not become hypocrites. Suffice it to say Audrey and all her girls were stunning and men and women came to them like bees to honey.

This is the female lure that I would now like to explore. The seduction of beauty that attracts us, then provokes us to respond, and then persuades us to submit. It is the power of her flower and it's pistillate.

Scott has seen man after man fall, corrupted by his lechery. Unable to resist the fallacy that he was just too weak to stand in the face of such over powering beauty. Brother after brother has crumbled in his self destructive lust to rub up against something pretty.

The ancient Greeks called the goddess of beauty and desire and love Aphrodite. We call anything that makes us horny an Aphrodisiac.

The Romans called her Venus, naming her after the brightest planet in our solar system. While she is the brightest, she is second in distance to the sun, perhaps the source of all feminine jealousy. From Earth, Venus with all her luster resembles a star that seems to herald in the dawn.

She is called the Morning star or Lucifer, the name of the fallen angel.

Could the brilliant giver of light, and the great deceiver really be a woman?

Maybe it's neither male nor female, a neuter, or maybe it's both at the same time, whatever it needs to be to beguile. Maybe even the great evil entices women in a different way than it seduces men.

In any case, Venus is also another name for the Dionaea Muscipula, a carnivorous plant known as the flytrap. The Venus flytraps flowers are unremarkable, unimpressive in comparison to other flora in botany, but at the apex of her leaves, she spreads herself open to feed. Her lips not unlike the labium or the vulva of a woman. Soft and alluring, sinfully sweet. Maybe she even releases pheromones into the air to attract her prey. No one really knows what causes the trap to snap closed. The flytrap has no nervous system, nor muscles, nor tendons. Certainly she is as mysterious and crafty as a woman. Her lies are soft and pink and deadly, irresistible to the flies, irresistible to the men.

The warmest place in the world is inside a girl.

Kelly sat on the edge of Aunt Audrey's bed. Scott watched her as she stared at the t.v.

He sat close to her, their legs were touching. His heartbeat raced and his mind could not help wondering down her body and wanting. Why was he so nervous? How should he proceed to make his move? Was she even thinking about being with him?

Then Kelly turned and looked at him with those beautiful eyes and said perfectly calmly," Show me what you kiss like."

And "With persuasive words she led him astray and seduced him with her smooth talk. All at once he followed her, like an ox to the slaughter, like a deer stepping into a noose till an arrow pierces his heart, like a bird darting into a snare, little knowing it would cost him his life." (Proverbs 7:21-23 NIV)

He leaned into her and kissed her deeply and she kissed him back sweetly. He ran his fingers through her hair and put his hands on her face, tenderly feeling her cheeks as he tasted her mouth with his tongue. As they fell back on the bed, her flavor was that of cigarettes and cocaine. She tasted bitter as medicine and she was as benumbing as the narcotics. There was a euphoria to the girl. Kelly was Scott's nasty idjit personified; a living breathing female version of his drug addiction.

Scott reached to touch her under her shirt, but Kelly pulled away. At first, he thought he had done something wrong or maybe that she was being a tease, but when he looked at her again he saw that her face was all red from his unshaven face scratching her.

"Go home and shave." she said

And here's where it started I think. Scott did what she told him, he went right home, shaved his face, got some more money for drugs and came back. Desperate to please her, he was like a lovesick puppy. This set a dangerous precedent for the rest of their relationship. Scott chasing after Kelly the insatiable, sacrificing everything to be with her.

Yeah, sure he came back to Audrey's and embraced her and bedded her. For the purposes of decorum we could say that they made love, but that wasn't quite it. What they did was more primal and carnal. Like animals.

Lest you believe that Scott was some big bad wolf who came down and drugged her and snatched her virginity, you should know that Kelly already had a son.

His name was Dylan and he was a beautiful little boy who looked as if he could have been Scotts. The kid had blonde hair and the same complexion. Once Scott took him and his mother to a Trenton Titans hockey game and the woman behind them said "I'm trying to decide if he looks more like his mother or his father (meaning Scott)"

This sparked something inside him and his vanity and he knew that Kelly must give him his own children. From then on Scott tried to impregnate Kelly every time he took her. It didn't take him long, for he had very potent seed.

Kelly told him that she was pregnant one night in the middle of a fight. Scott apologized to her for whatever he was arguing with her about. Suddenly everything was his fault. If Kelly had been hard to please before, now that she was carrying his baby she was downright impossible.

Still, Scott let her get away with it because he was overjoyed at the thought that he was going to become a father. He had no doubt that his child would be a son, a beautiful boy and that he and Kelly would reconcile all their differences for the sake of the baby. Surely they would learn how to love and then they would become a family.

What happened instead was that the fighting grew worse and sometimes Kelly would disappear overnight. It was a blow to Scott's pride that he could not control his women. She continued to want drugs throughout her pregnancy and Scott fed her addiction because he had his own demons to feed. And the world started spinning, and he was afraid of the future and he started to get dizzy. He thought crazy, irrational thoughts like, "the baby will come and force us to change, Kelly will be a great mommy and the baby will save me."

Instead, after a fight over drugs and money, Kelly disappeared for a week. Scott worried about her and the baby constantly. In a way, he loved her, though he wanted to punch her. Where the hell was she with his kid?

Then, on January 28, 2003, she called him from her mom's house on Division Street.

"Chip, it's me. I'm sorry; I had to go away and try to clear my head out. Are you mad?"

"I was worried about you and the baby. Are you O.K?"

"I'm fine, I'm at my mom's" She was starting to cry. "Chip, I . . . I'm sorry . . . I, I had a miscarriage . . . . I lost the baby."

Scott felt as rejected as the devil expelled from heaven and he cried out in pain, from the cold denial of his child, his blood and his vanity. "How fucking dare you do this to me!" He was cursing God on high, not Kelly. He screamed in his head silently.

Kelly spoke on softly into the phone. She had said it was a miscarriage, but he knew it was an abortion. She still wanted to be his girlfriend so she got scared and she lied.

"It's gonna be alright baby. I'll always love you, we can try again when you're ready."

Hesitation and then "Can you bring me something?"

"Yeah. I'll be over in a minute."

As Scott hung up the phone, the tears swelled up in his eyes. They raced each other down his face and he sat there a moment and he cried.

Chapter 4

Ariel Elizabeth
(written in the valley of sickness)

H E COULD NOT remember if it had been raining, snowing, or sunny on the greatest day of his life. Nor could he think back and tell you exactly what day of the week it was. I suppose he could easily look into the records and find out if he wanted, but really, it was irrelevant; pedantic.

What Scott could remember were new sounds and new smells. One sonance in particular was the sweetest noise his ears had ever heard. It was blissfully burned into his brain, inculcated into his memory, an imprint, he could never forget. It spoke to his soul about hope. Heaven and angels, and love. But we'll return to that sound later, for now, what Scott's nostalgia was reminiscing about was the smell.

It was the scent of soft soap and detergent, the hygienic aroma of disinfectant, sanitation, and cleanliness. Scott came to associate this smell with new born babies and the neonatal intensive care unit at Mercer hospital. He remembered the sterilization sink and using his teeth to tear open prepackaged iodine sponges used especially for scrubbing your hands before handling the babies. He also remembered stepping on a rubber pump underneath the sink and squirting foamy soap through this flexible plastic tube and into his hands. He forgot what that soap was called, but he did remember having to watch the clock and scrub his dirty fingers for a full one minute before he was clean enough to enter the sanctuary of new life. Was he more like a priest getting ready to enter the holiest of holies or more like a surgeon prepared to cut into some patient and poke around in their insides? Scott considered this and it didn't matter. Either way it was important to kill all the germs and bacteria before going into the room with all the babies.

Surgical masks were even available to prevent the spread of influenza.

The hospital that Scott was now in was not the same one that he went to for all his stitches, x-rays, drug overdoses or other such traumas. That hospital, while being a part of the same capitol health systems was on Brunswick Ave and this one was in the Hiltonia section of Trenton, sandwiched between Bellevue Ave and Rutherford. While it is true that both hospitals display the same general disrespect for the poor and uninsured, Scott had happier memories of his times at the Mercer campus. It was the hospital that he and his mother had been born in. Obviously he had no recollection of this, but this was the place where he first met his daughter. It was in this place that his baby was born.

If you were trying to drive to this hospital from Ewing, all you would have to do would be to come down Parkside Ave. off Olden. Once you got to Oakland, where Scott once came running out of the ghetto with his face pulverized, you would be getting pretty close. Next, you'd come to the intersection of Stuyvesant Ave, you would want to keep going straight here because if you made a right at Cadwaulder park, you'd be going the wrong way and if you made a left you might get carjacked, shot at or beaten. In fact it is entirely possible that you might just vanish in the blight, never to be heard from again. Sometime after the riots of 1968 set downtown Trenton aflame, this street and others like it became as dark and hardened as any you'll find in New York City or Baltimore.

The homes that line the sides of Stuyvesant Ave. are big townhouses that, legend says, used to be owned by doctors and lawyers. Rich Jews is usually how the story goes. Whether there's any truth to the legend, Scott never knew; it was before his time. But the buildings remain like vestiges. They are the boarded up, broken windowed ghosts of more hopeful times and glory gone transient. If it was true that this street once thrived, then something wicked must have come in and chased all the good people away because brothers sell drugs on the corners of this neighborhood today.

Let us go on to the hospital the slightly longer yet safer way. We come to the light at Bellevue and we bang a left. Up the hill and towards the hospital we go. We come to the intersection of N. Hermitage Ave. Again we stay straight, as a turn in either direction will lead us into another of West Trenton's badlands.

Finally we come to the hospital on the left and we pull into the parking lot. We push the button on the box by the mechanical arm and we receive our ticket. The divider lifts like the ones that protect us from the trains and we go in and find a spot. It's free to get in but to get out you always have to pay.

We walk across the lot and in the double doors. We say hello to the security guard who is friendly, fat and old. He gives us a clip on visitor pass and we make our way into the elevator. We push the button for two.

The double doors open and we are let out in the lobby of the second floor in between maternity and the NICU. We press the door bell to have someone buzz us in and as we wait, we can look through the window in the door and see Scott drying his hands. He rubs them together under the hot air of the blowing machine mounted on the wall by the sink.

All around him we hear the sounds of the subdued beeping of various machines; new born babies moaning softly in their sleep; nurses scurrying back and forth with bottles of breast milk or formula for feeding. Here and there, post-parturient mothers are holding their young ones, smiling and weeping.

And everything is so bright and antiseptic. Scott could not recall ever having been in a place that was so clean. It was a never ending battle against the microorganisms and bacteria that spread infection. Germ warfare, if you will. And oh how we hate those evil germs. Kill them all I say; bleach those bastards; drown them all in the chlorine.

What most people don't realize is that all of us originated from germs. We are just the evolution of such. A boy germ cell called spermatozoa meets a girl germ cell called ovum and they get together and grow. This is the process of germination, or conception, or impregnation.

Contrarily, the prevention of fertilization is called contraception. And the termination of germination is death or abortion. Nearly a year had passed since Scott and Kelly lost their first progeny to this painful process.

Scott thought about the nature of his creator. How does he know how things will grow? Which germs will become cancerous or viral, part of some disgusting disease? Which ones will grow to achieve angelicness, a beauty? How does he know which germs will grow to inherit a soul?

He continued to ponder the spirit of God and his holy ghost and how it must spend a great deal of its time in the hallowed halls of hospitals everywhere, on their respective second floors, where life so often begins and on other theoretical floors where it so often ends in a plethora of different deaths. He found it maybe even a little ironic how we celebrate birth, which is destined to live a life of disappointment and pain. And how we mourn for those dearly departed who have gone back to be with the Lord. We grieve for those who we believe are at peace; in a heaven unending.

It would not surprise Scott to someday discover that everything he ever learned from man about life and death and virtue had been entirely wrong. Furthermore, in spite of the fact that he believed God was ubiquitous, still he wondered if maybe this spirit wasn't somehow more contemporaneous on holy ground. Of the hospitals in general and Mercer in particular.

And was this spirit more in the church than it was in the hospital?

Kelly slept deeply in her bed in maternity, her chest rising softly as she was peacefully breathing. She slept in a blessed catharsis after the agony of childbirth and labor. Scott would never forget the look on her face; twisted and straining with pain. Or how helpless he had felt on that January morning. He knew that now and forever he would love her, she was his baby's mother. She would never understand what she had done for him.

He daydreamed further back to the night in late May, when in the backseat of his '98 Jeep, his daughter was conceived. He remembered the fogged up windows and the heat. Kelly moaning as they were wrestling and how sweetly she was sweating. His own sweat ran down his face in rivulets that dripped on her exposed skin as they convoluted and their passion intensified. They didn't kiss each other, they licked. He could remember peeling down her jeans and the jackhammer of his heartbeat. He ripped her panties off ravenously. They locked eyes and swam inside each other's minds. Kelly gasped when he entered her wetness and the sound of her misbreath almost drove him out of control. He lasted under three minutes if we are to speak veraciously. He ejaculated in the rapture of his climax and he slathered her uterus with his semen. The compartment was like a sauna and the two of them lay perfectly still. She seemed to have had an orgasm too, but Scott never knew. What was faked and what was true? He wanted to believe that they had come together, but whatever.

Even though Scott was incredibly attractive and virile, and the seed he implanted was stout and robust, he was still convinced that there was a divine miracle present in the scientifically explainable chemical reaction of germination. Of the millions of sperm swimming around in the ejaculi, only one of them could get at the woman's egg and impregnate her. Scott had to believe in something more precious than dumb luck in some genetic lottery. Obviously, the hand of God was involved in the selection.

Anyway the X and Y chromosomes of Scotts DNA struggled amongst themselves for survival in Kelly's womb. And of all of these, Ariel was the strongest. She was destined by fate or something greater to be his daughter.

Perhaps it is a sin for two young lovers to make a baby out of wedlock and the beautiful bonds of matrimony. Though Scott could not find where it says that in the bible. Maybe the reverends, priests, preachers and teachers are correct in their interpretation and definition of exactly what sexual immorality means. But there is a verse in Exodus 33 and again in Romans 9 that speaks about God, saying "I will have mercy on who I will have mercy and compassion on who I will have compassion." Certainly, the Lord blessed the birth of Ariel and if she was indeed conceived in sin, then maybe it was a venial one given it was late spring and they could sense the coming summer with its hunger and all . . .

After Scott slid out of Kelly and they had their inevitable moment of mitosis or fission, they wiggled up their jeans. Two again, they got dressed. Then, they went into Aunt Audrey's apartment (they had been parked outside her place) to smoke some weed and party. Kelly got high throughout her pregnancy. Truth be told, neither of them really even slowed on the coke and they ate painkillers (pancakes) to stay above the sickness constantly. Their life and their love were dedicated to the numbness of self and to analgesia, anesthesia and drug induced euphoria.

Ariel Elizabeth spent 8 months in the womb of this narcissism.

If it wasn't for some intervention from God, Ariel might have suffered some ill effects from the nicotine and narcotics that she was nourished with. I guess that's why they say that Gods grace is sufficient. Even in the grip of his addiction and sin, Scott knew that he needed to trust in the lord because the baby was in his hands. After all, the baby would belong to God more than it ever would to him. Scott in his narcosis put this fleece before the Lord. Scott had faith that God would send him an angel.

When his daughter was born at four o'clock in the morning his sleepy eyes would elate to adulation, weary anticipation would become jubilance and the spirit of God fill the delivery room with a presence that was energy; supernatural and electric. This presence was holy and it was the closest Scott had ever come to understanding its nature and purity. It was also the closest he ever came to true bliss and happiness. Try as he might he could not hold onto it.

Scott, like so many men, tried unsuccessfully to relive a few chosen well lived days over in his mind. It was his way of escaping pain and regrets that haunted him in his mind. Often he tried to return mentally to the NICU on that day in January 2004.

Regretfully, many memories faded off and were lost and some off the sweetest images were forgotten. Like waves wash the beach clean with their tides and erase footprints and sandcastles, so to rolls time robbing visions of their crispness.

So, too, it's true that many details got overlooked or distorted and the past is twisted and hazy. Memories are damaged or stolen by years of narcotics and television. Some of his reflections are sketchy at best. And imagination plays a perverse game with the sacred.

Still other experiences were branded on his heart with clarity. Things like the sound of Ariel's voice and the first time he saw her eyes, he was convinced he would remember these on his deathbed and beyond.

He would always remember the birth of his daughter.

Scott and Kelly got to the hospital one month and three days before her due date. Scott assumed that Kelly was merely pill shopping as usual and that this was just a false alarm. Indeed, while she was hospitalized, Scott brought her pain medication from the streets. Percocet's were nice little kickers to whatever the obstetricians had prescribed her.

Scott stayed overnights with her on a fold out cot beside her bed. The hospital staff even brought him his meals. Kelly had her adjustable bed and a remote control for the TV. They had their privacy and they smoked their cigarettes illegally in the bathroom. It was a little slice of heaven.

A beauty radiated off Kelly as she lay there with her big seductive eyes. She had tangles and knots in her long blondish bedridden hair. She could never seem to comb these away completely and Scott could recall how she brushed her hair obsessively. She was always so concerned about girlish things like split ends and she always said that she and he would always be best friends.

Scott put his head on her chest. He could hear her heartbeat and feel the softness of her baby inflated boobs. He put his hand on her belly. He could feel the baby kicking as he kissed Kelly on her tummy. I won't tell you exactly what was said but Scott talked to his unborn child.

This was so wild. They were both so immature. They were about to become parents and they were totally unprepared. Scott didn't know what he was supposed to do, so he just smiled. And prayed. He prayed to God for strength and that his baby would be born OK.

Scott held his girlfriends hand when the pain came and the doctor untied her flimsy hospital gown and exposed the bare skin of her sweet little ass crack. Kelly leaned forward and looked into her boyfriends eyes, squeezing his hand as the doctor injected a gigantic syringe of some kind of analgesic epidural for pain. Her eyes glossed over with high and she relaxed and laid back. Her head rolled to one side and she fell asleep. She seemed to be at peace.

Scott's mom and dad came to the hospital to be there for the birth of their grandbaby. Scott's daughter would be their first and they were rightly excited. They loved her already. They adored her before she was even born. But as the night wore on and the labor slowed and there were no signs of contractions on the EKG monitor, it became obvious that Ariel wasn't coming until tomorrow. Scott's parents reluctantly went home.

Apparently, God had reasons for wanting them to be alone.

After they left, Scott kissed Kelly's forehead and then lay back in his makeshift bed beside her. He grabbed her hand and then he closed his eyes.

When he awoke to the commotion, it was 3 AM and it took him a minute to remember exactly where he w as. Kelly's cervix had dilated to the point where his angel was ready to be born. Until a day or two ago, he was not even sure what a cervix was, although he thought it had something to do with your neck.

Anyway, the nurse in the room looked between Kelly's legs and said "OK I see the head! Don't push! I'm going to get the doctor." With that she ran out of the room.

Scott's heartbeat went prestissimo, near tachycardia, and whether the nurse got lost, couldn't find the doctor, or stopped for coffee, I don't know. But no one came back for several minutes. Again, it was as if the Lord willed them to be alone.

There was a tingly spirit present with them, Scott felt it. It was impossibly invisible and yet coruscated. Mysterious, illogical, and intelligent, it felt like wind.

In this solitary time, Ariel slid out of her mother and was born in a puddle of blood and fluid which ruined the white sheets of hospital linen forever.

Scott was the first to lay eyes on her. She was curled in a fetal ball in the mess and she was all wrinkly and purple. She was still connected to her mother by the umbilical cord which was an unnatural looking yellow; something that he had not been expecting. The color contrast between the yellow cord, the purple baby, and the red gore was startling. Scott's senses overloaded and he went into near shock and he stared at his daughter, shaking.

It was as if someone had pushed the pause button on the movie of his life. He couldn't move. There was no way this was really happening. His heart slipped into arrhythmia and his breath to momentary apnea. This was the total discomfort and panic of true bliss and happiness.

And then the doctors and nurses exploded into the room and Scott was pushed back into the periphery. He stood on his tippy toes to look over the shoulders of the obstetrician and the mid-wives. None of them seemed to notice the presence of the holiness which was flooding his brain with pure euphoria.

They handed Scott a pair of shiny, sterile, silver, scissors and instructed with where to ceremonially cut Ariel's umbilical cord. On the first attempt the rope sliced and slid between the blades, popping out, still connected by a thread and not completely cleaved. He snipped it clean and it severed on the second scission.

And the baby was physically free from all the bad habits of her mother. She would however, forever be ambivalently blessed and cursed with the genes of her beautiful, bi-polar mommy and with the blood of her father;

a heredity of heresy; of ever questioning. Some things were passed to her in the chromosomes, written in her genetic code, and carried in the very corpuscles of her hemoglobin. For better or worse, they were who she is.

The two narcissists had created a baby and God had made her an angel. And there was no doubt that God would always be there watching over her, protecting her and loving her.

Since Ariel was premature, the doctors were required to take her immediately to the neo natal intensive care unit. Scott suspected that they did this with every new born as a precaution but he may have been mistaken about that. Anyway, they put his daughter in an incubator to keep her warm and to help her fight off the jaundice. They put a little mask over her eyes to shield her baby blues from the harsh light of the heater and the hospital fluorescence. It looked like a smaller, softer version of the mask that Batman or Zorro wore, minus the eyeholes. They assured him everything was fine as he watched them wheel her out of the delivery room.

He turned to look at Kelly; his babies momma. It looked as if someone had slaughtered an animal between her legs. There was blood on her inner thighs and it mixed with amniotic juice and saturated the sheets with gore. There was a slight fetid scent to the vinaceous mess but it was ambrosial. He found this image beautiful and not the least bit disgusting. This was the most intimate moment yet, and he felt closer to her than ever. Kelly laying there exposed, ultra feminine, if you will. And would it be a sacrilege to suggest that Scott found it arousing and, dare I say, sexy?

He leaned over her again and kissed her forehead. He probably said something tender like "You did Kel. You made us a beautiful baby girl" or something along those lines. He could not remember.

He saw the redness and wetness in her eyes and she was still crying, though now she was also smiling. Whether it was from happiness or pain, Scott couldn't say, but for once in their relationship, he had no doubt that those tears were real.

The midwives asked him to wait outside the room for the afterbirth of the placenta and so they could clean up Kelly's girl parts and dispose of the hemorrhaged linens. Out in the hallway, Scott leaned with his back against the wall and he at last had a moment to think. He wiped his eyes, for he discovered that he too had been crying. He thought about his baby's momma and how he would love her forever. They were connected now joined before God in a way that not even marriage could bind them. He thought about this and he smiled.

His romantic baby name for her was Kelly Bella. Bella from belladonna, which is Italian for beautiful lady. Belladonna, ironically, is also a poisonous plant known as the deadly nightshade. Medically, it is used to stimulate the heart and to relieve pain. Kelly was a similar drug. Scott assumed that if you took too much of it, it would corrupt your system and kill you. The same could be said of his girlfriend; metaphorically.

Ariel was not named after the little mermaid in the Walt Disney cartoon. Nor was she named after the Uranian moon. And while it is true that Ariel means Lion of God in Hebrew, and that will probably prove to be appropriate, that isn't where she got her name from either.

In 1984, Paramount pictures released the movie Footloose, starring Kevin Beacon, John Lithgow, and Lori Singer. In case you missed it, it was about a righteous preacher who was mourning the loss of his son to a car accident. In the movie, Reverend Shaw Moore's heart has become hardened and was his daughter, Ariel, who shows her father the virtue of being a free spirit and how to enjoy the gift of life that God has given. Ariel pulls her father from his depression and grief and opens his mind to new ideas. Through his love for his daughter he reluctantly finds joy and enlightenment. A lesson in theodicy.

It is this Ariel that Scott's daughter was named after.

There was much that Scott hoped to teach his little girl and much that he needed to learn from her. There are some things that no one else could tell her because no one else knows them. Things like, how much he wanted to have her, how he had hunted for her mother, how much he truly loved her. And what he'd come to discover about the nature of God and humanity that others seem to have missed. And how she was special, different. What no one else was capable of telling her about her blood.

There is a myth that it always takes babies, especially premature ones a few days before they are ready to open their eyes. Scott found that to be a lie. He remembered talking to Ariel when she was just born. He was surprised by the softness in his own voice as he spoke to her, and tried to reassure her that she was safe and that this world was a happy place. He may have said "Hi baby, it's your Daddy. It's OK, everything is alright, I love you very much." But he couldn't exactly remember.

What he would never forget however was that at the sound of his voice his angel opened her eyes. She looked at him for a few precious seconds before closing them again and going back to sleep. They were the purest blue that he had ever seen and they held mysteries of the future that Scott had never pondered for they were so deep.

Strictly speaking, in the NICU you're not supposed to touch the babies. They say it gets them too excited. But what do they know about the divine? Scott ran the backs of his fingers gently across his daughter's cheeks. With her eyes closed she couldn't see her daddy cry, but she made this soft little moan that seemed to say "I know I'm not alone." And maybe even "I love you too, Daddy." That sound was the sweetest noise he ever felt.

When he left Ariel and saw that Kelly was still sleeping in her bed, he decided to go outside and have a smoke. He was so ecstatic; his feet didn't seem to be touching the floor as walked down the hall passed the security guard. As he floated passed the guard must have perceived something magical had happened to him and he said "Congratulations, sir!"

"Thanks' he replied and he felt like he loved the guy.

He walked through the double doors and he stepped outside.

He breathed deep into his lungs and the air was sweet and fresh. God was good in his heaven and he wanted to savor this moment forever. But whether it was raining, snowing, or sunny, he could never remember.

C.S.W.

Chapter V

Love and Needles

THE VENOMOUS ANATHEMA entered the bloodstream with the ritualistic and familiar sting. The cursed thing moved slowly through the current as the flow of plasma flushed all around it. The hemoglobin swept the heroin away from the lonely embolus with a speed best measured in megahertz. It took the opiates on a rollercoaster ride through the venous tracks of the vascular system. It was carried through the heart and lungs. It was arterialized and headed for the brain. The dope was metabolized back into morphine and ready to come crashing through the defensive blood brain barrier and shut down the production of the endogenous endorphins. Once inside its only mission was to tickle the opiod receptors and get the whole system high.

Did you know that Morphine was named after the Greek god Morpheus, the god of sleep and dreams? Myth logically, Morpheus slept in a cave on a bed of ebony and his cave was surrounded by fields of poppies. The Papaver Somniferum, opium poppies, producers of morphine, so named because of their power to induce sleep and dreams.

Anyway, the evil embolus in the bloodstream was burning with infection, all down his forearm near the site of the injection. And the leucocytes attacked the embolus, which was a small fiber from a cigarette filter, like a gang of racist Aryans jumping an unwanted minority in their neighborhood. They swarmed and threw punches. The embolus did not go down without a fight. There was the burning pain of the "cotton fever" and Scotts whole left forearm and hand were inflamed. It felt like someone had thrown boiling water on his skin.

"God damn it, Kelly!" Scott screamed "You did it again! You rushed the shot and you put something in me!"

Kelly had shot him up hastily and now she was hurriedly fixing her own. "I told you, you should have let me go first, and then I wouldn't have been so shaky."

"No, because then you get all noddy and sloppy and then you'll miss. When you pay for the shit you can go first."

Kelly wasn't really listening.

"Aw Christ, Kel, look at my hand" It was swelling up like an inflated surgical glove. "I can't make a fist and it burns. I can't move my thumb! Are you happy now, Kelly? Congratulations, you've killed me!"

"You're not dying, Stop being such a pussy." She was always saying sweet things like that. She loaded the hypodermic needle with the brown junk and went intravenous in her right arm. She hit the vein on the second stab. She pumped in the solution and enjoyed the warm rush, then she clean up the fixin's before her mother came down stairs and caught them.

Scott was convinced that he was going to need to go to the emergency room but when the diesel set in, he just passed out on the couch instead. It was just another day on Division street, now that they were junkies.

Sigmund Freud said that all human behavior falls into one of two classes, the life instinct and the death instinct. The life instinct he called Eros after the Greek god of love and lust and intercourse. Erotic Eros sustained life by compelling people towards pleasure and reproduction. Eros was responsible for love, attraction, desire, and social behavior, and also for baser instincts like thirst and hunger and pain avoidance.

Freud said the other drive was darker. He named it Thanatos after the Greek god of death.

He said "the goal of life is death and that all people have an unconscious desire to die". Evidence of this could be seen in the destructive nature of man. He cited examples of violence and war.

Another example of this would have to be drug addiction.

All over, humanity is drawn towards habits that they know to be harmful to them. Everyday people wake up and dream of playing with substances that have the potential to kill them. You could call this a disease, like the alcoholics anonymous believe. Or maybe you think it's called sin, like the Christians. Or maybe you agree with Sigmund, that we are all secretly longing to die.

Freud was a man who liked his cocaine, and when he died, when he succumbed to his Thanatos drive, he called up his friend and had himself euthanized. His drug of choice? Yup, you guessed it. Heroin. Smack. Dope. Diesel. He overdosed on the hard stuff.

Scott too had this sinful, psychosomatic disease, only he called it "the nasty idjit" and wherever it came from, there was one thing he knew; the fucking thing was always, always hungry.

This hunger was the reason that Scott sat in his car one evening with the engine running on the corner of Woodland Street where it intersects with Anderson. In beautiful drug infested Chambersburg. He was waiting for Kelly to cop them some Oxycontin or Morphine, but he would settle for some Percocet or Vicodin if nothing else was available. Pancakes! Painkillers for their hypochondria

He saw his babies momma turn the corner in his rear view mirror as she headed back to the car. He read the look on her face as negative. She got in, shut the door, shook her head and said, "Nobody's got shit."

"Fuck. Are you serious?"

"The only thing I can find is coke . . . . and heroin."

"I'm not wasting the money on rock, Kel. We'll be wishing we had pills in an hour."

"Let's get the H then."

And so it was that they started snorting the light brown powder up their noses. Processed opium grown in the poppy fields of South America. Harvested, refined, and shipped from Columbia. Then it was imported to New Jersey, where the dope is the purest, and filtered down to street level guys who went by aliases. Brothers with initials for names; like R. S. J. and Q (Cue). Others with names like Shay, Scales, Black, and Shady. The drugs found their way into the hands of the black ghetto denizens. Guys like Pezzie and Wab. Destined to be incarcerated or shot.

And then there was Dahlia, beautiful as the blackest night, diva of the Trenton dope game, and queen of those addicted to needles in exchange for their souls.

They took the diesel with them back to the room they rented in Ewing. The division of youth and family services, in their infinite wisdom, had decided it was in the best interest of the child for Scott and Kelly to live elsewhere from Ariel. Ari remained at Scott's mother's house. D.Y.F.S. pronounced die-fus, was always making such generic and uninformed decisions about what was best for everyone else. From the first day of Ariel's life on, the state had its ignorant hands and ridiculous policies keeping Scott from being her Daddy. We'll discuss custody and hypocrisy later.

Anyway things were beginning to fall apart for Scott and Kelly. It was summer and their relationship and their spirituality were deteriorating fast. They were both feeling empty. They clung to each other in desperation, a dependency disguised as devotion. They called it love, but only the dope made them feel alright.

Kelly held up the loaded hypodermic and the needle twinkled in the sunlight shining through the second floor window. She asked him the question for the first time. It was a question he would hear many times before he learned how to hit himself. "Are you ready?"

He tied his belt around his left arm. A tourniquet. He constricted the belt with his right hand and he pumped his left fist. A few slaps to his forearm helped bring his veins up to the surface.

This was to be his first time intravenous. She was about to bust his drug cherry, heroin virginity.

And this leads us back to the blood.

Kelly pulled back on the plunger of the syringe and with it came a bloom of red inside the chamber. Junkies call this the rose. The rose lets you know when you're in. Then she pushed the mixture of shit into his left cephalic vein at the crease of his arm, inside the elbow.

The injection hit him in his shoulders first, they got warm and tightened. A copper metallic taste flooded his mouth. When his shoulders relaxed on his next breathe, his whole body, mind, and soul relaxed with them. The high was indescribable; wonderful. From then on Scott was infected. Infected with knowledge of a euphoria that should have remained unfelt. He slipped through the taboo of shooting drugs with needles and experienced a bliss that was purely self satisfying and evil. He would never forget that sensation, the sweetest he had ever known. The ultimate rush, the believable lie, the illusive, seductive perfect high was to be found by pumping the drugs right into the blood.

He could never go back to his chastity. Something within him got lost.

Bela Lugosi, portraying Dracula, quoted the bible saying "The blood is the life." That's Leviticus 17:14. And just like vampirism is a corruption of the soul through the blood, so to do heroin addicts taint each other through blood. Each is a form of abhorrence and blasphemy.

Kelly retracted the syringe from his arm and she smiled. She was his seductress, his succubus, his vampire.

Did you know that the first vampires of superstition were supposedly women? Most people tend to think about Bram Stoker and Dracula when they think about the origins of the nasferatu and the undead. Some think that Stokers' Count was based on the true life accounts of Vlad the Impaler. But actually Bram was probably more influenced by a woman who predated the Count by twenty five years.

There was a woman named Elizabeth Bethory. She was every bit as bloodthirsty as Vlad. She supposedly drank the blood of peasant girls. She

C.S.W.

thought she was stealing their beauty and fighting her ageing and maintaining her youth. She was a woman of considerable wealth; vanity and dementia. She went crazy in her narcissism and psychosis; she supposedly killed six hundred women back in the early 1600's. She predates Dracula by almost three hundred years and is probably a truer influence on Stokers Dracula.

One other thing, while we're on the subject. 25 years before Bram's book there was another story, which he would have read, that tremendously influenced his writing. It was called "Carmilla". It was written in 1872; Dracula 1897. Carmilla was an earlier vampire, definitely feminine; suspiciously lesbian.

Furthermore, if we investigate deeper, we will inevitably be lead to the supposed source of all bloodlust and find; to not too much surprise, that again, the root of the evil is feminine.

Our research leads us back to the beginning. Back to Eden, in the garden, Genesis and creation. To the story of the first man and woman. Biblically, the first man is said to be Adam, but according to the legend the first woman was not Eve but Lilith.

Lilith was made from the same Earth as Adam and created to be his equal. And Lilith was a woman that refused to be submissive to the man. She would not lay down missionary and let Adam nail her. They got in a big fight and she cursed him and ran away.

The story goes that God punished her for her disobedience and cast her out.

She is said to have become demonic and the first vampire. A succubus of vanity and vengeance, who seduced weak and lustful men like a black widow spider.

Legend says, her spirit comes and entices men when they sleep, sexually sucking the life force out of them. She is the erotic demon of wet dreams and she only appears to be giving herself. Really she's taking. Really she's draining. She comes in many forms and all of them sweet. All of them dirty. The young girl child. The prostitute. The slave. The married woman in heat. Lilith comes in every kind of forbidden sexual desire or taboo. Supposedly the succubus laughs hardest when she makes a pious man come. She likes to fuck with priests.

And when he wakes up alone sticking to his underwear and sheets . . . then Lilith is nowhere to be seen. And was she ever really there? Was she only just a dream?

I looked Vampire up in the Random House dictionary. The fourth definition said a vampire is a woman who unscrupulously exploits, ruins, or degrades the man she seduces.

Kelly looked at Scott with her beautiful angel eyes, although her eyes were sunken now with dark circles under them and anemic white skin. She watched him roll over on his side; benumbed.

Scott heard her laughing as he drifted away with the dope. He knew in his mind that she had done something unholy to him and that he would forever be changed. He was different now.

V is for vampire. And there are a couple of other comparisons between the nocturnal demons and the junkies. They both are narcissists who selfishly steal from and hurt others and they are both infatuated with death and inevitably progress towards delusion and insanity. Both seek to satisfy an insatiable greed and they both puncture veins to feed. They sell their souls and thus become infected with evil. They are dependent on sexuality and ecstasy and are enslaved by the fallacy of their needs. They may claim to be motivated by love, but the truth is that their affection is a lie, used to justify their lusts. Their lust of the glorious rush that can only be achieved by fucking with the blood.

And narcissism is just another word for sin, the root of all evil. Only when we learn to think of others more highly than ourselves do we addicts ever have any chance of recovery and only then do we truly understand love. Only then do we begin to understand the nature of Jesus Christ who was without narcissism or sin. Then we learn to transcend ourselves and receive God's enlightenment and gnosis. Only through the spirit can the sinner be redeemed.

Beautifully, we are also cleansed by the blood. By our savior purified, if you believe in that.

On the night that Kelly took Scotts I.V. virginity, they were in a room they rented in Ewing township. Wallace Avenue, that was. What his sweetheart had done to him was consensual and yet as immoral as statutory rape. He knew from the first hit that he had been changed. Heroin would be the only thing that could fix him now, nothing else would be the same. And did you know that Heroin was originally designed by the Bayer aspirin company to be less addictive form of cough suppressant and pain killer? Alanis Morrisette might call that ironic.

Anyway, that night Scott's friend Kenny came over to visit and to play chess. Kenny, who had wisely walked out of Hoffman Avenue before the beat down. He was not yet a lawyer in Trenton but he was every bit as intelligent and argumentative as one. Kenny was Scott's atheist friend and beloved nemesis. He knocked on the door and Scott came outside to talk with him. Kenny and Kelly did not get along. None of Scott's friends or family liked Kelly very much for that matter.

As they walked around the jeep parked in the driveway of one Wallace on a beautiful and soft summer night, Scott confided in his friend how he had taken the cursed initiation that would portend his downfall. He said "Well bro, it's over for me."

"What do you mean?"

"For thirty years I promised myself I would never do drugs with needles. Even through all the cocaine and painkillers, I would never shoot up. Never I said."

Kenny looked at his friend and said nothing, just patiently waited, listening.

"Tonight, she shot me up twice. It's dirty and disgusting and evil, but I like it." Then, as if to accentuate the point, Scott vomited all over the gravel of his driveway. He curled over and hurled on his front lawn. He wiped his mouth with his sleeve, laughed as if the shit was funny and then he said, "Excuse me." It was an event that foreshadowed the grim future, an omen of his addiction.

Kenny said "I don't like it Chip. You're going to end up like Chris." Referring to the Chris who abandoned him in the Miller Homes projects, the Chris who would later die in his parent's house of an overdose. Chris who was sad and tragic and funny. "He's a straight junkie, the guys going nowhere. Do you want to end up like that? You're smarter than that."

But what Kenny didn't realize was that for better or worse the decision had already been made.

When his friend left, disappointed, Scott went back inside to his room and his girlfriend. He didn't want wisdom or council and he didn't want sex. What he wanted from then on was another rush, another high, another fix, another needle.

Scott and Kelly had their adventures on the dirtier streets of New Jersey's capitol. Their relationship bloomed like a bloody rose on Chestnut Ave, Gennesse St., Home Ave, South Clinton, and Broad. And no matter how much money got spent or how many drugs got ingested, it was never enough to sate them. The highs they attained, like the love they claimed were temporal and fading.

Now let's fast forward a flash into the future, maybe three or four weeks and let us look in on the progress of the disease.

Scott wakes up alone, naked under his filthy sheets. His woman had been with him when he fell asleep. They had gotten pretty high and the sex had been particularly sweet. Now Kelly's side of the bed was cold; perhaps she had gotten up to use the bathroom or went outside for some air. He reached on the floor and found his underwear. After he slid them on, he grabbed his jeans, but he heard no familiar jingling of loose change or his car keys. He searched his pockets to find that he had indeed been robbed. He ran to the window and looked out at his driveway. Sure enough, his sweetheart had stolen his jeep. Since she was not licensed to drive this was very unwise. Scott was disappointed to say the least. His mind began to fantasize about the fantastic beating he was going to give her when she got her skanky ass back home. Compounding his anger was the fact that she had taken his cigarettes with her.

Could he get away with burying her in his backyard?

Surely no one from his family would miss her.

As Scott waited for his bella to come home, the minutes turned to hours, rage turned to worry, and worry eventually gave way to sleep. Kelly came home at close to four in the morning. She ran right into the shower to wash off what she'd done. She hurt him worse than he could ever hurt her with his fists when she went out, whoring for more.

This would be another drug induced war.

She slid under the covers beside him and he kicked her out of bed and onto the floor. "You're not fucking sleeping with me! Are you crazy?"

'What? Why?" She looked at him with those big innocent eyes and it seemed like she genuinely had no idea what she had done to make him so mad.

"Listen! Gimme my fucking keys, Kel. You can sleep on the floor like the dog that you are and in the morning you can find yourself a new place to live. I've fucking had it!"

Again she asked the same questions "What? Why?" Only now there was a hint of fear in her voice.

"What? Why? You can't be that fucking stupid Kel. Where'd you go until four in the morning, pumpkin? Where'd you go in my god damned car?"

Of course there were no answers to these questions and Scott in his rage and frustration went downstairs and outside to get his cigarettes and smoke. He needed to get away from her and calm down. After he had had his smoke he came back to the bedroom to go to sleep only to discover that the wonderful bitch had locked the door. It was almost the straw that broke the camel's back. "Kelly, you must be out of your mind locking me out of my own room! Open the god damn door!"

"No, you're being mean, Chip." She said this sweetly like she was an innocent victim.

That's when he snapped.

"I swear to God, Kel, open this door before I count to three or I'll kick it in and beat the piss out of you!"

"Stop yelling at me!"

"One . . . ."

"No, you're gonna hit me."

"Two . . ."

"Awright, awright, wait I'm coming."

"Three!" And Scott kicked open the door at the exact moment his sweetheart was opening it. The door snapped through the latch and swung on its hinges so hard that it knocked Kelly backward onto the bed. Her boyfriend was on top of her in a flash with his fists raised ready to punch her in his rage.

She covered up and cowered like a frightened child and Scott read the terror in her eyes. That was what saved her. He never threw a punch. He climbed off her, no longer screaming. Deflated, he said "I mean it. You're not sleeping with me. Over there on the floor. You're not my girlfriend anymore."

And, as usual, Kelly was crying. "I'm so sorry. I love you."

"I don't care."

But the girl she knew her part. She was so much better at manipulating. At playing the game. "If you leave me, I'll kill myself."

"So do it. I'll help you."

"I mean it."

"Who's stopping you?"

So Kelly went into the drawer and took out a brand new bottle of Benadryl. It was the extra large size bottle with a hundred tabs in it. She tilted her head back like she was taking a shot of alcohol and dumped a mouthful of pills in. She spilt about a dozen of them down her shirt and onto the floor. She probably took about twenty of them.

"Is that all you're taking?"

"You're an asshole." She took another gulp of the pills and dry swallowed them. Then she drank some water to help her get the rest down. All totaled, she took about sixty of them.

"Have a nice death."

"I fucking hate you!"

"Hope that works out for you." And Scott rolled over, closed his eyes, and pretended to go to sleep. He would however remain very much awake. He was worried for her, even in his anger. She was Ariel's mother and he loved her.

It was close to six in the morning before Scott felt Kelly gently tugging on his shoulder. "Chip? . . . Chip?" She said timidly "I need to go to the hospital. Please take me. I'm scared."

So they got in his truck and drove to Capitol Health system @ Fuld on Brunswick Ave. The drama hospital. They took Kelly into the E.R. while Scott was parking the car so he didn't get to see them insert the endotracheal tube in her nose and snake it down her esophagus.

He missed watching them suck all the gunk out of her stomach until it turned clear.

He arrived behind the curtain of examining room 2 just after they had given her the activated charcoal. The theory was that any poisons left in her stomach would be absorbed by the charcoal and passed in the stool. Only that isn't what happened.

As Scott closed the curtain behind him, his girlfriend began to vomit up the charcoal into a little kidney bean shaped plastic throw up bowl. The spewage was black and as thick as roofing tar. It dripped slowly off of her chin and soiled the front of her shirt. And she heaved and she heaved and she heaved. She filled the bucket with the substance that looked like it had been coughed up from the pits of hell and the nurse handed her another one. You might have expected her head to start spinning three hundred and sixty degrees while a demonic voice screamed "Fuck me! Fuck me! Fuck me!" but fortunately that never happened.

"That was the most beautiful thing I've ever seen Kel, I'm glad to have been here and to have seen it. Thanks."

"I'm so sorry baby. I love you so much." She reached for his hand.

And he took it. "I love you too."

Scott knew all about forgiveness. It was necessary to forgive Kelly constantly. It was a requirement of the sick dependency that substituted for love in south Trenton. Indeed, Scott found it in his heart to forgive her when she stole jewelry from his mother to support her habit, even though she didn't share any of it with him. He even got over it when, after he made love to her and fell asleep, she got up, drank half a bottle of Vodka, and climbed into bed with his brother, Brian. His brother, of course, never fucked her, but oh the chaos; the beautiful bi-polar chaos. Even when his bella sucker punched him and he felt the pop of her knuckles on the side of his jaw, he forgave her. Yeah, Scott knew about forgiveness. He knew what it was like to be an animal addicted.

So anyway, let's leave this scene now and pan out. We'll let the lovebirds nurse their wounds and heal. We'll check back in on them in a couple of weeks, where we'll take another snapshot of the disease.

In three weeks time we still find them living on Wallace Ave. in Ewing but now they are two completely different people. We find, to no great surprise, that there are track marks up and down their arms and that there are dark circles rimming out the pin dot pupils of their hardened eyes. Eyes that have grown cold. No one really knows what happened to their souls, but if we are to read their faces now, all we can see is sickness and hunger.

Nothing matters to them now, not their family or their children, not their future nor their God. Unless you grant heroin as their God.

Finally the breaking point came one Friday when Scott was too dope sick cot to work. He went in, in the morning, picked a fight, quit his job, and got his check. Before two PM, he spent everything but his rent money on heroin and cocaine for he and his girlfriend. By two AM, the rent also went. Spent.

By Saturday morning, Scott and Kelly were packing up their shit to move out before the inevitable eviction. They robbed everyone in the house before they left. They took their electronics and money. They even grabbed this Christian kid's checkbook and forged themselves some checks which they took to the bank and cashed.

They fled Ewing in search of more high and they went to stay at Scott's uncle's house on Washington Ave in Trenton. They stayed in an empty room on the second floor where, for the rest of the weekend, they smoked crack, and fucked, and shot drugs. They were only dirty and soulless.

Eventually, the money ran out and the desperation set in. After the laughter and the good times, the high tide ebbed, then the nightmare of the realization that the sickness of withdrawal was coming and inevitably the druggies would reap what they've sown

And Kelly had an idea to save them. "You know, they'll give us a couple of more bags if you let them take your Jeep."

Perhaps you've never been dope sick. Maybe you don't know about the aches and the pain and the smells. Just in case, allow me to describe it for you. There is a migraine that feels like your brain is trying to claw its way out of your skull. A living organism of torment that has a pulse so pounding that it makes you want to throw up, just for some relief. There is the retching, twisting, discomfort of dry heaves, and after the agony of this labor, the birth of the vilest of bile. The bright yellow egg yolk of the heroin venom, given up so reluctantly. The yucky stuff.

Perhaps during this magical experience, there is a releasing of the bowels, but at this point you are really too sick to care. If only you had had the afore thought to put on a pair of underwear. And if only you had one more shot of diesel, you'd be strong enough to pick yourself up off the floor and take yourself a shower. You sweat wet with pain and the horror of knowing that it's going to get worse before it slowly goes away. Detox is at its worst on the second and third days.

"Take it Kel. Take the Jeep. Just get us some more." Scott agreed terrified and weak.

And with the merciful majesty of a holy miracle, his angel scored them some more. Four bags stamped with red stars. Two for Scott and two for his bella. And they shot the dope that Trenton junkies call diesel and it hit Scott in his sweet spot and he drifted off to sleep. To the land of nod.

Elsewhere, Ariel Elizabeth was also sleeping peacefully but she hadn't seen her parents for almost three weeks. She was living with her Grammy and her Pop Pop. She was well taken care of. She was happy and playful.

Her mother was an empty shell.

Her father was living in hell.

Scott had planned on sleeping for maybe an hour or two while the drug dealers used his Jeep to make their deliveries throughout Trenton. He fell into a near coma however and 6 or 8 hours had passed. When he awoke, Kelly, as usual, was gone. He looked around the dark room. He was still feeling OK from the dope, but was angered to discover that his vehicle had not yet been returned. He called his dealer on his cell phone. "Yo."

R. was still running the heroin back in those days and he was usually in a pissed off mood from dealing with the junkies and all the bullshit that they put him through with begging for fronts, lying to him, and calling him constantly for delivery service. This was before R. was sent to prison for dealing and his girlfriend Dahlia came to power. Neither R nor Dahlia was anyone to play with.

"Yo. What's up, Chip?"

"You tell me. What the fuck R?! We said two hours for the Jeep. It's been like eight. Where's my fucking truck? Don't think I won't call the police."

"Hey fuck you," replied an ungrateful R. "Talk to your girl, she made another deal for the rest of the night. We dropped off more shit an hour ago."

"You did?" Funny, Kelly didn't mention it or come in and share any of it. And where was his little love bunny anyway?

"Yeah we did. And don't forget who you're talking to, pussy. If you ever threaten to call the cops on me again, I'll come over there and stomp your white ass to death. You hear me?!"

Apparently Scott had made a serious miscalculation and forgotten his place. "Yeah, I hear you."

"Good." Click.

So, there was more dope. Scott discovered his babies momma was in the bathroom with the door locked. "Kel, open the door."

"Just a minute."

"I just talked to R and he said he gave us more shit for the Jeep."

"Yeah, he did."

"Where's mine?"

"Oh, you were sleeping so I did it."

And the fighting ensued. It ended with Scott saying to his sweetheart, "I don't care what you have to do Kelly, call them up and get my Jeep back." After all the money he had spent on her and feeding her addiction, it was unfathomable to him that she would get more dope and not share it with him. But that is the nature of the disease; selfishness and greed.

Kelly came up with a plan. She took the empty wax paper bags, this time they had the letters D.O.A. stamped on them, and filled them back up with ground cinnamon. Then she sealed them with little pieces of Scotch tape. Her idea was to sell them or take them back to the dealer.

In case you're not familiar with heroin, you should know that it doesn't look anything like cinnamon. The consistency is about the same, but the color and the smell are entirely different. Her plan had no chance of succeeding. Any drug dealer would decipher the deception immediately.

Metaphorically, Kelly had balls the size of grapefruits.

She took her beat bags with her and left Uncle Alan's house on Washington Ave. She disappeared into the Trenton night. It would be almost six months before Scott saw her again. Two days later, she was arrested for driving without a license and outstanding warrants. The Jeep was impounded and Ariel's mother was sent to jail.

Scott's father came and rescued him from his Uncles the next day. He took him to detox in his basement where he went through the nightmare of withdrawal for the next several days. Then Scott was sent to rehab in the New Jersey Pine Barrens for four months.

While he was gone, Kelly was released from the workhouse and sent to her own drug rehabilitation facility. The two junkies were now on the road to recovery.

Scott called Kelly at a rehab called Springhouse, where she lived with forty women. Every time Scott called Kelly, she was fighting with someone.

A phone call went like this.

"Hi baby, how are you? I miss you."

"Oh hi baby, I'm good, how are you? I miss you too. Hold on a second, honey." Then in the background. "Yeah, Yeah? Do it then bitch! Do it! . . . . Yeah, that's what I thought, Pussy." Then. "Hi honey, back."

"Kel, I thought you were trying to stay out of trouble? I can hear you starting shit with some girl."

"It's O.k. sweetheart, she ain't gonna do shit." Kelly was always so sweet and angry. And then, they talked of their recovery, their love, and their baby. And how everything was going to be pure in the future. How God and Narcotics Anonymous would save them from their Idjits and demons. And they pushed the monster way down deep and their every thought and breathe was clean. And soon the demons fall asleep. Like a Cancer in remission as we embark upon this mission. She with the recovering addicts and he with the Christians. They sought to suppress their inner evil, and didn't feed their lusts or greed's, or need for needles. But time and loneliness determines their fate. And deep down inside, the devil waits.

Scott was in love and illusioned. "We can do this baby. I know we can. We can stay sober and be good parents to Ariel."

"I know we can baby, I don't wanna get high anymore. I miss my baby so much, kiss her for me."

They had hope when they hung up the phone.

But two weeks later, Kelly got kicked out of the Rehab. Scott never knew why; as Kelly sometimes lied. He picked her up at the entrance and loaded up her luggage and he had meant to take her straight back, but before they even made it home, they were, the both of them sniffing dope.

And the two pillars of sobriety crumpled, like the Trade Towers and their hopes for tomorrow vanished along with their clean time. In spite of their dreams and their best intentions, Scott and Kelly were like poison when mixed together and the recovery came crashing down again.

Kelly was sufficiently high by the time she saw the apartment.

Two days later, they were back to injecting the serum. Again with the anathema of fucking with the blood.

Once again Scott held her in his arms and loved her.

And Ariel's mommy may indeed even be some sort of succubus or vampire. But love, like the drug, goes coursing through the blood.

And V is for the venereal that goes pumping through the vascular.

Chapter 6

Ethan Scott

S O, IT'S DECEMBER 25, 2005 and all around the world Christians are celebrating the long ago birth of their Lord. Outside, on the streets you can see decorations of various degrees, some featuring Santa Claus and others remembering the nativity scene. The faithful go to church and spend time with their families. There is lighting of candles and lighting of trees. There is gift giving, generosity, merriment, and peace. The spirit of the season calms the fighting and anger is abated, even on Trenton streets. It seems like lust and greed are temporarily suspended in honor of Gods holy day. All the children have been excitedly waiting for their gifts to arrive. With magic in their eyes, they look to the skies for Santa to arrive. (See how I just rhymed arrived with arrive? Clever, huh?) Anyway, it would have been the perfect day for many if it wasn't for the fact that it was raining.

The day was cold and gray and for Scott it was shaping up real shitty. He was in the grips of depression and he was mighty freaking dope sick. Usually he liked the way the raindrops sounded when they struck the windowpanes, but today they just made him feel sadder. He would not be allowed to spend this holiday with his daughter. Dyfus and the state had taken her away. Scott reluctantly gave up a half smile as he fantasized about building a bomb and blowing up Judge Superior and his courthouse. Fortunately for the state, Scott was just too lazy to build a bomb and so his revenge would have to remain a fantasy. With his luck, he'd probable just end up blowing hisself up. He had a tendency to do shit that was stupid.

He watched the raindrops resonate circles in the puddles outside on the street. He was home alone, without dope, and feeling as grey as the weather. What was everyone so afraid would happen if he was allowed to play with his daughter? Why couldn't he tickle her and tell her how much he loved her? The judge had ruled that father and daughter should be separated and it made them both needlessly hurt for nothing. And the bullshit laws they used to take her punished him with a pain unlike any he had ever had to deal with.

Scott pressed his lonely face against the window and it was cold. He remembered Christmases past and growing up with his mom and dad. They always had toys and food and laughter and a feeling of contentment and gratitude to God after. He remembered playing with his brothers; Chuck and Brian and he thought about how the strongest bond in life is ones family and how the sweetest thing in life is love. His mother, Nancy was like God's gift to Christmas. She always had a way of making things special. She was a wonderful mother.

Today, Scott might not even see her; he was so disgusted with himself. He didn't want to be around anyone. He turned down several invitations from family and friends and he stayed back at his apartment on Bruce Lane in Ewing when Kelly went to Trenton to spend some time with her son, Dylan and her mother.

Scott looked around his room and saw that it was filthy. He and Kelly were living like animals. The Nirvana poster that was hung where you'd walk in, in the kitchen signified a safe haven for junkies. Dirty clothes lay all over the floor, scattered and in piles. Uneaten food in bowls with cigarette butts and ash sat in place for days and turned moldy and disgusting. Thankfully it was winter time and there weren't that many flies. Empty bags of dope, broken syringes, and discarded Marlboro packs completed the décor. The room felt like it was haunted with a drug infested presence. The spirit of the idjit maybe.

And he began to daydream. He was trying to decide if this was his worst Christmas ever. Another twisted Christmas image came to mind. Once, when he was young and in rehab, he had gotten into an altercation with this kid and got himself sent to the Mental Health Unit. (Or pysch ward, if you prefer.) Here goes the scenario.

Scott was bullshitting with this kid and since Scott couldn't remember his name we'll stick to calling him this kid. In the course of conversation it came up that yes Scott was playing the system and when he got out he fully intended to start getting high again. In this kid he confided. What Scott did not know was that this kid was a snitch and that he had ratted him out to the staff. So Scott was going to beat his ass. Scott also had no way of knowing that the whole thing had been a set up to see how he would respond to the test of this kid running his mouth and talking shit like, "I told them you're not serious about any of this and how you told me that you're still going to get high."

"What?! Mother Fucker! Why?!"

"If you're not serious about this, then you should give up the bed to somebody who is."

""Fuck you, dude!"

"They are trying to help you, Chip. We all are." Sanctimonious little douche bag.

"You're a little bitch." Said Scott as he approached the kid with fists. "And this is what happens to faggots who get in my business." It was mostly just tough talk, Scott only planned on hitting the kid a couple of times. Anyway, security had been listening to the whole thing just outside the door, waiting to respond to the anger that they had provoked. They rushed Scott before he ever got his hands on the guy. As I said, the whole thing was a set up. Entrapment.

In their infinite wisdom they decided that Scott should be moved immediately to the Psychiatric Hospital for evaluation. They sent him there that night. It was shortly before Christmas, the exact year lost in his memory.

They locked Scott up in the men's unit with thirty lunatics. Everyone was all drugged and fucked up. One time while he was sitting in his room, in walks this crazy dude. He stomps over to Scott without introductions and without saying a word; he lifts Scott off his chair by his collar. He spins him around and slams him into the wall. Crack went the back of his head into the sheetrock. He held him by his throat with his left hand and made a fist with his right.

And our hero feared for his life. Something about this guy wasn't quite right. Madness was in his eyes and he was almost twice Scott's size. Scott was maybe twenty and this guy had to be at least thirty five. Someone had apparently gotten his dosage wrong.

Scott could remember the stink of the dudes breath, which if memory served him correctly was the scent of evil, decay, and death. Now he screamed at Scott and he spat at him when he did so, the spray landing on his face. He was frozen in fear and could not react or run away. Besides the unit was locked and there was really no place for him to go.

. So like a mouse frozen before a snake, or a woman caught in a vampires stare, Scott wasn't going anywhere. Like a deer caught in the headlights of a car, if you haven't had enough clichés.

Or if you prefer a Trenton euphemism like a little bitch, Scott stood there catatonic and waited for the lunatic dude to hit him. Bracing for impact.

That's when his roommate came to his rescue.

"Leave him alone."

And the monster turned his head, momentarily distracted.

"This ain't none of your business."

"I said "Leave him alone."

And the lunatic let go. What he did next, Scott would never forget. It was amazing how hard that crazy man caught that boy on his jaw. Dropped him with one punch and Scotts roommate started screaming as the guy grabbed him just like he had Scott a moment ago, left hand holding onto the collar of his shirt. And he proceeded to beat him senseless with repeated right hooks to his face. He got in plenty of shots even after the guys hands dropped away from defense and the screaming had stopped.

And out in the hallway the alarm went off. "Dr. Strong! Dr. Strong! To unit C"

The older of the two gentlemen punched like he was on steroids, while the younger was losing consciousness and being beaten mercilessly.

Scott was still frozen in fear, but now he was also fascinated as he stood in the presence of evil. The lunatic must have been possessed by demons to hate the boy so much without so much as a reason. He busted both his eyes and his nose and knocked out a couple of teeth, oblivious to the Christmas season.

When the guards came in to separate them, three of them tackled the dude. They held him down while a fourth shot him in his ass with a syringe full of Thorozine. Once he was drugged, they drug him away. Presumably to someplace with padded walls and shackles.

When they picked up the kid, he was all bloody down his chin and neck like a gruesome goatee. It stained the front of his shirt in the shape of a V. They took him to the infirmary where he would get some different medicine.

The room was emptied out and Scott still stood in the same spot where he had hit his head against the wall. He pondered what he just saw. He thought about how just a few days ago, he had wanted to beat up some kid for snitching on him and now here he was locked up and afraid. There was probably an important lesson to be learned here, but whatever it was Scott never got it.

Inside the asylum, they lead the kid with the busted jaw and pulverized face to the nurses' station dripping blood on the floor as he went. There was absolutely no reason for the beatings; that was the part that scarred him and fucking ruined his Christmas.

Soon after, Scott's mom and dad showed up at Unit C with presents and candy and best wishes from the world of the sane people.

Outside, down in the valley of the quaint little Norman Rockwell town, folks were hurriedly wrapping up last minute gifts of love and singing songs about God and goodwill towards man. While up the hill in the nut factory something was terribly wrong. No all was not well up there for those dudes. No, not at all.

It still ranked as Scott's shittiest Christmas ever.

"That there was a bad one." Scott said to himself as he came out of his memory and back into his apartment, dope sick on Christmas 2oo5.

His gallery, his shooting den smelled horrible, like vomit and piss. He climbed under the covers and crawled into a ball. He shook, and sweated, and farted. The unfortunate withdrawal was starting. There are a hundred cheesy metaphors comparing the burnt, semen stained sheets and Scotts existence. You see what I'm getting at.

Scott passed out and started dreaming.

His dad, Wes was driving him around in a taxi. The dream imagery wasn't that hard to decipher because Wes drove Scott to more places than anyone else he knew. Scott loved him and trusted him. He had a humbler, servant's heart; more than any Christian or Muslim he had ever met. A caring soul. And Wes wasn't religious, he was merely a realist. He never claimed to know an unknowable God and he was an honest man. The smartest wisdom that Scott had ever learned was that when it came to God the smartest thinkers can only answer I don't know.

As I said, they were in a cab, driving slowly down this driveway made of dirt and some stones. On either side of the road there were cornfields, row after row.

At the end of the driveway was a circular carport that drove around this weird angel man statue sitting in the fountain. Water was churning in the thing peacefully as Scott and Wes pulled up in front of the house.

The place was a plantation from the Georgian south, abandoned now as the last tenants moved out. Ivy grew up the sides of the house and all around were the sounds of crows, and locusts, and crickets.

Scott was getting out of the taxi to go up the front steps when Wes who was sitting in the driver seat looked back at him and said,

"You don't have to do this you know."

Scott looked up at the house and said.

"I know.' When he looked back at his dad, he was wearing a ridiculous taxi drivers hat and he said.

"Fifteen dollars."

"I'll pay you later, ok?"

"Sure kid, you know . . . you don't have to go."

"I know." Scott got out off the cab which was bright yellow, almost psychedelic in his dream. As he walked up the front steps, behind him Wes and the taxi vanished from the dream.

Scott watched the cornfields from the porch and he saw leaves rustling as some sort of small animal ran through just out of his periphery.

As he turned back to the front door it opened in front of him. Uninvited he stepped inside to the hardwood of the foyer. There were echoing sounds through the house of his footfalls.

To his right there was a dining room. It was furnished with a long wooden table and six wooden chairs. It appeared to be the only room in the house with any kind of furniture.

When he looked into the room on his left, the den was empty. Empty, except for a fireplace with a strange chiseled inscription in the masonry. He proceeded toward the fireplace for a closer look when, suddenly something jumped and knocked over one of the chairs behind the large table in the dining room. Scott turned around and went into that room to investigate. The only other way out of the room was an open doorway that led to the kitchen. As he walked into the kitchen, he saw that it was empty and still. Still, except for the door leading outside into the backyard of this haunted house. A small pet entrance was cut into the people door and the black rubber mat was swinging like a pendulum where whatever had knocked over that chair had just run through. Scott looked out the window of that door, while the pet door continued to move like a mud flap behind large trucks tires.

The kitchen was on the second floor and the house was on a hill. Scott looked down the slope into the back yard where he saw a solitary tree. It was a twisted, evil, leafless tree. Surrounding it were fields of the Papiver Somniferum. And somewhere down there, the idjit hopped through the poppies and made him crave morphine and oxy's.

He still had never gotten a really good look and the furry little bastard, as it also stayed in his periphery, and it was totally nerve wracking. There was no sign of it now as Scott surveyed the beauty of the wild flowers and he thought once again about the mythological entrance to Morpheus's cave.

That was when he heard the first of the low guttural laughing sounds coming from upstairs. The laughter was humorless, without mirth, and sinister sounding. It was mocking of Scott and accusing him. A shiver shot up and down his spine as he realized that it was calling him to find it. It was a diabolical invitation. The laughter, as I said, was coming from upstairs, but it seemed to emanate from the walls as if the idjit was the very heart of the house. It all made perfect sense though, there in the dream. He went back up the steps and made his assent and played hide and go seek with the spirit of his addictions. Furry little squirrel man, tempter, demon. And of course in the dream, his progress was hideously slow. It was a physical effort for him as he laboriously climbed the stairs. He could hear the wood of them crack under his feet, as if he weighed a ton or the idjit had done something to the gravity of the house. He heard the laughter closing in on him and he turned and looked back down the steps, behind him, towards the den. Bastard must have come back in through the chimney. It was covered in soot and ash when Scott came face to face with it. The day he met the nasty idjit.

The thing came at him; unnaturally blinking in and out of his vision like it was under a strobe light. He only saw three glimpses of the monster as it rushed for him.

On the first, it was about forty feet away, and Scott saw that the idjit was really very small. Its beard and hair were all nappy and squirrelly. It had red eyes and it spoke two words into the air and Scotts head as it approached. It said "Idjit Ijati."

Scott somehow knew exactly what that meant.

The idjit stopped about a foot away from him and it was only as tall as his waist. Scott looked down into its eyes and saw that they glowed red like a light emitting diode. There were blood stained tears matted to its eyelashes and whiskers. Then it lunged at him and tried to bite off his nuts. Fortunately before the thing could lock it's jaws around his junk, Scott woke up.

He didn't exactly scream as he sat up and nor did he wet himself, but still he was pretty shook up. It seemed he had snagged himself a demon. But what the fuck did it want? And what the fuck did it mean?

When he awoke, he was back in his apartment and it was still Christmas 05. He was shaking because he desperately needed some heroin. He was waiting for Kelly to come back home and bring him some dope. She was his only hope.

There was no magical holiday snow, only rain, but the grey sky seemed to brighten when his girlfriend finally got back. He heard her coming up the stairs. He brushed his long dirty blonde hair away from his face and thought about how long it had been since he had had a shower. Probably more than a few days.

Kelly walked in with a smile on her face. She didn't manage to get just the needed three or four bags, no somehow she managed to get eight. His beautiful Bella, his dark angel had brought home a Christmas miracle. And they got to mixing the fixins, hovering over the sacred bottle cap like witches over a cauldron.

Around 2,050 years ago, Christ was born in a manger in Bethlehem.

Almost three weeks ago, Ethan Scott was born in a hospital in Trenton, N.J. The same hospital his sister was born in. Same one his father and grandmother had been born in. And the same one that his "Uncle Tommy" would one day overdose on dope and die in.

Once Kelly and Scott got themselves right, they bundled up against the rain and walked down Parkside Ave towards Bellevue. It was only right that they weather the storm to go and see their beloved boy. He shouldn't be in the NIC-U alone, not on Christmas.

So they trod on the sidewalk and eventually they gave up on avoiding the puddles. Water saturated their sneakers and soaked through their socks to their feet. They walked on historic brick and cobblestone paths. Sometimes on newly poured concrete and sometimes on concrete poured before you were born. If you took this route and you wanted to you could probably count a million cigarette butts discarded in the street, flicked out of passing cars, some now floating in puddles, others caught in the stream as it headed for the storm drain.

They came a crossed Oakland Ave where it intersects Parkside. Scott could still not walk passed this spot without remembering the time he came running out of the ghetto with his face pounding. It was five years ago now, but he was still scarred from the beatdown. He remembered how he had laughed afterwards; nothing seemed funny now. He felt pity for his drug infested town. And the rain continued to pour down.

There was to be no Christmas snow and the day bloomed cold, wet, and grey; as ugly as Scott felt. He was high for his walk, yet this did nothing to lift his spirit. He knew that Dyfus was gonna come and take his son away, just like his daughter, and he knew that he was powerless to stop it. The dope helped with the pain and then it made it worse.

Scott thought about his son as he walked with his mother on this his first Christmas. He wished like hell he could reassure the boy that everything was going to turn out all right. The trouble was Scott really didn't think that it was.

They had given Ethan, Phenobarbital through a tiny I.V. to help with the withdrawal and the shaking. He was kicking the drugs that his parents had given him. Ethan came into this world hard in a state of heroin detox. For that Scott would be eternally sorry.

Nothing could ever erase the past or replace the loss. It was another cross that Scott would have to bear, another fucked up scar on his soul and "Ethan daddy's sorry."

Scott thought back to telling his mother that Kelly was pregnant with Ethan. The three words landed in the kitchen like a hand grenade. "Kelly's pregnant again." This was followed by seconds of silence and then, in disbelief, his mom said;

"No, she's not." Hoping he was joking. A look of fear on her face.

"Yeah, she is, Mom. I'm telling you it's going to be great."

And how things were shaping up now, with Dyfus out to destroy his family and he and Kelly both hopelessly dependant on dope.

Scott never looked at his son's birth as anything less than a miracle and a blessing. He was there when he was born and could testify to the sensation of angels and the spirit of God being in the delivery room. It was similar to the birth of his daughter; both were divine and magical.

Scott remembered Ethan's birth clearly. He had been so sinful and dirty. He brought the heroin to the hospital. Truth would never allow him to deny that. Kelly shot him up in the bathroom. They went two and two. And he fucked her, high on diesel, and the feeling was ecstasy, and yeah, maybe even demonic. It definitely felt a little evil. The dope flooded their brains and they were both feeling no pain. They both knew that this shit wasn't right, still, Scott never felt better in his life.

But the price he would pay for his sextacy would be catastrophically high, like a punishment from God. After the orgasm faded there would be regret and loss for many, many, days.

Whether it was the drugs or the sex that triggered Kelly's labor, it was impossible to know for sure, but she delivered his son to him that night. And all through her labor, she asked for more pain medicine. Even though her eyes were pinned from morphine and the doctors were reluctant to give her any more meds. But Kelly could beg and, as it was with Scott, she eventually got her way. The nurse went to go and get her the syringe and once again Scott and Kelly were alone in the room.

And Scott sensed something special when, just like Ariel, his angel, Ethan was born with no doctors present. A miracle in itself in this day and age, but of course, Scott and Kelly were poor and uninsured, so they weren't going to get the best service that the hospital had to offer.

Ethan slid out his mother in the bloody muck and landed on the sheet between her legs.

The boy must have shared in some of the numb of his parents, but his birth was none the less holy. The narcotics a non factor in the eyes of the Lord. No amount of sins from his parents could ever interfere with God's chosen blessings for him. And God judges much different from man. Gnosis knows this, but it doesn't take a genius to see it and figure out that His mercy and creation surround us.

Years later, while in therapy, trying to deal with his issues of loss and regret, Scott would confess to his psychiatrist how he was haunted about shooting up Ethan's mothers just hours before his birth. He felt crappy about doing her dog style over the hospital bathroom toilet. That time he had come like a machine gun.

His doctor assured him that the sex and semen actually helped Kelly to have the baby. It supposedly triggered muscles in her vagina or uterus or some shit. Still, Scott always felt rotten about it.

The doctor could find no way to justify or rationalize him giving his son the diesel and this lead him to ponder if his boy was ordained or if maybe he, Scott was just plain evil.

His thoughts lead him back to the days when Kelly had broken his heart. He remembered finding out that his beloved children's mother had turned to turning tricks to get her next fix. Sure, she shared what she got with him because he was her man and she loved him. Even as she ripped out his heart and she hurt him.

When Kel had told him she was pregnant with Ethan in the midst of one of their ever increasing fights, she said she could not guarantee that the baby was his. This sliced like a mother fucking knife, even as God assured him that the boy was his own blood.

Scott thought back to the time he had bought his first and only prostitute, after he found out about Kelly. How that girl had been meant as some twisted kind of erotic revenge.

He called up a service in the newspaper. Hookers are listed in the Trentonian, Trenton's daily rag. "Chinese fortune Cookies" the ad had read. Scott had never been with an Asian. Unfortunately, when the woman answered the phone, she informed him that she had girls from every race except for Oriental. A clear example of false advertising.

Anyway, the lady explained that a suitable white girl could be found to come out and service him for two hundred and fifty dollars. Scott actually had the money because Kelly was mostly sleeping out on the streets in those days. He was consequently sniffing cocaine through much of the day and so when the hooker arrived, Scott was sufficiently high.

The sluts name was Dana, or Danielle, or something like that. She was blonde and thin and skanky. She happened to be from Philly, but she just as easily could have been a Trenton girl. She was a little busted, but still sexy.

At the beginning of the session, she asked him a question.

"Do you mind if I smoke a little rock before we get started?" And she began smoking crack like a rabbit and soon Scott joined her in her habit. While he hit the shit, the girl undressed before him. She wore only white cotton panties and ordinarily it would have been driving him out of his mind; crazy, except that he couldn't stop thinking about Kelly. "So this is what she does with strange men." Disappointment. It really was only a job and this poor girl beside him didn't seem to be enjoying herself at all. Despite all the drugs, it was empty and she wasn't having any fun. It was almost like she was afraid of what was to come.

Scott sat behind her on the bed and he reached around her and started squeezing her breasts. He had after all just paid for her. As he tweaked her nipples, she shook her tits free of him, stood up, and said, "Not yet." Then she said, "Make yourself comfortable."

So Scott stripped down to his boxers. He had not been wearing them for too many days and so they weren't yet that disgusting.

But the prostitute smiled and said, "More comfortable than that."

So Scott slid down his underwear. The problem was that his faithful soldier was not ready for combat and his man part just lay there like a useless little mushroom. He was not too high to be completely embarrassed. The problem was that there was absolutely no foreplay and the whole thing was just business. And shady business at that. Truth be told, his mind wasn't really into it anyway. "Fuckin' Kelly, This shit was all her fault."

And so she blew him and he got semi erect for her while she did that, but when he tried mounting her, the thing just went flat. All the money he wasted on her and he never even got off. That was the truth of the story that never got told. (Don't tell anyone else, O.K?)

This was sort of shit that Scott thought about as he walked, reunited with Kelly, in the light Christmas rain, as they finally reached their destination. They were the both of them, soaked from head to toe and they were the both of them so high from dope that they didn't really feel the cold.

Neither did they notice his Brother Chuck's truck parked outside as they made their way inside the hospital lobby and tried to get dry. The boy was on the third floor.

When they got upstairs to the NIC-U, (where they have that cool sink, where you have to wash your hands for one full minute) they discovered that Ethan already had visitors.

Chuck and his wife glared down at the baby, sleeping in the incubator. If you looked into the woman's eyes, it was not hard to read that a plan was being devised. She loved Scott's children and she wanted them. The moment was awkward as Kelly and Chuck's wife never really liked each other. One Christmas, while Kel was pregnant with Ariel, Chuck's wife had told his mother that she would not spend the night at her house unless she made Scott and Kelly get out. So like Joseph and Mary, who could not find a room at the inn, Scott and Kelly felt unwelcome and sought refuge elsewhere. Scott would never consider her like a sister and he would never assign her any place in his family.

When it came time for them to leave the hospital and go their separate ways, there was no great feeling of brotherly love that Christmas. Scott could not remember if they even offered to give them a ride home. It didn't really matter as Kelly would not have accepted anyway.

So, the rift in the family was begun and Scott looked on Christmas 2005 as the beginning of the betrayal. His son and daughter were destined to be taken from him. Later, a judge would deem him unfit to be a parent and say that all this shit was in the best interest of the children.

But the simple truth that could never be denied was that Ethan was of his own blood and you could see it in his eyes. Beautiful, blue, eyes. Gnostic eyes. Aryan and proud.

Scott named the boy Ethan, after Ethan Allen Hawley from Steinbeck's book, *The Winter of Our Discontent*, It is about a good man who contemplates and overcomes corruption and evil. Ethan beats the devil.

It was also an angelic name, same as his sisters. Ariel and Ethan, beloved.

And so Scott and Kelly visited with "Et'n bug", (as Ari would start to call him), on this his first Christmas, but there was so much conflict and addiction that there were great overtures of sadness. Because of his own sickness, his son, was born high and dependant on heroin.

Scott and Kelly walked home the same route that they had followed here. They even had some shit left to stick in their arms. Soon they would have more dope and they would feel none of this. Nothing.

Little Ethan Scott lay in the NIC-U paying for the sins of his father.

Heaven forgive him.

Idjit Ijati.

Chapter 7

Many Failures

S COTT SCRATCHED HIS balls through the front right hand pocket of his jeans as he drove south down route 29 from Ewing towards Trenton. There was nothing unusual or remarkable about either of these events, as he drove on this road almost every single day of his life and his balls seemed to be perpetually itchy. Dissatisfied with the sensation created by the feel of fabric on skin, Scott pulled his hand out of his pocket. He sucked in his stomach and made room between his belt and his belly and he plunged his hand back in. He dove under the elastic band of his underwear for a good old fashioned scratching and the veritable bliss of nails on skin. He vigorously jostled his nuts, reddening his taint, testicles, and inner thighs.

He remembered back to the days when Kelly used to scratch him here, in his private parts. And it was near ecstasy too because Kelly had magic fingers. She knew instinctively how to rub, scrap, and tear to satisfy that tingling irritation ever present in Scott's genitalia. Now, as he drove past the water filtration building on his right he fantasized about his girlfriend and dug into himself with complete abandon. It was not masturbation, but close. He closed his eyes for a moment. "Oh, yeah baby, that's what I'm talking about." He said to the empty compartment of his car.

He turned onto the exit ramp that leads to the notorious Calhoun Street Bridge. He finished up with the business of scratching and put both hands back on the wheel as he came up the hill leading to the stop sign. There was also a sign at the base of the bridge that read "Alternate merge" which, when translated means "have some fucking courtesy." The road department tries to tell the people in Trenton to do the right thing using dumb signs, unfortunately it doesn't always work.

Anyway, Scott came up to the stop sign and waited for his chance to merge onto the bridge and over into Morrisville. That's when he first saw the guy. Again, I apologize for not remembering his name.

So, he was a black guy in his late fifties, early sixties and the reason that Scott took notice of him was because of the way he was walking. He was bent over in obvious pain. He was holding his lower back and moving around like a broken man.

Scott looked around and passed the guy as he motioned for him to walk in front of his car. Wherever he had come from, to get up to that medium on foot meant at least a couple of block walk. What was so important that a man in this much agony would get out of bed and walk through the Trenton badlands, over the highway, and across the boarded sidewalk spanning the Delaware River? What could possible motivate someone to endure that much pain?

If you answered "drugs" then you are probably right.

Scott having suffered from the torture of lower back pain knew about the agonies of spinal problems and pinched nerves and so he took mercy on the guy. "Yo, my man, Get in." Miraculously the line of traffic behind him didn't start beeping their horns impatiently. Scott was glad for that. He hated the whole road rage thing. His father had the worst case of it he had ever seen. He was always ready to fight to the death anyone who cut him off or didn't show him the proper driving courtesies. People like that got on his nerves. Just like the dumb mother fuckers that don't understand how to alternate merge.

"Thank you, sir, you are very kind" said his passenger as he awkwardly lowered himself into his seat. The guy really did look as if he ought to be using a walker. He was a friendly enough guy though, a likeable gentleman with gray hair. His countenance betrayed him to be a poor man. Scott hoped he had a good family that loved him and that he had plenty of grandkids who visited him and called him "pop pop." But Scott doubted that was the case. A different story was written on his face. An unhappy one. Deep lines and crow's feet told of a hard life. They were the scars of his sadness.

All of his front teeth were missing and obviously he wasn't the type of dude who had the dental insurance to get them fixed. He probably didn't have five bucks in his pocket and if he did it would be the total sum of his wealth. Anyway, speaking of those missing teeth, Scott had seen this look before. Most likely this guy was a long time crack smoker.

Scott's inclination was that this guy probably had no contact at all with any of his family. In spite of how nice and grateful he seemed, grandpa's aura was as dark as his skin and his whole existence seemed gloomy.

Traffic came to a halt and Scott was forced to stop dead center on the bridge. He looked down at the river and saw the sun on the water ripples glistening. It was a beautiful and cheery day and Scott felt happy to be alive.

C.S.W.

But two feet to his right, his passenger was looking at the same sight and he sat there close to tears and contemplating suicide. "You know sometimes I think I'd be better off if I just threw myself down."

And Scott trying to be a good guy attempted to lift the brother up. "Don't say that man. Shit will get better, it always does." Then he proceeded to deliver somewhat of a sermon on God's love and mercy. He compared the guy's pain with days of rain and he told him to weather the storm because tomorrow would be brighter.

"Yeah, I know." he goes.

The problem was that Scott didn't believe any of the shit he was telling him. Grandpa's life would probably be hardship from now on and he, being uninsured, would never be able to afford the necessary doctors to fix his back. He would most likely suffer that, deteriorating worse until he died. And who was Scott to say this guy was better off alive? Who was he to decide?

But he did feel bad for the guy. He dropped him off at his friend's house in Morrisville. It was only a couple of blocks out of his way. "Thanks for the ride, sir." said the nearly crippled guy. The white man and the black man shook hands and went their separate ways. Somehow Scott knew he'd never run into him again.

Still, he felt so magnanimous. What a great guy he was, picking up riff raff that you wouldn't pick up and giving them a ride. He was almost Christ like he was so fucking kind. And his generosity was really hard to beat as well.

Do you know what solipsism is?

It's the theory that self is the only object of real knowledge or that nothing but self exists. Perhaps this is the beginning of gnosis and enlightenment or maybe it's just egotistical bullshit. Who knows? The gospel of truth, which didn't make the cut to get canonized and is not in the bible, says "Therefore, he who is Gnostic is truly a being from above." Maybe we are all born with some God stuff in us and have a right to be vain about it. Maybe we are all God like and glowing. Perhaps we are all angelic and are here for some divine purpose. Scott sometimes thinks he knows this.

Anyway, as he drove away Scott thought about the black man he had just dropped off. Would he actually commit suicide? Would he jump off the notorious Calhoun Street Bridge when he tried walking home? For this there was no way for Scott to know.

Was this what his life had in store? Was he destined to one day cripple over with pain, hating the days? Poor, uninsured, and uncared for. His life wasted on drugs like a million other denizens of Trenton? Or was there something more?

Had Scott possessed the healing powers of Jesus he would have touched the guy and saved him, he would. Unfortunately, it just wasn't to be. They were both stuck here in reality.

Maybe Scott and grandpa were both equally growing older to death.

Scott reflected on grandpa's black countenance and he couldn't help but think about his old buddy Pez and earlier lessons. Pez had been a young man when they arrested him. Busted for cocaine possession, in case you don't remember. Scott hoped he would be released before he too got old and time robbed him off his strength. Before he too had gray hair and no teeth.

Or even more recently his dealer Wab who was taken into custody and sent away to be a guest of the state. Wabby; another great guy with a family, a sense of humor and a smile. He was a brother who loved to laugh and he held no anonymity in his heart against the past of long dead white men. He hated racism but he knew how to live and let live and he knew how to forgive. They sent that man to prison. For what? Yeah, you guessed it, drug offenses.

This made him think about God's compassion and justice and of the overriding goodness.

And about how we, all of us, are walking around thirsty for mercy. Be it from the hospitals with their healing or from the legal system for forgiveness.

Unfortunately money tips the scales of justice and if you are poor, then you will receive no clemency. And Judges rule the state of New Jersey. How many good men did they send away? How many futures have they stolen? How many non violent offenders rot in prison today? How many come out violent? How many never come out? They are the victims of the war on drugs and other laws that are equally stupid.

Anyway, since we are speaking bluntly, let's continue with the race words as they relate to our discussion of many failures. Once, when Scott was in therapy, his psychiatrist suggested that he read the autobiography of Malcolm X. He said it might give him some perspective and insight into the nature of race relations, looking at it from the other side, through the black man's eyes.

So he read what the minister did and said and he grew in understanding. He respected Malcolm because he always shouted out against injustice, regardless of what the consequences were or how much it cost him. Equally impressive about Malcolm was the fact that even though he originally hated white folk, his life and his journey eventually taught him that we are all brothers. God (Allah) had shown him the error of his ways and he was humbled by the true spirit of Islam. He was a man unafraid to say "I was wrong" "I'm sorry" and "Forgive me." Perhaps not in those words, but you get the gist.

Scott related to the persecution perpetrated on Malcolm by people of contrasting color. But every time Malcolm spoke of Aryans as "the white devil" it was like a slap in the face.

The fact that Scott may in fact be a white devil notwithstanding, he had never gotten together with any of his friends and swarmed and attacked any black man who was helplessly outnumbered. A crime that the black man had committed unto him. Likewise, he had never taken a knife or a razor and sliced open any dark skin. A black devil was guilty of that sin. Scott never fractured one of their skulls in a merciless and evil beating.

He would be lying if he said he never hated the men that attacked him or if he said he never called a man a niger, but he never put on a white robe and lynched anyone and he didn't go around lighting crosses on fire either. Nor had he ever put on a black robe and slammed a gavel and sentence anyone to prison, nor had he ever separated any man from his child. Like Judge Superior in his wisdom. No, Scott never did anything to damn any of them.

In fact it might be safe to say that he loved all the races the same.

People; no two alike, they're bound to fight all our lives, people.

Scott sat and remembered his incarcerated friends; Wabby, Magoo, and Pez. Guys convicted of non violent crimes and sentenced to ludicrous amounts of time. Sure, they had all been poor and basically lazy men, but they were also entrepreneurs and capitalists, making decent livings selling drugs and supplying the demand.

Anyway, enough with the digression about blacks and whites, jock itch and the courts, and other ramblings embarked upon. None of this, though needing to be said, leads us back to our story, so without a sufficient segway, we'll just jump back into it. Shall we?

So its bitter cold now with winter and the wind chill stings exposed skin and the air is frozen with a February freeze. There are very few black birds left in the trees and the road is covered with ice as we follow the streets back to the second floor apartment on Bruce lane in Ewing. A car pulls up to Scott and Kelly's.

Dahlia and her boyfriend Double R get out and slam their doors. The sound resonates in the ears of the junkies upstairs anxiously awaiting their product to fix. As the two make their way up the unshoveled and snowy steps, the inhabitants wait like little kids for Christmas.

Huddled around the coffee table are CJ, his girlfriend Donna, and their friend, a guy Scott and Kelly had never met named Rich.

Kelly lays on the bed which is a mattress on the floor in the same room as the coffee table. Scott sits on the floor as the apartment is very small.

The dealers enter through the only door which is in the kitchen. They pass by the sink filled with two weeks' worth of dirty dishes. Dahlia and her man enter the main room passed the Nirvana poster without ever even knocking. They do so to a chorus of happy drug addicts.

Now there are seven people in the room. 5 white and 2 black. 4 men and 3 women. The visit is relatively brief and the money and the drugs trade hands. This shit is called H.I.V. or Dope dick, or Larry Love. The junkies begin the process of fixin' before the dealers even leave. They all have important business to attend to and nothing else matters except taking the sickness away. Shaky hands rip open wax paper bags and spill the precious little powder into their spoons, cans, or lids. They bite a piece of cotton from their cigarette filters and they pass a cup of water around and they all dip in their syringes. It is the beginning of the daily ritual.

They spray their water over the diesel, the diesel most evil, and they begin to mix. Some use the plungers on their needles and some use the bright orange caps, anything really, it doesn't even matter. Soon the water is no longer clear. Now it is dirty brown. The filthy liquid gets sucked back through the cotton and loaded into the needles, the needles most evil.

Kelly cries to go first, but Scott tells her no. he pulls his belt tight around his bicep with the needle in his teeth. CJ. uses a shoelace and Donna the drawstring from her hoodie, but they are all tourniquets just the same. Scott sits on the floor watching the blood bloom in the needle and he pumps the poison in and waits for the rush. He has waited all day for this moment and it is pleasant and nice.

Kelly almost goes insane from hunger as she waits; again the blood lust is practically vampiric and almost unbearable. She feeds a greed she perceives as a need. She will share Scott's needle when he is done. This is their romantic little game; foreplay. In New Jersey something like 80% of all I.V. drug users have Hepatitis C. Scott and Kelly are no exception.

And the blood mixes with the dope in the various needles (called sets) around the room. And once they're in, they pump the dirty fluid and flex their muscles and relax. And the warm rush that envelops them renders them all useless.

Scott and the new guy Rich close their eyes while Kelly cleans Scott's syringe and begins her own procedure. Unfortunately, Kelly's veins are bad from shooting up so much and when she can't find one, she gets anxious, paranoid, and she cries. She asks CJ to hit her in the external jugular vein in her neck. CJ is not a doctor and has no medical training, but he has been on heroin longer than any of them and, so, he is considered the authority on drugs. You can trust that he will not blow your shot.

Soon, all around the room the junkies will be falling out and nodding. Soon Scott will open his eyes and everyone will be high.

If we were to set up a camera now in the center of this drugged circle and spin it panoramic, we would see a scene of sick and wasted humanity. First, if we zoom in for a close up on CJ's girlfriend Donna, maybe we notice that she too is having some trouble booting. She sticks herself for maybe the sixth or seventh time. She too is desperately trying to find a vein, feeling Kelly's pain. They have all been in this situation before. Soon, she will ask CJ to hit her, which he will do, if she gives him half a bag.

CJ sits back and he smiles. He booted his shit on the very first try.

Kelly comes back from the bathroom where CJ blasted the dope into her neck. They had to leave the room because no one wanted to watch it. She is high for a little while and she sits back down on the bed quite and satisfied.

It is only when we spin in the direction of CJ's friend Rich that we first detect a problem. The dude's head is rolled over to the side, resting on his shoulder. He does not seem to be breathing.

So Scott says "Yo, CJ what's up with your boy?"

CJ appears annoyed and starts yelling at his friend. "Yo Rich! Rich, wake up!" When this has no effect, he reluctantly gets up off the couch and shoves the guy three or four times. Nothing. Still the guy remains comatose.

If you are unfamiliar with this phenomenon, this is known in dope circles as "falling out" Heroin is a tricky drug to get the dosage just right and when you shoot it, you really have no idea how it is going to react. It was not unusual for Scott and Kelly to find one another unconscious and to have to wake each other up by slapping them in the face to resuscitate them. Scott could remember many times finding his beloved passed out on the toilet or bathroom floor and wondering to himself in a panic "Is she dead?" and "Dear God, don't let her be dead." This was not uncommon in their relationship. Such was their sickness.

Anyway, Kelly and Donna were relatively uninterested in whether or not Rich was dead. He did not matter enough to them to interrupt their high and ruin their nod. It was a buzz kill.

CJ didn't seem that effected by this either for that matter and he went back to the couch to sit down.

Scott, however, didn't need some guy he just met to drop dead in his apartment. "Yo, man, you better fix your boy."

"What do you want me to do?"

"Something."

So CJ (who has no medical training) drop kicks the kid in the chest and knocks him off his chair. Still, he drops like a dead man. "Fuck dude!"

The junkies pick him up and lay him on the couch. Unresponsive. Scott gets an idea and he runs to the kitchen. He grabs a dirty cup out of the pile of dishes that Kelly never washed and he fills it up with water. He comes back into the room and throws it in the kids face. It does not bring him back but some of the water splashed onto the coffee table and landed on the left over wax paper bags of diesel that they were saving for later.

Only now does Kelly take notice. Horrified she says "Watch what you're doing, Chip, you're gonna ruin the dope."

"I'm really sorry Kel, but I think this is a little more important right now. We do not need this guy to die in our apartment. That definitely will not be good for us."

Kelly ignored him as usual and began to carefully and lovingly dry the bags.

Now CJ gets up and acts as if he and Donna are going to leave. "Well, we gotta go."

"Dude, take him with you. He is not my problem."

"What do you want me to do?"

"Let's carry him out to your car." So CJ grabs the dude's wrists and Scott grabs his ankles. The plan was to attempt to carry him down the steps. Now, maybe you've never tried to carry a lifeless body before, but so you know, 200 pounds of dead human weight is a lot more awkward than you might think. Especially for two junkies with weakened muscles.

Fortunately for Rich, when they dragged him into the kitchen, he actually came to underneath the Nirvana poster. He regained consciousness by the sink filled with dirty dishes that Kelly was forever too lazy to wash.

It sounds comical, but the dude awoke with murder in his eyes and Scott let go of him and took a step back. The kid then recognized CJ and his expression relaxed. His first words when he came back, "CJ man, I need to get some cocaine." Drugs that make you go slow, then drugs to make you go fast. Again, the sickness.

So maybe by now you're wondering what's the point of all these little blips of story and what, if any, is the message that it's trying to convey. Well, hopefully it has entertained you with truth, written such as it is as fiction. But maybe it's more than just another war story about addiction and it might even speak about the human condition and the need for recovery and religion. Narcotics Anonymous speaks about the need for a higher power and for these distorted denizens of Trenton, heroin has assumed the role that normal people reserve for God. In fact, to take it a step further CJ and Donna and Scott and Kelly might even be involved in a demented love triangle with the drugs making up the highest point. They might not make love to each other like lovers in healthy relationships but they still have their daily orgies. A dark ménage trois.

Deuteronomy reminds that God is a jealous God however and a jealous God can seriously fuck with the sinner or idolater. Or the junkie if we fast forward to the prevalent crimes of today.

So where do we pick up from here?

Let's jump ahead shall we? To after the rent and electric went unpaid for days that turned into weeks and weeks that turned into months. After the power was shut off and they were forced to shoot their drugs by candle light. To after Scott and Kelly were inevitably evicted. After Kelly went to jail for the first time and Scott got sent to his sixth or seventh rehab. We'll pick up our tale on South Broad Street when they were reunited again after being apart for a while.

As usual they mixed together like poison, destructive, each to the other. He was killing his kid's mother slowly and after each injection he told her how much he loved her.

Anyway, Kelly introduced him to this dude Charlie and the girl who was staying with him at the room he was renting on the second floor on Broad, down the street from the convenience store called the pantry. That store will play a part in our story shortly. Charlie's girl friend, who was not his girlfriend, was named Christine.

Scott and Charlie hit it off instantly and within minutes of their meeting they were laughing and joking around like old friends. Charlie and Christine were crack smokers who only dabbled here and there with dope. Scott had never met a more generous crack smoker than Charlie. He shared hundreds of dollars worth of the stuff with Scott and Kel the first night that they met. That shit just doesn't happen in Trenton. Scott began to suspect that his new friend might even have some homosexual tendencies and maybe all the drugs had some strings attached. But Scott had no curiosities and so that shit was never going to happen. Still, Charlie was funny and high and generally a really likeable guy.

Scott got along much better with his new brother than he did with his women that night as it was not uncommon now for he and Kelly to fight.

It was always over drugs. There were four bags left and even though Scott had paid for them, somehow they ended up in Kelly's pocket.

Outside Charlie's place on the sidewalk the fighting began with Scott trying to get his two bags. Kelly was reluctant to share his drugs with him and she tried to pull a fast one. They just got out of Scott's van, a green Chevy custom job which we'll discuss more later, when this jerk off walks up to them out of the darkness. He knows Kelly from somewhere and he wants her to cop some drugs for him. Kelly can't wait to get away from her boyfriend and disappear down Home Ave. or Chestnut with this guy. She did not however want to give her lover his share of the dope regardless of the fact that she still had two bags of her own or the fact that Scott had paid for it all.

"Here" she says, handing him an empty cigarette pack. "It's inside. Don't open it on the street."

Yeah, right sweetie. He checks the shit immediately before she can sneak away with this scumbag. As expected the cigarette pack contains only their empties. "Kel, don't fucking play me. I knew you were gonna try that shit."

"Oh, sorry, I thought they were in there. Wait until I get back, I'm just going around the corner to cop. I'll be right back."

The dude was standing there waiting impatiently.

"Kel, if you think you're leaving here with my bags than you're crazier than I thought."

Now Kelly's new friend speaks up. "Dude, we'll be right back."

Scott was indifferent about the guy until now, now he totally hated him. "Yeah? That's nice." He turned back to his babies' momma. "Kel, don't make me take the shit off you right now cuz' I fucking will, right here on the street."

The guy obviously didn't want to intercede and protect her so Kelly was cornered. "Maybe you should just give it to him" said the dick.

And since she was really out of options, she finally gave him what was his. "Here Chip. Damn you're an asshole sometimes."

He probably said something sarcastic to her after that like "You kids have fun." because he really was an asshole sometimes especially when it came to drugs and getting high.

Then the dirty mother fucker disappeared from his view with his women and he had no way of knowing what they were going to do.

We touched on the topic of trickin' before. If Kelly had sex with this guy for money or not, Scott never knew, but once he had found out for sure that she had done it, the suspicion never left him. It broke his heart because he loved her, he really did. Every part of her; her insanity and the chaos she brought with her. Her body, her eyes, her ass and that anything for the next high mentality.

How many times had she saved him from being sick with prostitution? It was like how many licks to get to the tootsie roll center of a tootsie pop? The world may never know.

And yes he took the drugs she gave him gratefully only to look disapprovingly at her after.

Scott had a friend named Jack, who was also a heroin addict, and many times when he was unemployed or just too sick to work, his wife Maria would do what needed to be done to get their next fix. "Listen, Chip . . ." Jack had said to him "You gotta look at this like a business. It's just a job for them. They have no feelings for these guys. Don't think about it. Hey listen, if girls would pay you to fuck them, you would right?"

"Hell yeah." he bragged. But definitely not. And no matter what C.J. or Jack ever told him, the thought of what Kelly felt she needed to do always hurt him.

Anyway the night Kelly disappeared down the street, Scott went upstairs to party with Christine and Charlie. He promptly shot his dope and then he smoked crack for the rest of the night with his new best friends.

From the second floor window we can see Scott's van parked, unlocked on Broad Street. It must have been about 2 am when Kelly finally came back. They watched her go into the van and they could see inside the constant spark of her lighter. Charlie went down to invite her in. When he got there, he found Kelly sifting through the garbage in the van, fiending for a forty dollar piece of crack that she had dropped. This is a common condition for the crackhead. Charlie helped her look for it for a few minutes, offering her suggestions as to where she might have lost it. What Kelly didn't know was that Charlie had already found it on the sidewalk and that it now rested safely in his pocket. A few minutes later, he comes back upstairs and says to Christine' "You should go downstairs and talk to her, she is pretty upset." So Christine leaves.

When she is gone, Charlie smiles at Scott. "Dude, guess what I found?" And he drops the glorious pebble on the table. "Fuck them bitches" he says "Me and you are smoking this shit, cool?"

"Cool." And Kelly never found out that her boyfriend was upstairs getting tore up on the crack that she was still downstairs desperately looking for. It was a beautiful little boulder too.

Anyway, soon enough morning came and the cocaine let go its hold on them enough that they were finally able to fall asleep. Scott and Kelly on the guest bed and Charlie and Christine on the master bed by the T.V.

When he awoke, all hell broke loose.

Christine was shaking him violently and Kelly was gone. "Wake up" she screamed "Your bitch of a girlfriend robbed fifty dollars off me while I was sleeping. I know it was her too, look! She cut a hole in my pocket!" And sure enough, someone had made a razor slits in the sweatpants she was wearing. It seemed like there must have been easier way to rob her and that Kelly had gone through a lot of trouble with all the cutting. But whatever.

"I'm sorry. Are you sure it was Kel?"

"I fucking know it was her! She left here with Charlie. Watch when they get back. I know she's your girlfriend and all but when she comes back, I'm kicking the shit out of her!"

All Scott could say again was lamely "I'm sorry. You see how she gets. I'm not even sure she's my girlfriend anymore." So, while Scott and Christine were waiting for Kelly to come back and get smacked around, Scott's eyelids got heavy and he drifted back into dreams. Sometime later, he heard the door open and Christine began screaming again.

"You mother fucker, you stole my money and went out with that skank!" Charlie had come home alone.

Scott pretended to sleep through this, but he shot up quickly when he heard what came next. "Here" Charlie said and Scott heard a soft thump as something hit Christine in her chest. "I shouldn't even share this with you, talking to me like that."

"God damn, Charlie! What did you do? Rob a bank?"

"Shh keep your voice down."

Now Scott was fully awake. He was dope sick but he loved the sound of that conversation. Surely his new friend would buy him some heroin with all the money he had stolen. Provided that Kelly hadn't fucked up his chances that was. And where was she anyway? She should be here getting in on this.

So, one of the things that a dope fiend will do is play up how sick they are. Even a junkie that has just fixed will act as if they are miserable if someone with money or dope comes in. Drug addicts are great liars and better actors than those you see on T.V. Scott put on his show for Charlie. "Yo man, I don't feel so good. Buy me some dope and I'll drive you wherever you want to go."

And again he was amazed by the generosity of Charlie. "You know it bro. We're gonna get tore up from the floor up." The air crackled with excitement and anticipation. So Scott's new friends made some calls and stocked up on their narcotic provisions. They ended up in a park in Trenton by the Delaware River. They all shot heroin and spent the day walking around in the summer sun smoking the crack and cigarettes that Charlie supplied in abundance.

The biggest problem for any addict with drugs is that no matter how much you have, eventually you run out. Such was true for our trio that day. Soon they needed more. Fortunately, Charlie still had plenty of money.

They were forced back into the city to meet the man with the dope. The deal was set up at the convenience store called the Pantry on Broad. While they waited for the guy, also named Scott to deliver the dope, Charlie tells our Scott to buy whatever he wants.

He comes back to the counter with a coke and a pack of Ho-Ho's. Now, the other Scott, who was the dealer arrives and joins them. Since selling heroin in Trenton is basically a black man's trade and because we already have a main character called Scott, we'll differentiate the two by calling this one White Scott.

Anyway, at this point, Charlie pulls out a knot of obviously stolen money from his pocket to pay for the cokes and Ho-Ho's. The rolled up bills are roughly the size of a McDonalds Big Mac. White Scott pushes down his hand with the cash and says "Damn, Charlie, put that shit away. People can tell it's stolen. You gotta keep that shit on the down low. Now, how much do you want?"

Our hero Scott takes his soda and chocolate cakes outside into the parking lot to leave the two alone to talk business and set up the deal. As he took his first bite, he noticed that things were about to go horribly wrong.

A car pulls up behind his van blocking it in. The cops in plain clothes jumped out from both sides with their guns in their hands and their badges hanging from chains around their necks. They ran passed him like he wasn't even there. They burst into the store and started screaming.

Scott thought to himself "Please God, let them be here to bust the dealer." He knew where else to get drugs. He did not know anyone else with fifteen hundred dollars that they would be willing to spend on a drug spree. His prayer to God went unanswered and a few minutes later, they brought his new brother Charlie out of the Pantry in handcuffs.

Fuck.

Charlie was no longer smiling and he did not look Scott in the eyes as the police lead him by. Nor did the cops ever question Scott, they just took Charlie into custody and he never said goodbye.

This was not Scotts first time having a friend get arrested and he already knew the drill. He would never see the dude again. A Trenton lesson taught to him by guys like Wab, Magoo, and Pez.

Apparently Charlie did not get away clean with his crime which turned out to be robbing a restaurant and not a bank. He got close to two grand but someone had seen him and the witness lead the cops to stake out the Pantry and wait.

When they took him to jail, Scott and Charlie's girl friend who was not his girlfriend had the same thought at exactly the same time. "Shit, now how are we gonna get high."

A few minutes later, White Scott snuck out of the Pantry looking guilty as sin and relieved that he was still a free man. He moved like a rat as he looked around to see who was watching before running down the alley that lead along the side of the store leading to Adeline Street. He was so obviously a criminal that it was funny. If you had seen him sneak away like that you would have laughed.

It was completely understandable to Scott why guys would fear going to jail so much. For all the crimes he had committed and even sometimes been caught for he was always spared going to jail. Scott had to believe that God had a plan for him that didn't include prison and for that he was always grateful. Kelly had once said to him "You don't really know the streets because you've never been in jail."

To which he replied "No, I've never been in jail because I know these streets." This of course was bullshit. If wasn't for some divine intervention, he'd be sitting in there with his friends wasting away. And probably somebody's bitch as well cause really he wasn't that hard.

He'd known guys tougher than himself so scared of going back to the cell that they took their own lives. Ernie, his uncle's friend and Coke dealer that I told you about in chapter one was a bad mother fucker who probably would have ruled in jail. But the thought of going back drove him to shoot his self in the head when the sheriff's boys came for him. May he rest in peace Amen.

Christine looks at Scott with the customary Where am I gonna get my next fix panic in her eyes. She says "I think Charlie left some of the money under his mattress. Take me there and I'll try to get in."

So they go back half a block down Broad St. from the Pantry to Charlie's apartment. Christine goes inside and argues with the landlord but the guy refuses to unlock the door and let her in. She comes out and tells Scott to take her around back so she can scale the wall and try and break in through the second floor window. A few minutes later, she comes back unsuccessful and she and Scott are sufficiently screwed.

They drove around Trenton coming down off the drugs and not sure what to do next. That's when the devil came through with what seemed like a miracle and Scott saw his angel walking down Chestnut Ave. They pulled the van over and his babies momma got in. She had scored four bags of diesel and Scott wanted two of them. Kelly, however, only wanted to give him one and again the fighting ensued.

"Fuck that Kel, when I get shit, we split it right down the middle."

"So? You had dope all day long. These are the first bags I got; plus I'm sick and you're not."

It was true that he wasn't technically dope sick but his brain was polluted into dogshit and so he was acting like a dick. "Kelly, you're gonna give me two or so help me, I'll jump over this seat and take them all off you."

"I fucking hate you."

Christine in the passenger seat finally chimed in. "This is the way you talk to each other? I thought you loved each other."

"I don't give a fuck about him." Said his princess as they pulled up on Division across the street from her mom's house. Scott was a little blurry on what happened next but at some point he had both of his hands around her neck. He was choking his children's mother, the woman he loved, just to get more of the drug. That wonderful drug.

Elsewhere in Trenton, Charlie was spending his first of many nights in a cage.

And Ariel and Ethan were warm in their beds sleeping; protected under their blankets provided by people who were not their father or mother. Scott and Kelly were both twisted by idjits and possessed by rampant addictions.

"O.K, O.K., here Chip." His hands on her throat did the trick and she handed him his shit, so he would calm down when he fixed. Then she said sweetly, "Honey, at least let me go first, cuz' I'm sick."

And Scott relaxed with his bags said "Alright, but hurry up with my set." He was after all a great guy and magnanimous. He handed her his needle and she got to mixing up her heroin there in the back seat on Division St. They were desperate, suffering, and young. Their emotions see-sawed from lust to violence in a heartbeat. One second they wanted to kill each other, the next they were completely in love. And everything they did, they did for the drug.

This night was not over yet though and high in the sky the moon still cast its cosmic purplish glow. It was bright for night but on Division there was only darkness. From up in his heaven, God could see his children Scott and Kelly; selfish and sinful. It was not the first time He'd seen them fight. Perhaps something inside them was broken or as Kurt Cobain would say "there was something in the way."

So while Kelly was attempting to boot up, the minutes crawled like hours and an eternity seemed to elapse while Scott waited for her to pass back his set, infected as it was with dirty blood laced with Hepatitis C. Her arms dripped red and the dope was pink in the set, and yet, she refused to push on the plunger and run it. Maybe he was still paranoid from the coke that he smoked earlier, but Scott was convinced that the police would be there any second to bust them all. This was a little irrational because it seemed like the cops almost never came down Division.

"Come on. Kel, you're taking way too long."

"Wait! I can't get it." Kelly cried and the tears ran down her eyes and the needle stung every time she tried. But still she tried and tried and tried.

Finally, Scott gave up on waiting and he sniffed his shit up his nose. Now every junkie knows that snorting heroin will get you off E and it might even get you high, but you will not get that rush. That delightful warm rush they all want. "Fuck, Kel, are you happy now? I had to sniff mine." And he was enraged and out of his mind.

Later, Kelly would say that he had hit her and that the left side of her face was black and blue for days. If that was true, Scott never knew. It didn't really count anyway because if it happened, it happened in a blackout. Besides, strange as it sounds wasn't there some part of his Bi-polar girlfriend that secretly liked this? That wanted to get hit? That found it exciting? Is this really what she wanted? Did she believe that she needed to be beaten? Is that why she seemed to ask for it? Oh Jesus. Could she be that sick?

Scott jumped on her and they wrestled around in the back of the van cursing at each other. "You dirty bitch, get the fuck out of my truck!"

"No! You fucking asshole." Christine had gotten out of the front passenger seat and Kelly reached up front and ripped a piece of decorative wood off the consol around his outdated cassette player. Motivated by hate, she threw this at her boyfriends face. She wanted him dead.

Scott dodged the throw and grabbed her, in an attempt to pull her out the side doors of his van. He screamed "I said get out, now!" But Kelly wasn't cooperating and she had herself turned upside down. Her feet kicked at the track lighting that lined the ceiling and she clawed at him as he finally was able to drag her out. He managed to push her onto the sidewalk. "I'm so fucking sick of you! This shit is over!"

Commotion like this is not uncommon in Trenton and nobody in any of the nearby houses bothered to come out.

Scott got back in the van and was about to drive away when his sweetheart jumped in front of the car. "Move Kel. I should run you the fuck over!" Her face was the shade of red that one associates with extreme rage and she grabbed the plastic grill on the front of his van and snapped that off as well. When Scott put the vehicle in park and got out to remove her, she threw the grill at him too.

"My purse is in the van" she said "You're not leaving with my pills." She had medicine for her various conditions; Scott wasn't sure what they were; Xanex, Clonapine, Valium, or Pamprin. Whatever. He went in the van and grabbed her pocketbook from the back. Then he flung it down the street where it spilled its contents from 710 Division Street to the corner of Hewitt Street.

"Here" Scott smiled at her as he watched the horror in her eyes. He had a sadistic side.

"Mother fucker!" Kelly chased her purse as the pills and beauty products and lighters and paraphernalia spilled everywhere. When she went to retrieve them, Scott made good on his escape. As he was starting to drive away, Christine opened the passenger door and said "Can I go with you?"

"Yeah" he said "Get in." And she did.

When Kelly saw this, she flipped. "You fucking bitch! You're going with him?!"

Earlier, when Christine thought that Kelly had stolen her money she had said something about kicking her ass. When they picked her up however Christine stayed quiet and never mentioned anything to her. Truth be told Kelly was crazy and if it came down to it, Kelly would fuck Christine up. Trenton and the devil had made her tough.

Anyway, a few blocks down, Scott stopped the van and told the girl to get out. His life was out of control and he needed to go do something about it. And all his life's education was in drugs and rehabs. Recovery and relapse.

So Scott left Kelly at her Mom's house and was gone.

Now I don't know if it's because they were so codependent; addicted to each other as much as the drugs, or if they really did have an everlasting and indestructible love. But for whatever the reason this madness was far from reaching its end.

Scott and Kelly would be together again.

Chapter 8

Judge Superior and the hypocrisy of the Good.

YOU SHOULD KNOW, too, that in this town there are ghosts.
There are the kinds that haunt us all, collectively as a society. The ones that endure throughout history. They are born from racism and resentment and from spirits tormented. They seek retribution or redemption, and they remember atrocities past, long forgotten by the future souls they cry out to of injustices done. These ghosts shape the course of current events like puppet masters behind the scenes. They sweep us along like a river flowing to the ocean. Being mostly unaware, that these ghosts are even there, they are beyond our control and they take us where they want us to go. Everyone gets caught up in their inertia. There are no exceptions. These ghosts are discontentment.

Then there are the kinds that haunt the individual. These are much more personal. We inherit these from our ancestors, and our fathers. Some of them are passed to us genetically, given to us along with our race, hair, and eye color. Some are born in our lifetimes. These are the memories behind our scars, be they physical or emotional. These haunt our self esteem and our dreams. These ghosts can corrode our very souls.

In this chapter we will look at both of those types of ghost.

To understand the spirits that linger in the city of Trenton, perhaps it would be best if we took a quick history lesson. And yes, some of this shit may not be entirely relevant.

The city was named after William Trent who came to New Jersey with the Quakers. The Quakers settled in the Delaware Valley in 1679, their name meaning friends. Now it is impossible to know what kind of guy William was, if he was kind to children and animals or if he beat on his wife, but we do know that he came here seeking freedom and he brought with him his slaves as was the custom of those days.

William and the Quakers wanted to get away from religious persecution, so they came here as an escape. Almost immediately upon their arrival the native Lenape' Indians were displaced. Scott could not find out much about how they drove the Indians out, but he suspected that the dealings were shady. He could imagine the white man trading trinkets for land before losing patience with commerce and trade and taking to weapons to drive the Lenape away.

Anyway, William was one of the richest landowners around and of the fact that he was a swindler, Scott had no doubt. The city was named after him in 1721. Originally it was called Trent's town. This was back in Trenton's conception and infancy.

If we were to follow Trent's legacy further through history, we would discover that after he died of what historians believe was probably a massive stroke on Christmas day 1724; three of his slaves were executed for his murder. They hung the three Negroes twelve years after his death. At this time, there would be no forensic evidence on which to convict or condemn these men. Yet they offered the brothers up to the god's and three malcontented ghosts would go on to haunt the Trenton landscape.

How many more were murdered in racisms name remains a mystery, but perhaps the most famous slave owner in American history was none other than the father of our country, George Washington. He came to Trenton for his greatest victory (arguably) of the Revolutionary war in 1776. George aimed the artillery down King Street, which is now Warren Street and Queen Street, which is now Broad. He directed the battle, presumably, from a position of relative safety. A well protected General, like an unassailable king in a game of chess. Never put in check or threatened. In any case, the future first president was not hit by any of the Hessian's bullets. Another future president who was at the battle was not so lucky though. James Monroe took one in the shoulder, for he was a soldier. The musket ball severed an artery and he was fortunate that doctors were able to clamp it, lest he'd of bleed to death. Welcome to Trenton.

Today, there is a monument in the heart of the city, where the north and south wards meet, to commemorate where Washington commanded his epic battle. A bronze statue 13 feet high sits atop a pedestal 150 feet above the street, surveying downtown Trenton, which became the state capital in 1790.

Historians also say that Washington was conflicted about the morality of owning slaves and being the leader of the free world and democracy. Despite his inner contention and ambivalence, George did nothing to set the black man free. He lacked the courage of his convictions and that is his hypocrisy.

The very same dilemma was faced by the next fifteen presidents for eighty some years. As you know, it wasn't until 1863 that Abraham Lincoln signed the emancipation proclamation and finally freed the slaves. But even then America went to war over the issue and the racial tensions lived on long after Lincoln got himself assassinated for signing it.

Maybe even guys like William Trent and George Washington are the reason that there is still so much animosity between blacks and whites in the north ward. Maybe that's why Scott had to have his ass beaten so badly on Hoffman Avenue, two hundred and some years later. Though to his knowledge, he and those dudes were in no way related. In any case, he never saw dime one of their money.

The racial time bomb exploded in Trenton some time after April 4, 1968 when down in Memphis, some crazy white man shot and killed Dr. Martin Luther King. The riots that ensued almost destroyed the city.

Four years before Scott was born, all hell broke loose in his eventual city. The scars left by the riots could still be felt as he was growing up and curiosity lead him to investigate the event. He couldn't help but smile as he pictured the images described in newspaper and internet articles. Supposedly, looters broke into a furniture store the day more than 200 downtown businesses's got ransacked. One reporter said it looked like sofas and love seats had grown legs and were running down the streets. Scott, who wasn't there to witness this mayhem, thought this shit was funny. Even more hysterical to him was the story of how the brothers broke into a sporting goods store and stole the golf clubs so they could drive golf balls at the approaching riot police. They placed guns on the rooftops and many of the businesses were burning.

Fortunately, as far as Scott could find out, there was only one fatality.

Harlan Bruce Joseph was a name that Scott had never heard before. He was a divinity student who returned home to Trenton following the death of Dr. King. He was supposed to have loved reading God's word and he had plenty of friends. In the midst of all the chaos and violence, Harlan ran into the street with the hope of calming the madness and restoring the peace.

The police officer who shot him said he was just trying to fire a warning shot into the air when a looter bumped into him and the bullet hit 19 year old Joseph instead. Scott's research did not tell him if the cop that shot him was white or black, but most likely he was white. Either way, the boy was killed just the same. Harlan Bruce Joseph was a hero and it is a shame that history has seemed to have forgotten his name. No 150 foot statue stands to commemorate his life, but Scott thought the boy sounded very much like a saint. A real life mother fucking martyr out of the North Ward, killed four years before he was born.

You best believe that his spirit is still here to this day, with his hope for racial harmony and peace. Latent yet ubiquitous and yearning for the goodness in man to overcome the evil.

Unfortunately, nothing lingers in this life like pain and memories of racism and the civil rights fiasco also remain. These are the ghosts that haunted the black youth and the reason why they jumped and beat Scott and other white dudes in the hallway at school. And yeah he was scarred from the violence. They hated him for his white skin. It was what you might call reverse racism, if such a thing exists. Scott labeled his attackers as mindless animals. He, himself never owned a slave and he had friends from just about every race, but still he took what he got from the black man in retaliation for what somebody who looked like him in history did to someone who looked like them. For the record it was never a fair fight.

And the ghosts perpetuate the cycle and the cycle never ends.

Scott knew too many black people that he loved however to really ever develop a blanket hatred for the whole race. Plus he has had his ass kicked by plenty of white people too. In fact, (and on this point he was probably on the same page as most of the brothers he knew in Trenton)

The only group of people he could honestly say that he despised were the police.

Please pardon me this diatribe and forgive me as I digress off on this tangent.

To quote N.W.A "Fuck the police." Scott had never met a cop who wasn't on a complete power trip and who didn't feel like he was so much better than everyone else. Two cops had married into his family; one to his cousin and the other his sister. Both of them ended up breaking their vows and cheating. One of the scumbags left and filed for divorce and the other got caught and promised never to do it again. But he will, Scott had not even a shadow of a doubt about that, for he was police and of predictable character. Scott's animosity was so absolute that after his sister had married the cop, he couldn't help but think less of her. She deserved the tears that she cried because she couldn't see him for what he was before their wedding and she lacked the courage to leave.

In the fifteen or so rehabs that Scott had been to, he must have met a million drug addicts (All of them 10x's cooler than your everyday cop) and you would be surprise to find out how many times five-oh would send a man to jail and then go and hit on his wife or girlfriend. Nothing is off limits to them. They take what they want, hiding behind their badges, with a feeling of supreme entitlement. These simpletons walk around carrying guns, believing their own bullshit, and they are not subject to the same silly laws you and I are. Everyone who would become a cop lacks the intelligence to question. Question which laws are just and fair. Question which Captains and Judges are crazy. If they were ordered to kill you, you best believe that they'd kill you. Allow me to reiterate; "Fuck every single one of them."

Can you feel it? The noose tightening around your neck as the government tightens its grip on its citizens? Tell me you don't see the same corrupt system as me. Watch as our freedoms are slowly stripped from us. Watch as they tax us beyond reason and take away the ones we love. It is ludicrous to consider that we are still a democracy.

For instance, the authorities may believe that they have the right to insist that you wear a seatbelt. If you don't then they can pull you over and write you a ticket for ridiculous amounts of money. Then they run that bullshit at you about how they really give a flying fuck about you or if you get killed in your car. That way it's about more than just the revenue and they can justify their extortion.

You probably don't remember voting on whether or not you thought this seatbelt law was a good idea, and that's because you weren't asked you were told.

And since nobody stepped up and fought this ridiculousness, now they can also fine you for talking on your cell phone. At this rate, it will not be long before you are not allowed to smoke cigarettes, listen to the radio, or masturbate while you drive.

Pretty soon, most of us will not be able to afford to drive anyway, between the insurance companies and the division of motor vehicle with their surcharges and fines. And the inevitable five dollars a gallon for gas.

Anyway, my point is this. Remember when Jim Florio was the governor of New Jersey? With his corruption and ties to organized crime? You must remember hearing about Governor McGreevy, humiliating his wife and state with his gayness, and cheating fagotry. Well' Scott never voted for either of those douche bags who felt that they were qualified to lead us as a people. He did not respect their positions of authority over him and he was convinced that this must be some sort of sick joke from God. How he likes to let the morons run things. Like retards behind the wheel of a car.

And all up and down the ass fucking that is the Trenton legal and political system, they look down on Scott and John Q Public as weak and stupid. If you question their laws and authority then they come back at you and question your patriotism. As if America hasn't been fascist for a very long time.

When was the last time you felt like you were being represented by congressmen?

Scott had no idea who his congressman was or where he lived, but somehow he was sure that the guy was a dick. And that he did not have the mentality to represent all the pissed off people in Trenton. He sure as holy fuck did not represent him. As if we could ever actually elect someone who didn't go to their schools and come out democrat or republican.

You see what I'm saying?

Scientists may say that there are more stars in the universe than there are grains of sand on all the earth's beaches. And we all believe them. But the thing is, we don't really know that now do we? I mean, maybe after so far out the stars simply stop, never to start up again. What we come to believe in as truth is really just somebody else's theory. One guy gets an idea and he tries to get his friend to agree with him. Then they take the theory to others and the movement is begun.

The preacher may feel that he is closer to God than you, but we have no way of knowing if this actually true. He is in the same boat as the scientist, forever rocking in a river of uncertainty. Puzzlement and wonderment. Maybe the way God intended it. But Christianity, Islam, and Buddha are all eager for us all to agree and believe as they believe, because let's face it; they know the fast track to get in good with the God. But it's a nasty pill to swallow.

Where do you think you will find more segregation in the world, in the prisons or in the religions? And what has been the number one reason for combat throughout history? People are constantly fighting because of their opposing understandings of the Lord. Perhaps it's even the reason that God doesn't come around much anymore. Maybe he's sick of all the conflict and he's had it with our holy wars.

The devil, however, is still here. Scott might have even bought dope off him a couple of times. If you think that the Papiver Somniferum is not a blessing from Satan, then you are mistaken.

Anyway, the law is an invisible thing beyond understanding. It's a trip how they make defendants swear on the bible. Books mutilated through time by the Jews and the Catholic Church with their debates on canonization to the point of making it unreliable and inaccurate at best. Totally perverting it at worst. And what would weigh more on the scales of justice anyway, man's laws or the commandments?

It's hard to know exactly what or how much gets stolen by the Trenton legal system, the state. Sadly, there are some ignorant people in charge of the welfare of the children today. Remember in the bible when it speaks about the Pharisee's and Sadducee's? See they never go away. Scott would love to sucker punch every single mother fucker down there at division of youth and family services when he thinks about how hard they persecuted he and Kelly, while elsewhere in the city kids were being beaten and raped and were starving. Stories from Dyfus are almost comically disturbing, but I am speaking of an even higher state of dysfunction than that. Enter the courtroom. Enter the lawyer.

And the judge who stands in for God figuring he's the best suited to do it. But whoever gave this guy the right to judge him? When did any of us sign on for this shit? To once again quote the bible, Jesus said "Judge not and you will not be judged." And "Let he who is without sin throw the first stone."

Unfortunately, the state needs that revenue and so God would just have to overlook some of that shit about compassion and justice. Mercy and forgiveness just aren't that good for business. And the judge sits in the highest seat, with his agenda, and his gavel. With his black robe bulging and his misunderstandings that inadvertently destroy other people's lives. See the judge figures that everyone he plays God over is only miniscule and pathetic. He is the most sanctimonious and he, like the police who work under him, considers all the defendants as less than. He knows neither gnosis nor any great truth and so he does not consider the truth to be a threat to him.

What could he possibly know about God's chosen and the blessings that he has passed on to Scott and his family? Quite frankly, he just wasn't righteous or even smart enough to understand. And so this judge along with the imbeciles at dyfus stepped in with their system and fucked everything up. They inflicted a punishment intended to crush him when they took away children, his heart. They sentenced him without honor as hard as they possible could, as if they knew anything about God's will or the greater good. So obviously the legal system is cold and broken and horrible injustices are the norm today. And yeah lady justice is blind, but she's also shallow and stupid.

Talk to Ariel and Ethan about what's fair. Tell them how compassionate it is for the law to step in and say that they don't have the right to know their father. Or their real mother for that matter. And Scott would say "fuck you" to anyone who agreed with this holier than thou mentality.

That is not to say that Scott has not made a plethora of mistakes. For example, when the courts first started persecuting him, he was able to pass the first two drug tests they hurled at him, but on the third he came up hot. He remembered the phone call from the social services woman clearly.

"Mr. Westcott?"

"Yeah."

"It's (so and so) from the division of youth and family services."

"Yeah."

"Mr. Westcott, it appears that you were not completely honest with us when you said you hadn't taken any drugs for the last three months. Your U.T. came back positive for cocaine."

"No, it didn't."

"Yes, it did. It was very slight, but positive."

"Fuck." Third time was the charm for dyfus.

And Scott felt like the biggest loser alive. Why couldn't he just live the way everyone else did? If it was possible to feel any worse, he would in a few minutes when he had to tell his mother that he had failed their test.

"Mom?"

"Yeah."

"I have to tell you something."

"What?"

"I failed the drug test."

"No, you didn't." At first she thought he was joking because Scott had a tendency to tease his mother. "Chip, don't play with me."

"I'm sorry Mom, I got high on Friday, I thought for sure it would be out of my system by Tuesday." And the disappointment in her eyes was far worse than her anger, though there was plenty of that too. She understood the implications of this and how the state now had the ammunition it needed to keep his daughter from him. This was back before Ethan was born, before the prescription medicines lead his mommy and daddy to heroin.

Scotts memory then flashed forward to another day in court and how two hours before he arrived, Kelly had said to him, "Baby, take two of these Xanex before you go, they will keep you calm." She knew how the judge tried to push his buttons. "Nothing they say will upset you if you're on these." Unfortunately, the pills seemed to have the opposite effect on him, than it did on women. In fact, when he sat there in court, he could not remember ever being more pissed. He sat there enduring their condemnation and judgment and he was dripping with contempt.

When "his honor" had finished telling him what he had decided would be best for his family, Scott had only three words. "Are we done?"

"Yeah, we're done." said the mighty one.

And Scott got up in his rage and kicked the little half door separating the defendant from the people in the gallery. The gallery where Scott's parents sat horrified at their sons behavior; behavior that was about to get a lot worse. He stormed out of the courtroom.

Nancy and Wes followed him out; as the judge decided that Scott's exit was too disrespectful and he sent his bailiff to fetch him back in.

The bailiff met them at the elevator and put his hand on Scott's shoulder. He momentarily snapped and shrugged the black man's hand off him. To everyone's astonishment and shock he said "Get your fucking hands off me, niger!" (More apologies, that would never come were probably in order.)

But the judge had sent for him and he would have to go back in, there was simply no way around it. The judge was also black and so his racial slur probably wasn't going to help his cause. Fortunately for him, the bailiff gave him a break and didn't say anything to the judge about his outburst in the hallway. In hindsight, he should have been thankful for the guy keeping that quiet, but at that moment he wasn't feeling very grateful.

So he went back in for another helping of shit, which he ate with a smile on his face and pretended not to be furious. He would have to thank Kelly for those wonderful Xanex later. When the verbal raping was finished, Scott walked humbly from the building. He imagined himself assassinating the judge, though he owned no guns. He even dreamed of constructing a dirty bomb and blowing the whole building to kingdom come, but he knew nothing about manufacturing explosives. Still, these fantasies remain with him to this day.

Now, you would be right in saying that Scott had no one but himself to blame. However, sick with addiction, it would be many years until he himself would see things that way. By then of course it was way too late. His kids were taken away. And only more heroin could kill the pain.

Finally, when everything was lost, he came to understand just how much heroin cost. It was much more than the meaningless financial fortunes that he spent many times over. He didn't really give much of a fuck about the money, but it cost him eternal heartache.

Scott could write a million elegies (mournful, reflective poems) about how badly he missed his babies and it would never be enough. He missed them learning to walk and talk and read and write. He missed them saying their prayers and tucking them in at night. He missed hearing them laugh and watching the squirrels. He missed the hugs, and the bugs, and the love, and the wonder. Scraped knees and baby teeth. These were Scott's lamentations.

By the time he and his parents went back to court for the last session, he was a complete and utter junkie. The idjit had taken control of his soul and every waking moment he fiended for heroin. When they went there that day, it was so the city and the system could take his parental rights away.

The judge said to him, "Hey, you are on drugs. You can't be a father to your children."

This was a premise that Scott disagreed with. His plan actually was to have his Mom and Dad raise the kids, because he knew how much they loved them. His mother had always wanted a daughter and Ariel was like an answer to her prayer. In his plan, Scott would be allowed to see his children all the time, while still being able to go out and be wild. He figured his brothers and their wives could even lend a hand and everyone would rally together like a family. But that wasn't to be.

Then the judge said to him, "You can't be trusted to make good decisions." O.k., the guy did have a point there. Obviously, his decision making wasn't right on target as he was shooting heroin several times a day. No one could disagree with the judge on this one, facts are facts, and Scott was on a lot of drugs.

But here's where the legal system gets twisted. They say, "You are not of sound mind, we are taking your children from you." (And "Watch your temper as we do this or we can tack on anger management and contempt of court charges too.")

"You are not of sound mind, you are going to hurt the kids." And "You are not of sound mind to do this" and "you are not of sound mind to do that." I mean they really tried to hammer home the point that he was not of sound mind. He must have heard that term twenty fucking times. Then they say, "Do you; Chip Scott Westcott, being of sound mind, want to sign away parental rights to your kids?"

And there sat his brother Chuck and his wife wanting to adopt them and promising that if he signed, he could visit his baby girl Ariel and his son Et'n bug all the time. They told him that this was in the best interest of his children and if he truly loved them than he would want the best for them. Which he did. Even in his addiction, he always loved his kids. Then they told him that they needed him to sign the paper so that they could get the medical insurance and benefits they needed to take Ethan to the doctor.

So Scott was really out of options.

Chuck, his wife and the representatives from dyfus sat huddled beside each other in the courtroom. They were a unified front to Scott's right. All were well composed, under control, and smiling. It was all very pretentious. There was no way for Scott or his parents to know that the whole thing was contrived; ostentatious, disingenuous; a show.

Chuck's wife was deceitful beyond reason though. If Scott had been in a better frame of mind, he might have been able to detect that her concern for his family was a charade. And that her goodness was feigned. Her affection was an affectation like an actress in a play. She had a devious plan, though no one in the courtroom suspected it that day.

Plus Scott and his mother implicitly trusted her son; his brother. They thought that there was no way that they would ever be betrayed.

Scott looked around the courtroom for his babies' mother, but Kelly was never there. His court appointed lawyer sat in her chair. He told Scott, "You're going to lose this case eventually, since you don't have a place for your kids to live and their mother is gone. You know that they'll be better off with your brother and his wife. I really don't think that there is any way for you to be able to keep these kids." (Not once the mother fuckers from Dyfus had stepped in.) His lawyer told him he could not win. And all Scott could think about was the pain he felt, how much he missed his girlfriend, and how badly he needed to fix.

So with tears in his eyes, Scott signed the cursed papers saying he was of sound mind, but he wasn't. It was the biggest mistake of his life. One that can never be made right. He is ashamed before God for signing their paper. It is one of the crosses he bears.

Now, you can say what you want about Kelly with her bi-polar and addiction, but she never for one second considered signing her rights away and she never put her name on that paper. His Kelly Bella. His rattlesnake.

It would not be long after that, that the adoption would go through and Scott would be denied visitation with his kids. Legally, Scott could be locked up if he even tried to see them. Chuck and his wife taught Ariel and Ethan to call them mommy and daddy and Scott, if his name came up at all, was referred to as "daddy chip." An afterthought.

So this is the end result of Scott's addiction and failure. It was the main reason behind his despair. Why he got high every time he felt bad, and felt bad every time he got high. It was also the reason behind the angry tone of chapter eight, as all that he had left was depression and unrelenting words of rage.

In the beginning of this we spoke about Trenton's ghosts. Well Scott, he had his own. He never wanted to be like his father; absent from his children's whole youth. He never wanted his kids to wonder what happened to him. And worry that they would never have a chance to meet. Now that reality haunts him anyway, as history repeats itself.

This is Scott's hypocrisy.

Even if it is true that the Lord lived up to his end of some unspoken agreement and blessed Ariel and Ethan throughout the drug infected haze of Scott and Kelly's insanity. Even if He was there the whole time preventing any disaster in the craziness of their mothers pregnancy.

And even if divinity itself sent it's spirit down to the delivery room and saw to their being born safely, . . . that didn't change the fact that a man in a black robe came in and took his angels away.

Now Scott can only dream of some kind of intervention from above, to prove to him that God is still a god of love. He doesn't hold out a great deal hope for this miracle however, because like we said before, God doesn't come around much anymore.

C.S.W.

Chapter N

CJ's Story / Dayton Street

LEST YOU BELIEVE that the mayhem of Scott and Kelly's adventures are isolated and unique, and lest you get the impression that theirs are the only two lost souls in the city of Trenton, I write to you the twisted and tragic tale of Charles Joseph Grifter. I submit it for your review and perusal.

CJ as he is known to his friends is a Piney. Meaning he was born and raised in the New Jersey Pine Barrens. We briefly explored this area before when we went searching for the devil. Anyway, the term Piney is a derogatory one, much like the racial slurs hurled at minorities to keep them down, dehumanize them, and remind them of their place. And much like the blacks, Puerto Ricans, and poor white trash cracka's took their affront and embraced it and wore it like a badge of honor, so too did the pineys. For example, if you were from the Pine Barrens and you walked up to another dude from the Pine Barrens, you could say "Piney! What's up my Piney?" or even "You know, you's a piney ass piney." However, if you were fortunate enough to have not been born in those godless shit sticks, you might want to shy away from such comments.

Perhaps the mere mention of the word piney has conjured up in your mind a mental image of what these genetic misfits look like. If so, that makes the job of describing CJ a little easier on me as he is the veritable epitome of the New Jersey piney. He is tall; even lanky and skinny; even malnourished. He has an elongated face, with less than perfect teeth and he has wild, untamed, insane eyes. They are the eyes of a man who has spent a great deal of time outside. Even if he were wearing a suit and tie, CJ's eyes would seem uncivilized.

In 1912, psychologist Henry H Goddard did a case study on the Kallikak family, a clan living in the Pine Barrens. He called his work a study in the heredity of the feeble minded. Goddard was eugenicist who demonized the pineys and depicted them as idiots and criminals.

Eugenics is the belief that we can improve the quality of the human species by discouraging reproduction of persons with undesirable inheritable traits. Incidentally, the Nazis also subscribed to this way of thinking; this pseudoscience. Anyway, regardless of whether or not there was any truth or merit to this argument, CJ's parents decided not to take Henry Goddard's advice and on April 28, 1977 their baby boy was born.

And a stranger dude than CJ, you will not meet.

But CJ was cool; hard working and loyal to his friends, to an extent. He was also popular with the ladies. Chicks really seemed to dig CJ.

As I said, he was born in the pinelands, in the town of Chattsworth, specifically. Chattsworth is what is known as an unincorporated area, meaning that it is so rural that it is not a part of any municipality. It was under the jurisdiction of only the state police. Piney's fostered stories of how terrible it was in the barrens or how violent they were in the hopes of keeping law enforcement out. The notorious Pine Bandits were the evolution of the dregs of society living in the barrens. They were poachers, moonshiners, fugitives, deserting soldiers and such. Stories such as theirs and that of the jersey devil were meant to scare outsiders from entering.

The early settlers who came to this region of pitch pines and cedar trees called this land, roughly the size of the Grand Canyon, the barrens because the soil was unfavorable for growing any kind of profitable crops. Because of its sandy acidic soil the farming sucked. That meant, no corn, no cabbage, no potatoes, And no mother fucking tomatoes.

Despite the inhospitableness of the area, parts of it were really quite beautiful. CJ loved the isolation it provided him. He was proud to say, "My nearest nabour is five miles away." Because of its remoteness there were no power lines run out to CJ's Chattsworth house and so everything; lights, water pump, TV, were powered by a generator. And because this was how he was raised and all that he knew, it became who he was and it was his home, where he was happy and it was a property that he loved.

From a young age, CJ could be seen tearing up the trails between the pitch pines and scrub oaks on his 400 Ex Honda Quad, or later, his beloved 99 Husqvarna 610. Speeding through the flats and launching over dunes CJ could also boast about kicking up roaster tails of sugar sand 8 feet high and 15 feet long. He had to ride fast so his momentum would carry him past hollows where the sugar turned into quicksand. The spray of the ultrafine silt off the back tire of CJ's dirt bike pelleted the trees and mixed with the debris of millions of fallen pine needles. He cruised through swampy cedar forests where the water appeared almost red because of the high level of iron ore in the soil.

CJ learned to ride his "Husky" to the point that it became like an extension of his body and he knew all the trails around the goose pond and hidden lakes like he knew the back of his hand. He was truly a man at one with his land.

The house that he lived in for 20 years was left for him to live in after his parents got divorced and went their separate ways. CJ's girlfriend, Donna moved in with him and as she was incredibly sexy, they both seemed satisfied and happy. Supposedly, Donna gave a fantastic blow job plus she had a tight little body. They both enjoyed having X (ecstasy) raves around campfires in the woods. There was always a party. CJ sold weed to the locals for money and they had lots of friends and marijuana a plenty. For years, he and his women lived like this and he described it as bliss.

Everything changed for them two days before Christmas. It was the holy holiday season and the air was calm with a festive peace. There was a slight wind, 5 mph and chilly. This breeze swayed the millions of pine needles on thousand of branches on hundreds of pine trees. All was serene.

Inside his Chattsworth home, CJ and Donna were alone. He was playing on his playstation on a color TV powered by the genny. But there were no flashing Christmas lights outside and they had no holiday tree inside. They were unnecessary. Plus they drew too much of the precious electric. CJ sat on the floor in the living room much too close to the screen. He was playing Grand Terrismo3. Donna was upstairs in the bedroom. Whether she was sleeping, reading, or eating, we have no way of knowing.

At 9 o'clock on December 23 there came an obtrusive knock on the door. Perhaps a jovial band of Christmas carolers? No more likely a pesky customer needing some weed, some Yule tide bud, just a guy looking to score.

When CJ answered it, instead of one guy standing there, there were four. All of them wearing black ski masks to hide their identities.

One second later he was struck in the face with a baseball bat. He was knocked backwards as his heartbeat raced with terror and panic. The first concussion cracked his skull on his zygomatic bone. It was the same place that the Hoffman avenue boys busted Scott's skull for him that day in Trenton. Only while Scott's nightmare lasted under five minutes, CJ's attack would drag on for over a half an hour. This was only the beginning of his beating. His skull would fracture in two other places before the violence was over.

CJ tried to think. Shit was going so horribly wrong and happening so fast. He tried to run to his room where he kept a loaded Remington 1187 shotgun. His plan was to start blowing holes in people. There were four attackers and his semi automatic Remmy held five shells. It would be more than enough to get the job done. He also owned a sawed off double barreled shotgun with a pistol grip. This was his favorite weapon but it was upstairs in the closet. If only he had known that these guys were coming over. If CJ had been able to make it to either of these guns, than I'd be telling you a different story.

Unfortunately, one of the intruders, the guy with the bat, tackled CJ before he could make it into that room. "Get the fuck out!" was all he could say as he flipped over and grabbed the bat. Before he had the chance to get up, the other three cowards attacked. In between kicks and punches and bat beatings they screamed, "Give us the fucking money!" and "Give us the fucking weed!"

Nobody outside could hear the sound of glass shattering as the Louisville slugger that fractured CJ's skull three times went about smashing his color TV and his fish tanks. The guppies and goldfish that came pouring out of the destroyed aquarium hit the living room floor and suffocated in the air til they quietly died. CJ's "nabours" were not close enough to hear the shouting or the smashing of the glass.

"In the pines, in the pines, where the sun don't ever shine."

If we were able to somehow push a pause button now and freeze frame the violence, we would be able to pan out on the worst ass kicking that CJ Grifter ever received. We could momentarily leave him there curled up into a fetal ball, miserable and suffering. We observe the pain and fear written on our beloved Piney's face. We cannot however, read anything of the expressions of the ski mask clad attackers. We cannot even tell their race.

Not that it matters I suppose as we've come to believe that the same sinfulness and evil lives in the hearts of all men. For the sake of the story, and with no evidence or truth to support it, we will say that one of the guys was white, one Spanish, and two black, because, let's face it, blacks are scarier. No, on second thought, I take that back, I didn't mean that. There are just four dudes mercilessly kicking the shit out of our friend. You can assign them their races from your own experiences or imagination, if that kind of thing is important to you.

Anyway, since we as Americans always want more, let's say we push play on our hypothetical tape and watch more of our ultraviolent movie. We love it, even as it turns our stomachs. We see one of the guys in the black mask wind up and swing the bat like he's trying to hit a homerun over the green monster at Fenway. The impact lands with a crack on the upper left side of CJ's torso. The noise we hear is the sound of two of his ribs breaking. It was alright though, CJ was no pussy, he could take a punch. It only really hurt when he tried to take a deep breath. It wasn't nearly as bad as the shot that busted his eye socket.

While CJ was still reeling and trying to recover from the damage done to his face and his chest, Manny Ramirez wound up and swung again. This time he connected full on with our friends knee cap and he completely blew it apart. Sweet Jesus and holy mother of God did that hurt. CJ let out another pitiful and broken scream. Was this shit really happening?

While the other guys ransacked the house looking for valuables, the guy hit CJ again for good measure.

CJ's blood leaked out of him from whatever holes it could find in his body. It was running out fast and staining everything. One of the last things he got to see before losing consciousness was his girlfriend Donna coming downstairs to see what the commotion was about.

When Donna saw the man that she loved pulverized on the floor and broken she was hit by a wave of stunned disbelief. No way was this really happening. "Oh my God" she thought "Please let him be OK." When she tried to go over to him and assist him and provide comfort, one of the ski masked men stepped in her way and stopped her. They wanted to have sex with her. Terrified, she cried now for her own safety. "Please, don't hurt me" she pleaded "Please, I am having my period. Please, please, don't." Donna wiped the tears from her eyes.

"You're having your period huh? Prove it." said one of the gentlemen.

So Donna undid the button on her jeans and unzipped her fly. She gave the men a full view of her panties which were baby blue. She slid her delicate, creamy, vanilla milk colored hand under the little bow on the elastic waistband. There was a soft contrast between the pink of her fingernail polish and the blue of her underwear. Her hand wiggled around her crotch like, (and pardon another baseball comparison) a major league pitcher adjusting his cup or shifting his junk. When she pulled her hand out, she held a dirty maxi pad. Humiliated, she held it out for the men's inspection. It was soaked dark red and disgusting. No one wanted to get close enough to smell it let alone touch it.

Fortunately, because she passed their perverted test, the men decided not to rape her. I suspect this had to do with a strong Christian upbringing. Or maybe they were ravenously homosexual. Or perhaps the sight of her blood was enough to make them sick. Too bad for them in any case because as every man knows period sex is one of the most decent feelings that this life has to offer. The men didn't seem to have too much of a problem seeing

CJ's blood however and one of the dudes gave him another kick. This one would dislocate his jaw and doctors would later have to wire it shut so that it could heal properly. He would always have the severe under bite of a true New Jersey Piney.

The fact that the guys decided not to rape Donna did not stop them from groping and fondling and ass grabbing her as they lead her through the house looking for marijuana and money. Unfortunately, Donna did not know where any of that stuff was,

CJ could have told them, but he was beaten unconscious.

Alright, so the guys were having a pretty good time as far as that goes. Anything they wanted, they could put in their pockets and steal. Anything they wanted to destroy, they could smash with their bats or throw against the wall. The only thing that really sucked was that it was so hot inside with those masks on. They each build up a sweat from the adrenaline rush and exercise they got kicking the shit out of the kid. Most people didn't realize that it was hard work fucking someone up properly. It was interesting how little any of them cared if the kid lived or died. One of the attackers enjoyed what he was doing so much that he was actually smiling. Thankfully, no one could see the sadistic bastards face through the mask that concealed his I.D.

After about forty minutes of this, the fun started to wind down like it always eventually does. The intruders gathered up the things they were going to steal; CJ's playstation, two of his guns (the Remington and the sawed off), plus a little over three hundred dollars in cash. After all that, they never found his stash. Perhaps they were pissed off because of this, or maybe it was just for shits and giggles but before they left they decided to break CJ's elbow.

He was slipping in and out of consciousness when it happened, having lost a lot of blood already. He was on the verge of passing out from the pain when the bat cracked the back of his elbow. It broke in three places, a compound fracture, and the noise it made was like that of a dentist ripping a tooth out from the root. If ever there was an unholy sound it was this. The noise of bones being crushed.

And so CJ fell asleep for a couple of weeks. It was a very deep sleep, the kind that doctors call a coma. I can't tell you what CJ was thinking about for all that time while he dreamed, but I can tell you that he slept through Christmas and nor was he awake to see January 1st 2001. He missed the birth of the baby new year.

Donna watched as the last of the attackers left through the front door. "Good night," he said "Thank you." Manners are very important.

When they were gone, Donna ran over to check on her man. He was in very bad shape. She was scared he was going to die. They had no phone for her to call 911 for an ambulance or the police. Donna needed to get to a phone, so she left CJ and drove 5 miles to the nearest nabours house. Once there, she called the ambulance and the state police. It took them about forty minutes to get there, about the same amount of time that those four dudes beat him.

Donna came back to the house with the nabour, who was CJ's friend. The two of them got all the marijuana and paraphernalia out of the house and stashed it in the trunk of a junk car before the cops and EMT's arrived.

When they finally arrived, they took the Piney to the Atlantic City Trauma Center, but since Donna had CJ's blood on her from trying to help him, the police, super sleuths that they are, determined that she had something to do with his assault. They took her back to the station and grilled her for three hours with questions. Your tax dollars hard at work. The whole time she had no way of knowing if her boyfriend was alive or dead.

As for the perpetrators, of course, the police never caught them. They got away clean and chances are they still get together and laugh about the time they beat that poor kid to within an inch of his life. Presumably while they fondle and have rough cowboy butt sex with one another.

When CJ awoke almost three weeks later it was in a hospital bed. He had bandages around his left eye and his knee and elbow were elevated and in casts. He looked like a mummy. His jaw, as I mentioned, was wired shut and he had tubes running drugs and fluids into him intravenously. There was a catheter shoved up his dick because he could not get up to piss. Plus he had a terrible case of double vision. The pain was very great. Doctors would ask him to rate it on a scale from one to ten. 10 being excruciating. His pain was easily a 15.

"That's when they gave me the morphine." CJ would later say with a dreamy, faraway look in his eyes. One could mistake that look for love as he reflected back to the feeling.

MORPHINE (MOR feen) is a pain reliever. It is used to treat moderate to severe pain. This medicine may be used for other purposes; ask your health care provider or pharmacist if you have questions.

"What a feeling that was. It was the only way to kill the pain."

That was when, I think, CJ's idjit, that nasty bastard of suicidal addiction was born.

After a couple of weeks, CJ could walk again, kind of. He moved around slowly like an old man. The nurses removed the tube that was up his instrument so he had to walk the eight feet from his hospital bed to the bathroom to urinate. Walking was still painful, so he would let the piss build up in his bladder until the pressure was near maddening before he would endeavor to get up and drag his portable I.V. cart with him to the toilet. The room was carpeted so that wasn't so bad. The tile floor of the bathroom was cold however and so he was thankful that the hospital had given him some totes. More than socks, but not quite slippers. Totes had the soles on both sides for traction so there were no tops or bottoms. You just slid them on and you were ready to go. Only a real moron could put Totes on improperly. Once CJ's feet were toted, he was then prepared to go pee. He got out of his Craftmatic adjustable bed, the one with the controls for elevating his head, knees, and feet and the volume and speaker for the TV built right in. CJ's feet were nice and toasty warm, but there was a slight chill as he hoveled his way to drain the main vein, as the paper hospital gown was not tied right in the back. Passing hallway nurses would be able to see his underwear, if he happened to be wearing any on that given day.

The narcotics masked the pain and he had a nice buzz going on, but the opiates also made him itch. Especially so under the casts on his elbow and knee. He was clever enough to have saved a plastic disposable fork from one of his roommates meals and he used that to scratch under there. It was blissful relief. It really worked quite nicely.

Unfortunately, the hospital bills were adding up and CJ had no insurance. It was figured that he owed them as much as eighty thousand dollars. It might as well have been eight hundred thousand because CJ had no intention of paying them either way.

Soon it came time for him to leave and CJ had nowhere to live. He could not go back to his Chattsworth house after what happened there. Those guys were still on the loose and yeah, CJ was scared. That kind of violence changes a man and he was not the same person he was when he woke up on Dec. 23, 2000. The emotional scars would take a lot longer to heal than did his body with the physical ones.

So, anyway CJ left the hospital and went to live with Donna at her parents' house. Unfortunately, about a month after he got there, her mother died of lung cancer. After that their drug addiction escalated and the pain killers were cripplingly expensive.

Then came the inevitable proposition. A friend told him that Heroin was "just like the medicine they were prescribing him but a lot cheaper." And CJ stood at that great precipice that many a junkie before him has teetered on. The decision; should he take the evil drug or not. It was the moment of a decision he would come to regret. That fabled moment we all look back on and wish that we had a chance to do over. To make the right choice.

CJ decided to take the plunge. Not the great disastrous plunge with the spike and the plunger, but the decision to start sniffing the "heron". He toyed with the dope, minus the works, AKA the gimmick, AKA the set, AKA the rig, AKA the syringe. Even though he only snorted the diesel for over a year, from that moment on, the needle was just around the corner.

Donna went with him for the ride.

Soon enough, they moved out of her parents' house and began living in a motel. They burned through the six thousand dollars that CJ had saved, plus the $280 a week the Donna earned working at WaWa. It was not long after that before they began stealing cigarettes from Donnas' work and selling them to help make ends meet. It helped them out for a few weeks until they got busted. Donna lost her job and they each received one year probation for their crime. No jail time. Through it all, their dependency on drugs grew at an alarming rate. Like many lovers of junk before them, Heroin was now their God.

We spoke before about how this kind of relationship forms the shape of a triangle. Interesting because I've always found love to be more of a circle than a pyramid. Love is a bubble actually. Inside it's comfy, and cozy, and warm. Happy, protective, and familiar. But when a couple breaks up and the bubble finally bursts : . . . . it fucking hurts. Then you walk around feeling all used, spent up, and empty. As used up as yesterday, you could say. Then the memories that used to make you smile, make you wanna cry.

But again I digress and I'm getting a little ahead of myself.

CJ and Scott met when Scott came to work for the same construction company that CJ worked for. At their boss's behest and under the threat of a lawsuit their bosses name will not be mentioned. Suffice to say that the guys got paid in heroin every day. You should know a couple of things about their employer however. First of all he was a gigantic black guy; 6'4' or so and around 250 pounds and he was infatuated, like a lot of black guys, with white women. He had had sex with a very great number of south Trenton Skanky ho's; prostitutes or women addicted to crack or dope. He called these girls "chickenheads". He even fucked CJ's girlfriend one time. Part of his addiction was to take from his friends. Donna was a pretty girl but I suspect that the fact that she was CJ's girl made her even more desirable to him. Scott was never sure whether or not his boss ever banged Kelly, but he put the estimation at somewhere near an eighty percent chance that he had. Some questions are better left unasked.

Anyway, their boss loved only one thing; money He owned several houses in Trenton and they provided great locations to bang his chickenheads in private when cheating on his wife. He hired junkies mostly to work for him and he underpaid them every day in drugs. Guys like CJ and Scott and a few others became his slaves. They worked 10 to 12 hour days, seven days a week straight. If they didn't get up and go to work then they were dope sick that day and that was a nightmare none of them had the balls to face. The boss man would ration the dope out to them throughout the day and if you asked him for more than what he wanted to give you, he would say "Me, I'm not Santa Claus dude." As if anyone would ever mistake this giant negro for saint Nick. There was absolutely nothing jolly about him. Ebenezer Scrooge would consider him a greedy son of a bitch.

Anyway CJ Grifter had succumbed to the needle by the time he started working for this guy and he and Donna came from the Pine Barrens to the city of Trenton where they rented a room in one of his boss's houses. This one happened to be on Dayton Street.

I would suspect that CJ being attacked left some sort of paranoid effect on him and after an incident like that he probably never felt safe or secure anymore. Maybe that was the reason for the security cameras he had mounted on his front porch. Nobody was going to sneak up on him ever again. He always knew well in advance who was approaching his front door. Images of Dayton Street could be viewed constantly in a smell picture in picture box on the lower right hand corner of CJ's television screen. It came in handy when one was anxiously awaiting drug dealers. It also served as some protection when avoiding them because CJ owed them money. He was frequently in that position too because he had the habit of getting his dope fronted. "Let me get four more, on the arm, until I get paid tomorrow." was not an uncommon expression for Mr. Grifter.

Most of the dealers who came to Dayton were just kids and not really dangerous. The junkies used to call them the young bloods because the oldest of them was only about 14 and they belonged to the bloods street gang. In Trenton at this time the bloods had all but eradicated their enemies the crypts. Having defeated the guys who preferred to wear the color blue, the guys who preferred to wear the color red divided themselves up into sects, segregating themselves based on the neighborhoods they lived in. Then they began fighting amongst themselves.

In years to come the war between different factions of the bloods would escalate until the sex money murder (SMM) gangsters accidently shot down an innocent thirteen year old girl. Tamrah Lenoard was killed in a drive by shooting at a block party attended by rival set Killa Gangsta bloods (KGB). Tamrah would become another ghost of innocents lost to violence lingering in this city.

The four young boys who came to CJ's house were bound to be drawn into this lifestyle of senselessness. It was sad to think about how these kids had no promise and no future. They were still young and just trying to fit in and have fun, but within the next five to ten years three of them would probably be in jail or dead and the other most likely involved in drugs in one form or another. Their names were Mir (like half of mirror), DayDay, K-Shawn, and Brian.

Brian, being too white a name for an up and coming dealer and gangster would soon have to pick an alias. Any letter from the alphabet would do. He could be "B" the obvious, uncreative choice or he could try and be clever and go with a cool three letter tag like Wab, Boo, Cue (Q), or, still my personal favorite Pez.

Anyway the young bloods were always a blast to hang out with. They brought low grade dope with them but, being kids it was easy to talk them out of it. The stuff would work you just had to take a lot more of it. Sometimes they'd front CJ and then he'd convince them that they hadn't. These guys were rambunctious and full of angst but they were not violent. Being kids, they just wanted to play. Mostly big kid games like slanging. (Drug dealing) All the young bloods smoked weed and a couple of them smoked crack but they stayed away from heroin and needles even though they sold it. They were fascinated however with watching the junkies shoot their dope. The main reason that the young bloods came to CJ's crib on Dayton street though was because CJ had hookers working out of his house. There was one girl in particular who everybody thought was hot and they would all take turns on her.

When Scott first met Angie, she was walking around the house in a bright red bra and a pair of skimpy Daisy Duke cut off shorts. She came from Atlantic City and how she ended up at CJ's house remains a mystery. Angie had dark hair, pretty eyes, and a perfect body. Perfect, except for the track marks that traced her veins up and down her arms.

At this point, Scott and Kelly were separated and Kelly was dating a new guy who she said she met in recovery.

Scott was very attracted to Angie but the fiasco with the only hooker he ever tried to get with still left a bad taste in his mouth about the whole business. Plus the thought of the four black kids running a train on her kept him from pursuing her. Oh yeah, and Scott was dead broke and could not afford to buy her anyway. The dollar fifty in his back pocket probably wouldn't be enough to get a look at one bare tit.

Scott remembered one time when he brought this dude he met in his own recovery house to Dayton Street. The guys name ironically was John. John wanted to get laid and Scott told him all about Angie, the Atlantic City beauty. John promised Scott forty dollars if he would set him up with her. It was the closest Scott ever came to living up to his lifelong dream of becoming a pimp. Unfortunately, when they got to the house, Angie had already gone out trickin'.

Scott went into CJ's room and said "Yo man, my boys lookin' for some sex. He'll give us forty bucks to get high with if we can get him laid."

"Angie went out," said the Piney "But Donna's home. I'll ask her if she'll do it." Now a lot of people might not understand how a man could ask his girlfriend to have sex with another man for money. Those people would not be junkies, they would not know about the sickness or the obsession. Plus it should be pointed out that CJ and Donna were broken up at this time and that Donna was now a full time prostitute. That was the direction that the drugs had led her. Like so many before her.

So the deal was struck and John and Donna went into the bedroom next door to where Scott and CJ sat. They closed the door behind them and proceeded to do the thing. Even though CJ had arranged their little rendezvous, Scott thought he could read sadness in his friend's eyes.

He could relate to that pain as Kelly had put him in similar situations many times before. He knew how much it hurt to have another man touching his girl. He could have said something to him to console him, cheer him up, and try to make him feel better. Instead, he said "Damn, man, he's really laying it into her isn't he? He's in there poundin' on that shit. What's it been like half an hour?"

John had not yet given Scott the forty dollars he promised him for drugs, so they had to wait until the business in the next door bedroom was finished before they could get high. This seemed to make time go a lot slower. Scott and the Piney watched the clock as John hit CJ's ex doggy style. They were in there for over an hour. Both of the dudes in the other room were losing their patience. They started raising their voices and made comments loud enough for them to hear. They said things like "Alright,

John let's go! She's a trick, you don't have to try and satisfy her." Or "For the love of God man would you hurry up! We got shit we want to do too." Or "Pump, pump, squirt, dude! You're not starting a relationship in there."

Anyway, while this was going on, Angie came home.

Eventually, John came out of the bedroom and rejoined the fellas in CJ's room. Donna was still in her room getting dressed and recovering. With a big shit eating grin on his face, John turns to CJ and says, "Yo bro, Donna told me that you guys used to go out and that you only recently broke up. I'm sorry man; I never would have done that if I had known." This was an outright lie. John would still have done it even if the two of them had been married. He probably would not have cared if CJ sat on the couch in the corner of the room watching them screw, crying his eyes out. John was pretty horny.

That's when Angie sauntered in. She slid her soft Italian ass in between John and CJ and before they were even introduced, John leans over and whispers in Scott's ear "I want to have sex with her too."

When John made this comment/ request it sent Scott's mind reminiscing about the time he actually watched Angie performing her trade. Tricking, that is. CJ as I mentioned before, had all these video cameras set up around the house. Mostly, they were used for security, so that he would have ample time to hide when drug dealers came over to collect for drugs that CJ had been fronted. One time, however, while Angie was at the store, CJ hid a camera in her room and ran the live video wire under the hallway carpet and into the TV in his room.

As luck would have it, when Angie came back, she was not alone. She came into CJ's room to tell him that she had a date and she said she would get he and Scott high when it was over. Then she went into the room with the guy and shut the door behind her.

The positioning of the camera could not have been better, the angle was perfect for some free real life pornography. The guys saw everything.

First the money changed hands. This guy trusted her and paid her up front. Scott always thought that this was a mistake, but this seems to be the new rule in Trenton. Angie put the money in her back pocket, then she got down on her knees and unzipped his fly. While she blew him, Scott and CJ watched from the other room. They giggled immaturely like two adolescents though they both were in their thirties. Think Beavis and Butthead, not Einstein and Freud.

Anyway, after about 2 or 3 minutes of this, Angie got up off her knees. She stood with her crotch directly in front of the camera, giving CJ and

Scott full view of her front and the dude, now taking his pants the rest off the way off, a good look at her ass. She wiggled out of her jeans and in the second before her shirt fell over her private, the guys could see that she was completely shaved. Then Angie crawled on her hands and knees and stuck her butt up in the air for her client to plug in.

Again, as I said, the camera angle could not have been better. And this is the part that Scott would never forget, the part he thought about every time he looked at Angie from then after. The guy was really trying his hardest. He was pumping her like Ron Jeremy, or Peter North, or some other extensively trained porn star. He even through in a couple of spankings for good measure. Extra credit.

But the voyeurs could read the expression on Angie's face clearly. She was bored out of her skull. This guy could nail her like that until the cows came home and she was not going to have an orgasm. Her mind was elsewhere. She looked as if someone was reading her the new income tax laws or directions on how to repair a toilet. Maybe the book of Leviticus. She even snuck a couple of looks at the clock.

To make matters worse for the poor schlep, she didn't even finish him off. There was no audio feed to CJ's room so there was no way for the guys to hear what happened, but one of them, him or her I don't know, pulled away and broke the connection. The humping stopped abruptly. Angie got up and put her clothes back on, while the guy grabbed his equipment and started masturbating. The junkies in the bedroom never found out how much the encounter, which had to be a letdown to him, had cost. Nor did they see if the guy ever busted on her bed and had himself a big finish. After Angie got dressed, they kind of lost interest.

They heard her coming down the hall towards CJ's room and they quickly changed the channel on the TV. A knock at the door and then "CJ?"

"Yeah?"

"Can you call R and tell him to bring us some dope?" She meant Dahlia's boyfriend RR in between stints in jail.

"Yeah, I'll call him." CJ replied. This was good news because Angie was always pretty generous with her drugs. The rule in Trenton is you always have to give at least one to the house. Since CJ had been renting his room on Dayton for the longest, he qualified as the house. As for Scott, Angie just shared with him because she liked him. She was not obligated to. For three consecutive nights Angie had given him dope and climbed into bed with him. She said "I get scared and lonely sleeping by myself in this big house."

Like I said before, Kelly was involved with someone else at this time, so Scott was free to sleep with whomever he chose. Angie was very sexy and her body was warm and fun to cuddle with, but despite how attractive she was, and the fact that Scott had plenty of opportunities, he never tried to have sex with her. Perhaps he was too high, but mostly the thought of her letting all the young bloods take turns on her was a major turn off. That and the image of the bored look on her face while that guy tried his hardest slamming her was enough to see to it that Scott slept with his clothes on. Plus, God knows what other grimy shit she had gotten herself into. Scott liked Angie and he tried not to judge her. He held her at night like she was his lover but whatever diseases she was carrying, Scott didn't need them.

John had no such concerns. He wanted his turn with her. He asked Scott "How much does she charge?"

Scott informed him that he could purchase the full package, complete with happy ending for the low price of fifty bucks.

John paid Angie the money up front, but he still needed a few minutes to recharge his batteries after his tryst with Donna. Angie promised John that she would be back in ten minutes. She just needed to go around the corner to cop and then they could go into her room when she came home. But Angie never came back. She lied to him like all Trenton girls know how to lie. John waited for her for over an hour before beat, he asked Scott to give him a ride home. He was not the first guy to get scammed out of money by a female and he was not the last. The day was not a total waste for him anyway; he did get to bang the shit out of CJ's ex-girlfriend.

Donna, who would later fall in love with one of her clients and marry him, left the house for the night. When Scott got back from dropping John off at his recovery house, he would sleep in her room. In the same bed the deed was just done in.

Her room was the typical dope users room. All heroin dens end up looking the same. It was identical in décor to Scott and Kelly's apartment on Bruce Lane. There was garbage everywhere. There were the crushed, empty packs of cigarettes, butts spilled out of ashtrays on the floor, piles of laundry strewn about, bowls of leftover food and literally hundreds of empty ripped open wax paper baggies. The later representing every type of heroin to come through Trenton in the last six months. There were too many colored stamps to list all the different brand names that Donna had injected. In the corner of the room was her single bed with a bare mattress; no sheets, dirty pillow, no pillowcase. Scott hoped that the stains he was seeing were from split drinks or maybe just body sweat but he knew better. He found a blanket and put it under him so he could lie down. The blanket had not been washed in a while either so it was not much cleaner. Not that Scott himself wasn't a filthy junkie. He was no poster boy for hygiene, but all those germs and grim beneath him made him feel creepy. Again he would sleep with his clothes on. Although sleep probably wasn't the right word for it. He would slip into an unconscious state after nodding into a dream; usually while holding a light cigarette or scratching hisself ravenously.

Whether or not Scott ever picked up any of Donnas dirty underwear out of the never ending pile of laundry and sniffed them is irrelevant and not really the point of the story. He could have wrapped her panties around his face like a perverted, albeit sexy surgical mask and that wouldn't change the fact that he and his friends were all slowly dying of a progressive and incurable disease.

Anyway, one night after everyone had left and the house was empty except for CJ and Scott, the boys sat smoking the last of the days cigarettes. They each had a little dope left and so they went about the ritual of fixin'. Perhaps when they finished, CJ would walk down Dayton and go to the KFC on Broad Street to beg the girls working there for some free food before they threw it away. Neither of them had eaten since he went and did that yesterday.

As the room filled up with smoke, they spoke. The conversation was mostly only bullshit, just words cutting through the silence, killing time, and said for no real reason as they went through the process of getting high.

Scott poured water from a needle on the powder in the spoon. "You know bro, I'm thinking of writing a book about all this."

"You totally should." CJ said. He was trying to be encouraging and supportive but he probably didn't believe that Scott would ever follow through on such an endeavor. People say things like that all the time while high and usually they believe it when they say it, they mean it, they are not lying. This turns out to only be a dream or a delusion of grandeur as junkies don't usually have the dedication or stictuitiveness needed to see anything through to the finish and writing a book is hard. If you've ever tried it, then you know that it is amazingly draining. And sometimes the research required can kill you.

"What's the book going to be called?" asked the Piney.

"Nigaz and Crackaz." said Scott without really thinking about it. Nigaz and Crackaz; not a bad title actually, it had the necessary shock value and was definitely "in your face" intriguing. It would not stand up to further scrutiny however and that title would have to be scratched. No matter, something clever would come to him.

"Cool." said CJ "You know, I'm thinking of writing a book myself."

"Really?" replied Scott "What's it about?"

"Your Mom." The two guys had one of those really tight relationships where they could say anything to each other. Nothing was off limits.

"Fuck you."

"No, I'm serious dude. I'm gonna call it "Chip's Mom" and she goes out and has all these adventures. Sometimes she comes back with the money, and sometimes she doesn't. It doesn't make any difference though, because she's always your Mom and you love her."

"You're an asshole." Now it was Scott's turn to throw some jabs. "Listen bro, I need you to do me a favor."

"What's that?"

"I need you to overdose on heroin and die."

"What?"

"Yeah, just hear me out. Somebody always has to die for a story like this to be successful. People love tragic stuff like that." These words intended to tease his friend would later come back to haunt him, as not too long after he said them he would lose a very good friend to this insidious disease. When he later heard of Kelly's brothers death, his mind would flashback to this conversation and he would be ashamed for uttering these words.

"Fuck you dude, I'm not gonna die. You die."

"How could I write the book if I'm dead? Besides, you're probably going to O.D. anyway. At least this way you'll be immortalized. I'll write something nice and sad about you."

CJ thought for a moment and then said hopefully "Are you gonna buy me the dope?"

"Yeah, but you gotta do it all at one time, I'm not buying it so you can stay high for the next few days." That was just talk too as Scott didn't have enough money to pay for even his own habit. He had no idea where his next fix was coming from.

The dope that the fellas were shooting tonight was ironically called "Sudden Death", but that was just another case of false advertising as neither one of them dropped dead from injecting it.

So like I said, CJ and Scott were good friends and they could joke about anything with each other. They were still men however and they never talked about their feelings or the things that hurt them. And being friends didn't mean that they wouldn't steal from one another. Once, when they were both dope sick, Scott came up with twenty dollars which he gave to CJ to go cop for them. CJ would get one bag for going to get it and Scott would get one for coming up with the money. Money he most likely begged his parents for. CJ went ahead and did both bags and claimed that he got beat when he came home hours later high.

Scott might have done the same thing to him if their roles were reversed. At that time, he wanted to kill him, but in hindsight, he held no animosity, he understood.

They were both slaves to the substance.

They both shared the same sickened beliefs. Maybe this is even the gnosis of the junkie; disillusionment. Neither of them held any belief in the great religions or their fallacies. And in the pursuit of any inalienable rights, they likewise don't believe. Being empty, they don't think that there is any such thing in this life as true liberty and maybe even life itself is overrated. They know that happiness is a goal that's unattainable.

They disagree with the Christians who think that there's some great banquet table waiting for us after we've deceased. Nor have they any interest in streets made out of gold, or diamonds, rubies, and precious stones. These things have no more relevance to the dead then do seventeen young virgins or food.

That isn't to say that they don't have a healthy respect for death. Gloriously, when they're gone no more drugs will need to be consumed. Then they can rest from the never ending, relentless quest. No more awakening to chase the insatiable. That is the true blessing, they suspected.

And the idjit, the master that owns them is only evil.

And the nightmare is the obsession with the Heroin, that diesel.

And they inject a slow death with their sets, those needles.

And what started out as a want or a lust has turned into an undeniable need.

Anyway N is for the narcissists. See how they feed.

Chapter 10

Kelly in Custody

D ESPERATION LIES AT the cold, ugly, core of the thing. The sweaty obsession and the sickness. Desperation can be felt in the very air of this city. Look around, and up and down, Division, Tyler, and Pearl streets with their crime and all the debris and you'll be sure to catch the sensation; of desper-fuckin'-ation.

It moves us, the addicted, in ways that the sane can never understand. It directs us to do what they cannot fathom or forgive. Like animals; so lowly. The drive; unholy.

Kelly and Kenny walked down Hamilton Avenue, where it cuts across the East Ward like a dreadful surgical scar connecting Chambersburg to St. Mary's hospital and Trenton high school. They were high earlier in the day, but that was over now and they were chasing it. The drugs, still in their systems, were compromising their morals and logic, and motivating them to attempt a crime with no chance of succeeding.

Scott wasn't there that day, as he wasn't there when most of his friends got arrested for doing something stupid, but he could tell you this; it was probably Kelly's idea. That was the kind of girl she was, amazingly crazy and ballsy. At this time no one could hold her or control her. Kelly's addiction was all consuming.

It was December again, when it happened, only the second day of the month. There was winter crispness in the air and it was raining, but the frigidity went mostly unfelt as the hopelessness and recklessness waged a unrelenting war in Kelly's mind. And soul. The chemicals in her system threw off the delicate balance of her Bi polar disorder and the serotonins and dopamine in her brain went all screwy. Perhaps at this point she was incapable of rational thought.

But still, she had a plan; it was not a good plan by any stretch of the imagination. It was all she could come up with, however, and so she went with it. Kelly carried with her a small brown handled folding knife. The blade was only about three inches long. She stepped out of the wetness and grayness of the day and into the He Yuan Chinese restaurant.

She walked up to the young Chinese woman working the register and ordered an eggroll, while she mustered up the nerve to do what she felt compelled to. Then with a shrug of her shoulders and a complete disregard for her whole future, she said to herself "Fuck it" and pulled out the knife. Out loud she said "Open the fucking register, bitch!" Then the mother of Scott's children jumped over the counter and put the knife to the throat of the terrified Chinee. At that moment, the woman at the counter didn't matter. She was not a person so to speak; irrelevant were her hopes, and dreams, and family. Unfortunately, for Kelly the woman didn't speak English very well, so it was hard to tell if she was stupid, staling, or just too scared, but for whatever the reason she could not get the cash drawer opened. Seconds passed like minutes as Kenny, her lookout, nervously waited at the door. Kelly punched and slammed the machine frantically as she tried to wield the blade in one hand and get at the money with the other. But the thing just would not open. The situation deteriorated rapidly.

And the caper took too long and containment was lost and it was too late to turn back, a line had been crossed.

Then came the angry men out of the food preparation area and kitchen. They were screaming in what would have been a comical Cantonese under different circumstances, but as it was they were agitated like a swarm of bees. Kelly shook their nest when she fucked with the money machine. Two of the dudes, flailed their arms around like they knew kung fu. One of them held a meat cleaver and the other a butcher's knife.

At this point, the realization of the seriousness of the miscalculation must have set in, because Kenny ran from the door where he was standing guard, jumped over the counter, grabbed her, and screamed "Let's go." If anything good could be said of Kenny's actions here, it was that at least he didn't turn and run and leave her there. Almost the hero, he pulled her out the door into the rain and the gray and the pain of the Trenton day. The fugitives fled down South Olden Avenue and back onto Hamilton toward South Logan where they disappeared out of sight. Kelly and Kenny would have no money tonight.

We can only imagine the commotion and chaos they left behind in the restaurant. I suppose, we shouldn't find this funny.

Police were called and they broadcast a description of the suspects.

An anonymous concerned citizen called the east precinct the next day and provided information (ratted) regarding the whereabouts of Kelly and Kenny, thereby, cleaning up the city of Trenton and making it safe for everyone.

C.S.W.

When the cops came to the rear apartment at 1215 Hamilton Avenue to bust Kelly, she was sitting around her place smoking cocaine. Kenny had escaped justice for a while because he was fortunate enough to be at the store buying new crack pipes (called stems) for the festivities, when the police (called pigs) arrived.

Scott would later ask Kel to describe how she felt when the boys in blue came for her and she summed up her emotions in one word, "fucked". They lead Ariel and Ethan's mommy into the squad car in handcuffs. She was taken into custody without incident.

Months afterwards, when Scott got his hands on the police report and read the words "following an extensive investigation by police" he couldn't help but laugh. They got a phone call and came and got her. It really wasn't like trying to solve the Lindbergh case.

Trenton's finest took Kelly to the station on North Clinton and wrote up her charges, which were threefold. First degree Robbery, Third degree Theft by unlawful taking or moving, and Third degree Weapons possession for unlawful purposes. Unfortunately for Kel, these were not her first charges, she had "prior's" and now they were coming back to bite her in the ass. Three times she had gone to municipal court; twice for harassment and once for loitering. These charges were dismissed, dropped but not forgotten. The thing that really stung and left a mark however was her arrest for Third degree Burglary (B&E) and Theft a little over a year ago. That one had gone to superior court making this her second upper court conviction.

Kelly sat at the Trenton police station until later the next day when they drove her to her new home at the mercer county workhouse. She would reside there for the next year. While inside the prosecutor would come at her and offer a "deal" of six years in the Edna Mahan Correctional Facility for Women in Clinton. Her other option was to take the case to court and fight it. The prosecutor explaining to her that if she took that course, Kelly could be looking at twenty years, inside. Since she knew she was guilty and the prosecutor could easily prove it, Kel signed the plea agreement and got ready to spend the next 2,190 days in jail. Or 52,560 hours, if you prefer breaking it down even further. Sometimes numbers can be a nightmare.

Now, as I said earlier, Scott was not around when his girl, (who I suppose was technically Kenny's girl at the time), got into all her trouble. He liked to think he could have protected her from this, although given their track record that was probably just wishful thinking. Scott would not find out about Kelly's plight until she was months into her dilemma; quandary, predicament, her pickle.

Scott remembered how he found out about it. He just came back to Trenton after being away for the last six months. He did five in what was probably his twelfth rehab. In Milwaukee, Wisconsin that had been. And his thirteenth for a month in Shedd, Oregon. While away he had started writing and he was anxious to see Kelly and show her what he had embarked upon. The recovery he had attained while he was away was wearing off rapidly, evaporating like water on a duck's feathers, as he walked his old streets, hunting for some excitement and his girl. He came to Kelly's mother's house on 710 Division Street looking for her.

Over the years Kelly's mother Colleen had become like a second mother to Scott. Her family, his family. She was grandmother to Ariel and Ethan and she took care of Kelly's first boy Dylan like he was her own son. She raised him and loved him above all. Colleen had a good heart and she had tried to raise her children right. Things became very hard for her, however, after losing her husband to cardiac arrest/ heart attack in 1997 and watching her kids sink into the grief and depression that set in, in its aftermath.

Scott never got a chance to meet Kelly and her Brother Tony's father, he died before they met. Kelly would have been about eighteen when he passed away and Tony a couple of years older. Now, on top of her own grief about losing the love of her life, Mrs. Cambell, Colleen, had to try and hold her family together as best as she could. Unfortunately for her, they were both young adults living in the heart of Trenton. A step out the front door and off the porch put them into the world of dealers, and hookers, fights and crime, cocaine and, yes, Heroin.

A sadistic Satan was just waitin' for the Cambell kids outside their door. He knew all about their pain and he was there for them with the cure. Needles were just around the corner.

That is not to say that Kelly and Tony ran right to the drugs. No that would be inaccurate. They tried to deal with their loss as best they could for as long as they could, but the neighborhood deteriorated around them, becoming more violent and dirty as days went by. It was as if Chambersburg itself was reflecting the way they felt; helpless, and hopeless, and lost.

Scott joined their family tentatively, as there was never any official marriage or wedding ceremony. Their bond was sealed in things more real, like babies, and blood, devotion and love. And yes, there were a lot of drugs. I suppose, also, that it would be fair to say that Scott felt more comfortable at Mrs. Cambell's house in her east ward neighborhood then he did at his own parent's home, safe in suburban Ewing, because the drugs were readily available there and he didn't have to hide the fact that he was high. Everybody was fucking high; you were free to do as much as you wanted. Nod out on the couch; pass out on the porch, smoke crack out back, whatever, didn't matter. Ironically, I think it was that freedom and liberation that would eventually enslave them. But again, that's another tangent.

Also, it would be untrue and unfair to say that Mrs. Cambell approved of the drugs. Nothing could be further from the truth. She hated them I suspect. She saw what they were doing to her children. It's just that she was only one woman with a full time job and a young grandson to support; there was no time or way for her to make the world outside a better place. She had to tolerate the drugs, because, that's just the way it was. There was really nothing she could do.

Colleen tried to protect Dylan and raise him safe. To shield him from this shit. It was a noble and loving endeavor to be sure, but I think the little boy gave her more than she gave him. He provided her with hope. He needed her and loved her and he gave her promise for a brighter future. He was something good to anticipate. Her own children were lost and broke her heart and would never live up to her expectations.

Can you feel what I'm sayin' about drugs and desperation?

Scott leapt up the three steps that led to the front porch of Mrs. Cambell's brown row home on Division Street. The porch was about four feet wide by maybe twelve feet long. There was a painted white wooden railing encompassing the porch and it was connected to the four by four posts that supported the roof. On one of these posts Scott had once graffitied a heart in green sharpie marker. Inside the drawing he had written his name and Kelly's. Underneath this he wrote Dylan's name and Ariel's. The ink was faded now because this had been inscribed years ago before Ethan was even born.

Scott knocked and waited for Kelly's brother Tony to answer the door. Eventually, he did. "What's up, my brother from another mother?" They were like brothers by choice and connected because of mutual loves and family, but not by blood.

"Hey, Chip" Tony smiled "When did you get back?" The two dudes gave each other a hug, something they had rarely done.

'Two days ago." Scott noticed that Tony was moving around all gimpy and wincing in pain as he walked. 'Yo, man, what happened to you?"

And Tony explained how his stomach was all fucked up and how he had just had surgery two days ago for Diverticulitis. Doctors had stitched him up he said and then he graphically explained what an ordeal it was for him to take a shit. It was information Scott could have done without. (As I'm sure you can, I'll spare you the nastier details.)

They had given him medicine for the pain and Tony was abusing the script as usual. He was not even close to taking the recommended dose. You could see in his eyes that he was more than sufficiently high. In just a few days he would be through his thirty day supply. After that, the sensation of desperation would be back.

Remember that feeling as we will return to it several more times in this chapter. It, being the underlying theme of this thesis, moving the characters and driving the story; always just beneath the surface like an undertow or current.

Now, there was a difference between the progressions of the disease in CJ. and Tony. When CJ went to the hospital after his beating, he was introduced to morphine and painkillers and his brain learned that opiates could help him escape both physical and psychological pain. CJ would slowly and steadily increase his dosage and his tolerance until his drug hunger grew like a magic mushroom.

Tony's journey was sadder and darker. His, I think, was born from his situation; the hopelessness of his surroundings and the devastating loss of his father. Whatever the case, Tony already had a dope habit when he went under the knife. He was no virgin; he already had a need for that needle. His brain didn't really care what kind of medicine it took it only knew that it always wanted more. There are alcoholics, and there are junkies, and there are crackheads. People who don't have a preference and just want to ingest everything fall into a different class. They are known in NA and on the streets as Garbageheads. Our friend Tony C was one of these.

Born and raised in Trenton where the streets can be rough, the violence toughened Tony up. He had been in more than his fair share of fights. Sometimes, he kicked a little ass and other times he got beaten down. That's just the way things go in this town.

One Christmas, when the desperation set in, Tony tried to steal a stereo out of this guy's car on Hewitt Ave. The owner of the car was a large guy who caught him. Instead of calling the police, the guy punched Joey in the jaw and broke it in two places. There was some speculation that the guy might have had on brass knuckles or at least something solid in his hands, though that could never be proven. What we know for sure is that Tony had to have his jaw wired shut and he had to eat his meals through a straw for a few weeks. Shit like that had a way of ruining Christmas and making the depression seem inescapable. On top of all that, nothing got jacked, and so Ton had no way to pay for the drugs he needed to feed his addiction.

Sometimes, arguments would escalate because Tony got too high or drunk, but mostly he was a good guy and peaceful. Mostly, he just fought if he had to, he never really liked to. In this respect, he and his sister were different.

Kelly, at heart was a fighter.

Scott asked Tony 'Where's your sister? Has she been around?" Then Tony proceeded to tell him pretty much the same story I just told you, minus a few details which wouldn't become known until later. Scott was saddened and shocked, but at the same time, not really surprised. He knew the last time he had seen his Bella, she was out of control. Her life was definitely headed in the wrong direction and she was going too fast. She was destined for some sort of crash.

Even though Scott was upset that his babies Momma was behind bars, he couldn't help but let out a sigh of relief. At least she was off the streets and still breathing. He was afraid that while he was away someone was going to find her ODed in some crackhouse, abando, or alley.

While Scott processed this, Tony added this, "You know, I was thinking that since you got to have sex with my sister, it's only fair that I should get to have sex with yours."

Scott couldn't help but let a little smile slip as he thought about some of the stuff he had done to Tony's sister. He said "I can maybe set you up on a date with her but I can't promise you anything else beyond that. Besides, I don't think your man enough for KoryAnn."

"Oh, I'm man enough" said the boy from Division Street "Believe that."

As things turned out Tony and Kory became very good friends and they did quite a bit of drugs together, but to the best of Scott's knowledge they never had sex. KoryAnn would actually fall in love with his buddy CJ instead. And oh what a mess that had been. We'll get back to KoryAnn and CJ later.

For now though, let's take a ride, shall we? Let's get in the car, you and I, and head north from Trenton towards Lambertville on route 29. Maybe it's Saturday, mid October and sunny. The leaves on the trees by the Delaware River and Raritan canal are red, orange, and yellow. It's comfortable outside with a slight breeze and as we head out of the city and into the country we start to believe that the world is really quite pretty. Perhaps even because of the beauty of nature, we start thinking about God and give thanks to our maker. We are feeling glad to be alive as we take our little drive. R.E.M. is playing on the radio with Michael Stipe singing about how "with love come strange currencies" For some reason this seems to be the perfect song for the moment and maybe all at once for an instant we understand everything. And we roll the window down and feel the wind on our face. We begin to enjoy ourselves even though we know we are on way to an ugly place. Kelly is in the workhouse and it is visiting day.

As we approach the rock quarry, the trees on either side of the road form a canopy over the street. When we emerge from these, we can see across the water to Pennsylvania, where Bowman's Tower is perched high on a hill to our left. This tower was built back in the revolutionary war times so that soldiers could watch the movement of enemy troops through these same trees.

We can't see the jail from our vantage point at street level; it is obstructed from our view by more trees and an old deserted barn and across the driveway a dilapidated old mill. Mercer County Corrections sits at the end of a winding drive atop its own hill. As we make our way up, we are bound to notice the giant black birds hovering and circling in the air. We can see some of these horrid things picking at the carcass of a dead animal by the side of the road. We don't stop to inspect and identify the road kill as it is starting to decompose. Possibly a possum or raccoon.

The Turkey Buzzards are not imprisoned by the eight foot high chain link fences that surround the facility. Nor are they intimidated by the razor wire loops twisting around the whole perimeter. They are free to come and go as they please. In this respect all the inmates must envy them.

Looking at these foul creatures makes it easy for us to believe that all existence is bleak and we must be careful not to let this place suck us in to that mentality. Even the color orange losses vibrancy and becomes listless. Yes even the carroty colored jumpsuits, that all the inmates are made to wear comes off somehow depressing. How can the color of orange juice, mornings, and pumpkins manage to look so flat and unhappy? Kelly would say "When I get out of here, I never want to see this color orange again."

The guards at the gate make you sit outside in your car for a minimum and mandatory half hour wait. Scott hated them. They treat the visitors like they are also criminals, guilt by association I guess, and they herd them in through the metal detectors and they make them put their wallets, car keys and valuables into a locker in the waiting room. These lockers cost you a quarter.

And these guards judge the family members and loved ones of the incarcerated with the same condemnation that they have for the inmates. They are no different in their hypocrisy than the police; we are expected to believe they are guilty of no sins, wrongdoing, or law breaking.

When the guests were finally led in, they went into a corridor separated from the gymnasium and the population by another chain link fence. There were chairs placed about three feet away from that fence on both sides. The guards watched to make sure nothing was passed between the fence and that there was no physical contact. And people shouted to be heard over the people visiting a foot to their left or a foot to their right.

Scott was led passed the gym with all its commotion and into a smaller room off in the corner. In this room, which was cut in half by a Plexiglas wall, there were six or eight cubicles. A telephone was connected on either side of the glass in each. Scott took a seat at the one at the end all the way to his left. He waited to see his girlfriend, who I suppose was still technically his ex at the time.

She came in and saw him, sat down and smiled. She even managed to look kinda cute dressed in that horrible orange jailhouse garb. Kelly's smile was as infectious and heartwarming as her laugh. Scott found her more than a little seductive and bewitching. He looked at her through the cloudy plastic glass that separated them. That smile, while genuine at the sight of him, (he was the first visitor she'd had in months) was still forced and it was not hard to read the pain and sadness behind her girl eyes. It was easy to tell that she had recently been crying. Kelly could break his heart without really trying. He thought about how it was going to be a long time before he could touch her and make love to her again.

Anyway, they had to talk to each other through these phones. Kelly picked up the receiver on her end and said "Hi baby. It's so good to see you."

And Scott grabbed his own phone and put it to his ear, equally happy to see her. "Hey girl, it's so good to see . . . ." But he didn't get a chance to finish his sentence or his thought because a cataclysmic event so personally traumatic it bordered on the apocalyptic had occurred. It seemed that the last person to use the phone had spit a particularly juicy ginker of yellowy phlegm onto the mouthpiece of Scott's receiver. It was gross beyond all understanding and it defied reason. Horrified, he pulled the phone away from his face and beheld the thick abomination as tendrils of it clung to his skin in thin strings that only reluctantly snapped and gave way. And yes, sweet Jesus, some of the mixture, which was easily the most grotesque thing ever created, got on Scott's lip. I really cannot stress to you enough how fucking disgusting this thing was. It would be fair to say that he freaked. "What the mother fucking fuck!?! Why?!! Why would somebody do that? Fucking animals!" He dropped the receiver and began frantically wiping the spittum off his mouth and chin with his sleeve. This side of the glass was supposed to be for the civilized folks on the outside.

Kelly laughed at him from the safety of her side of the glass. It was a deep hysterical feel good kind of laugh that can only come from something unrehearsed and unfortunate happening to someone else. Scott's anger and disgust abated as he listened to the sound of her laughter. It soothed him. Like I earlier mentioned, it was infectious. He was glad for the chance to lift her spirits even momentarily, as she sat waiting in Mercer County Corrections for her chance to be sent to the women's penitentiary in Clinton.

Scott would not let the loogy ruin his visit, yet now he thought he knew what Moses meant in the bible when he talked about dudes being "ceremonially unclean." He would scrub his face frantically like a true germaphobe when he got home. He would feel dirty for days.

He found some tissues in his pocket and wiped the grossness off the phone. He never held it closer than two inches from his face as he put it back to his ear and continued his talk with Kelly.

Kelly, who was only now starting to get her giggling under control,. "I'm sorry, baby. You'll be OK." She was still on the verge of losing her composure to the laughter.

"I'm glad this pleases you, honey." He said this sarcastically, but the truth was, he was glad for any chance to make her feel better. Seeing her again after all this time reminded him how much he loved her; Ariel and Ethan's mother.

And they reconciled there, in jail. They talked once again of the beautiful future, married and drug free, reunited with their family. Scott forgave her when she apologized to him about her indiscretion with Kenny and he told her that he would be there for her for the next six years, helping her out with letters and money. She could call him whenever she needed to talk. He wanted her to because like I said he loved the sound of her voice. He even agreed to pay for that.

There were those who said that Scott was a fool for taking her back, given their history and the situation. His devotion and dedication to her came from his twisted interpretation of love. It was what it was and not even close to the stupidest thing he had ever done.

In addition to the letters that Scott wrote her, he also started sending her his book.

He'd send her one chapter a week for her review, which she'd send back to him along with her love letters. She read the first six chapters of his book in jail and she passed them on to her friends. Sometimes, the girls locked up with her would attach notes to her letters telling him how much they loved the story and how they couldn't wait to read more. His book might not have ever gotten written if it wasn't for the early encouraging words of criminals. His Bella included. He ate up their praises and it totally fed his ego. Though, when it came to writing shit, Scott knew he was good and blessed. That much was obvious. Of his writing prowess there could be no doubt.

But you already knew that.

So, anyway, Scott and Kelly rekindled and picked up their relationship where they left off. Like ambers glowing after a fire, their feelings for each other never really died out. It was not a question of distance of separation or length of time. She was always his girl in his heart and mind.

Sure, this would be the longest stretch since they'd met that he'd have to go without touching her or getting to hold her. But even that was Ok too; he had gone without pussy before.

Besides, if he got hungry enough, Kelly probably wouldn't have minded if he got himself a whore. I mean let's face it, it was 2,190 days, and under the circumstances what could she say? Not that Scott would tell her if he slipped; no need to rub it in her face. Theirs had never been the kind of relationship that didn't have its lies and secrets.

Maybe to you this sounds like a nightmare, but there was something about Kelly that affected Scott like no other girl ever had. It was much more than sex, the way they connected, truth be told, he found something addictive and bewitching in the very Irises of her eyes. If the eyes are truly the windows to the soul than Scott had seen inside her as surely as he had been inside her. And Kelly had big eyes that captivated and enchanted. Scott could get lost looking into them and forget the sadness of his own self. He lived for the moments when their eyes locked, regardless of whether it was in love making or combat.

Glossy, near tears, always were the wetness of Kelly's cornea. Light easily reflected in that vitreous shine was the spark of life and you could read every emotion she had ever had there. And yeah, it's also true that she knew how to use that look to play you. Kelly had bad girl eyes too sometimes, lest we forget and think her always the victim.

Anyway, did you know that in Greek mythology Iris was the rainbow goddess? She was also the messenger of the gods.

The irises of Kelly's eyes were hazel; brown and green; (speckled pretty) and they hypnotized Scott when they contracted and let the light in. He suspected that it was here, in this space, in those colors that she cast her spell over him. Though that may be overly romantic or completely superstitious, what we know for sure is that perforating those irises were the black circles of her pupils. The desolation at the dark center of her eyes may tempt us to make a comparison between her pupils and the desperation that lies at the cold, ugly core of the thing. But since there can also be great deal of beauty in the absence of light and the night, and since maybe we can still see a little glimmer of hope left in her imprisoned eyes, maybe this analogy doesn't apply either. Forget I mentioned it.

As the lovers stared at one another through the glass of the corrections center, Scott wondered what she had seen with those eyes that had hurt her so much. Where did this precious despair that she held onto come from? What images were pulled through those black portholes and burned through her retinas and lenses? What visions of Trenton's streets had been so grim that they traveled through her optical nerve to her brain and scarred her? Scott could never know all of Kelly's ghosts.

Once, when they were both high at home, years ago on Bruce lane in Ewing, Kelly had shown him her poem. It immediately captured his mind and he read it and thought about it over and over. "Damn, that's good, Kel."

"Stop making fun of me." She thought he was patronizing her.

"I'm not. I mean it, I love it. It's perfect." Rambling and disorganized; it spoke eloquently about sickness and addiction. Metaphorically, Scott deciphered spiritual emptiness in those few words as well and there were all kinds of dark connotations. It implied more than it actually said, it was simple and beautiful because it revealed more than was intended. She likened her apathy to losing her eyes.

"Eyes away from me. It's dark at night and I can't see, drugs took my eyes from me. I don't care whether I can see drugs or not, they took my eyes away. I wish that I could see clear today, but that's just the price I pay. Drugs took my eyes away."

One time, when Scott was away at a Christian rehab, he was reading the bible and he came across a passage written by the apostle Paul. Scott related part of his letter to the Ephesians to what Kelly was talking about; that spiritual void. Paul wrote in Chapter 4 verse 18 "Having their understanding darkened, being alienated from the life of God, because of the ignorance that is in them, because of the blindness of their heart, . . ." In essence Paul was saying that depression comes from being separated from God, a theory that jives perfectly with the Narcotics Anonymous belief in the need for a higher power.

Allow me to interject my own opinions and commentary into verse 19 which continues "Who, (Scott and Kelly) being passed feeling, (high on morphine) have given themselves over to lewdness (were fucking like jackrabbits) to work all uncleanness with greediness (and shooting heroin).

He then goes on to mention Emanuel (God with us) as the savior and salvation from sin, saying in verse 20 "But you have not so learned Christ." And Paul was a guy who supposedly knew about having his eyes taken away. If you believe what it says in the good book, he was literally struck blind for three days when he met up with God on his way to Damascus.

C.S.W.

Indeed, even, Jesus once restored the sight of this blind dude by spitting on his eyes. You can bet when the messiah's saliva landed on the guys face, he did not respond by screaming out "What the mother fucking fuck!" like Scott, our protagonist had done. No, that guy was probably so happy to have his sight restored that he was eternally grateful. For a few hours at least.

Anyway, all this divine enlightenment is great in that it gives us a glimmer of hope in an otherwise dark and dismal place. And maybe it even gives us a little peak at redemption and recovery, with God acting as the lighthouse or beacon. Like the sun breaking through the clouds.

But that's not what this chapter is about.

We were speaking of the desperation that lies at the cold, ugly, core of the thing.

Through the dirty glass at jail the junkies sat there staring and both their eyes were empty. Scotts were benumbed from too many drugs and Kelly's emptiness came from being incarcerated for so long in a place that was filthy. It is true that Kelly herself had not been high for many, many months, not since she had gotten locked up, but ask any addict and they will tell you there's a big difference between abstinence and recovery. Kelly's disease was only in remission, the demon sleeping in her mind, waiting, biding its time.

And yay, though the Trentonians deluded themselves with talk of a clean and sober future, the here and now was what they actually had. Scott promising he would always love her. He'd wait for her forever; he'd support her and take care of her. But when he left her, he was going home alone to his needle.

Kelly would sit here in orange for a long time, working as a runner and doing stupid errands for the CO's who were just as pompous as the police on the outside. She moved easily through the jail and the bloods who were down with her respected her because she came from the same streets they did. That's not to say she didn't get into the occasional fight, this is after all Kelly were talking about. But even when they tried to get her to join their sets, Kelly stayed 550. (550—not in a gang, civilian.)

Awright, lest we start letting this place depress us, and since we are free to leave, let's do so, we'll go and let these addicts be. We'll pick up with them again in a couple of weeks. When the weather has turned colder and the days have turned grayer. It was the second week in November when Kelly called Scott on the phone and caught him at home.

"Hey baby, how's it going?" she called to check on everyone; Scott, Dylan Tony and especially her mother, who was now in the hospital. No one knew about the extent of her cancer yet.

"Everything is fine Kel; I just got back from visiting your Mom a little while ago. I'm not a doctor but she seems Ok to me. She was sleeping when I got there but she woke up and we talked for a while. I bought her some ice cream."

"That's good, honey. What about Dylan and Tony?"

"They were going up to see her later." Scott told her on his cell phone. That's when the house line rang with Tony Cambell calling in. That's when everything fell apart. "Hold on babe, I got another call." And Kelly listened as Scott talked to her brother and the situation escalated. She only heard half the conversation but it was all it took to tell the story. She heard "Hey Ton, what's up?" "Oh my God, what happened?" "I just saw her and she was fine." And "I'll meet you at the hospital." This obviously was enough to panic her,

"What is it?! Oh my God what's wrong with my Mom?" she pleaded and cried.

And Scott had no answers and no way to lessen her pain. God, up in his heaven was so fucking unfair. Kelly would not get to see her mother to say goodbye. This was not the way a loved one should die. Maybe this was the unbearable price she had to pay for letting drugs take her eyes away. She would lose her mother, her last parent, while she was frantic in jail.

"I'm so sorry honey. I'm going to the hospital now. Call me back in a half hour," If Scott didn't get off the phone with her now, they might not have enough time left on their account for her to call him at the hospital, when time and words would be more important.

"Ok baby, I'll call you back. I love you."

A feeling of dread got to the hospital ahead of him. Grief moved like a presence in the room and somber was the mood in the intensive care unit. Mrs. Cambell had been moved here from her private room. She had not been breathing for a while. Just how long? The nurses never knew. When they found her she was turning blue. And now the truth was coming to light, Colleen Cambell's body was riddled throughout with cancer and she would not live the night. This was all as surreal as a dream. This could not be happening. Not like this. Not tonight.

Scott's sister KoryAnn brought Tony there and the three of them hovered over the deathbed. Each of them looking down in love and loss and wonder. There were sniffling noses and runny eyes as they each took their turns kissing her forehead or cheek and saying goodbye.

Doctors had decided to flood her system with morphine so she would be at peace. It dripped from a dangling plastic bag and went into her body through a tube IV. She was resting comfortably.

C.S.W.

Dylan was spared seeing his Grandmother like this. He was now in the custody of his Godmother Melinda. Scott couldn't help thinking about how much Dylan loved his Grammy and how much the boy would surely miss her. Scott could relate to this, he still had his grandmother and he still loved her. He was lucky enough to have her in his life for 37 years. Dylan, poor kid, would lose his at age ten.

Tony was a product of Trenton and so he didn't like to let people see him cry. He tried to suppress his tears but they fell anyway. We have to respect him for trying, even though we've learned this is one of those times when it was ok, as his mother lay there dying.

Kelly called Scott back on his cell and Scott put the phone to her sleeping mother's ear so she could talk to her for the last time. Scott didn't have to listen in to know what was being said. Apologies and gratitude. I love you's. It would have to do. Mrs. Cambell would never regain consciousness.

When Kelly got off the phone, the room was quiescent with pain. Scott and KoryAnn looked at Tony and neither of them knew what to do. Scott noticed the morphine dripping into Colleen's arm and he saw how it provided her with relief. Would it not do the same thing for Tony, his friend, and fellow junkie? He knew that everyone in the room held their own sets. He and his sister still even had a couple of bags left. Everyone was going to need them tonight. If ever they needed to be numb it was now.

The dialogue was just a silent nod from Scott to Tony to the morphine bag on his right, hanging there unguarded on a stand. And in that quiet gesture Tony knew exactly what to do. He took his needle from his pocket and stabbed it into the medicine and pulled back on the plunger and withdrew the solution. He then disappeared into the bathroom to inject it. When he came back he went to the nurses' station and said "I need some alone time with my Mom. I want to say goodbye."

And even if the nurses were suspicious of such a request, they had no choice but to honor it. So they left Tony and Scott and Kory alone with Mrs. Cambell and her morphine. And Tony took another shot out of the bag and wiped it where a little bead of sweat ran from the puncture hole. Then he turned to his two friends and made his own silent gesture which implied "free drugs, take what you want."

Fortunately, Scott and KoryAnn both had some heroin left and so they weren't nearly as tempted. They could still take the moral high road. Plus Scott never wanted it to get back to his sweetheart that he had stolen drugs from her mother on her deathbed. But understanding the nature of the sickness of addiction like he did, he had no doubt that if he and KoryAnn had been out, the verdict would have been different.

Now, I know that it is also true that some of you, who do not know about the desperation that lies at the cold ugly core of the thing, may find this sin unforgivable. And only a real scumbag could steal from his dying mother. All I can say is be very glad that you cannot understand this madness.

Scott and KoryAnn however were afflicted with the same sickness. They had witnessed this and yet there was no judging or condemnation of their grief stricken friend. They understood the greed of the disease, that undeniable need.

In fact, a year later to the day of Mrs. Cambell's death, Scotts own grandmother would pass away, and before she died, Scott had stolen some of her pain medicine from her. It was not as dramatic as what happened in the ICU, but the principle was still the same. It was not a question of whether or not he loved her, he did and he would cherish her memory forever. It was just that living inside him (them) was a monster and it wanted to be fed regardless of the situation or perhaps even more so because of it.

Scott knew what it was to need to escape that pain by any means necessary. He learned this lesson up close and personal when his own beloved MomMom died a little over two weeks after her 97th birthday. May she be with the angels forever, amen.

Scott lost his grandmother on November 11, 2009.

Tony and Kelly lost their mother on November 11, 2008.

Ariel and Ethan would grow up not remembering either of them.

Scott would receive the honor of being one of Mrs. Cambell's pallbearers.

Kelly was still incarcerated and was not allowed to attend the funeral.

Colleen Cambell was 57. May she rest in peace forever, amen.

Chapter 11

Tyler Street
(Many failures revisited)

I GUESS WE COULD proverbially say that in Trenton, all roads lead to Tyler Street. If you ask any junkie in the east ward, they could tell you exactly where Tyler Street is, what this expression means, and what you could find there at any given minute. And yes, as you've probably guessed when we say this, we don't mean "all roads" in the literal sense. Obviously we are not talking about the actual asphalt, broken with potholes and outlined with concrete curbs and sidewalks when we say ":all roads." No, if you'll follow me through this analogy, you'll see when we say "all roads," what we mean is the narcotics addiction that they all seem to be afflicted with. Specifically the opiates injected by the lost souls embarked on this journey. Those of us committed to walking this dark path.

And when we say lead to Tyler Street, we speak symbolically of where we all end up when in the grips of this disease. It could just as easily be a street in Newark or Camden. Harlem, Brooklyn, or the Bronx. Regardless of the physical destination, it is all slavery. It is all a form of captivity. Whatever the city, it is all Babylon.

For the purposes of our narrative and the twisted group of antiheroes we are discussing, however, the place they were drawn to was actually Tyler Street. 277 Tyler to be exact. The place that Caroline and her boyfriend Eddie were renting.

Like bugs in the darkness on a hot summer night that are inexplicably drawn to a glowing purple light, that's how they all came. Even as, like the bugs, who witnessed friend after friend hit the element that shocked them dead, still they kept coming.

In case you missing it, here is the explanation of this parable. The light at the end of the tunnel is the pursuit of the perfect high, euphoria, that unholy lie. And the element that kills them is the shit that stands in their way. Anything that deters them from their quest. In could be a little thing like a fellow junkie overdosing, or it could be the police. It could be getting jacked, it could be getting beat. None of these factors however could open their eyes and teach then any kind of lesson, in spite of any deterrent, they are incorrigible. And just like those bugs of summer, so to do the junkies return to their streets.

Once again, maybe we are reminded of Sigmund Freud and his theory of the Thanatos drive. Maybe they all wanted to die. They kept coming back again and again, despite their deteriorating health, the loss of their children, or the deaths and arrests of their friends.

It's true too, that the journey was geographically and spiritually shorter for some than others. Like Kelly's brother Tony was destined to find Tyler sooner or later. Addicted as he was and he lived on Division which was only a couple of blocks away. He could easily walk to the cop spot.

Even Scott's boy CJ was within walking distance from his house on Dayton Street up North Clinton.

Scott's own trek was a little longer as he was now living on his parents couch in the nearby suburb of Ewing. He would eventually gravitate to the same place as the rest of them though; that Heroin den, the shooting gallery.

Scott's sister KoryAnn came from the farthest. Of all the people we've talked about, and with the possible exception of his Uncle Alan, KoryAnn was the most like him. They had the same mentality running through their heads and like so many members of his family, she was riddled with addiction.

KoryAnn grew up in Lambertville, miles away from Trenton, up Route 29, and she didn't meet her older brother until she was about twelve years old. They were not raised together as they had different mothers. Unfortunately for them both, and with no disregard for the importance and influence of the nurturing love and care of the maternal, the bloodline was passed through their father. The same genetic defect was inherited by Scott and Kory in the written code of their DNA. To put it a simpler way, their twisted characteristics were running through their blood.

And it always comes back to the blood, doesn't it?

The life is in it, Jesus supposedly shed it to save us, and junkies were always tainting it when they played with it.

The sickness within it was what connected Kory and Scott.

Yes, KoryAnn came up in a different neighborhood and, like I said, they had different mothers, so if the bloodline isn't passed through the fathers genes, I would be hard pressed to explain all their similarities. Brother and sister both loved drugs and could, on occasion, be a little crazy. Kory's right arm was all scarred up from putting her fist through a plate-glass window, once when she got into a fight with her boyfriend and he locked her out of the house. She had her father's rage

In spite of the fact that their mutual father and KoryAnn's mother would later try to blame Scott for their daughters addictions, the truth was that Kory was a slave to substances long before she and her brother ever hung out. This is a thirty something year old women we are talking about.

Before Kory came to the city, she had already had her tribulations with narcotics. Once, a friend of hers overdosed on painkillers and alcohol and died in her bed. The death of this dude really fucked Kory up and she knew about losing people she loved to this disease more intimately than her elder brother did. For the record, Scott was not even around when that shit went down.

Anyway, sometime after that tragedy, KoryAnn called Scott, while Kelly was still in jail and said, "I think you should meet a friend of mine. Her name is Jeanine. She is twenty three, sweet, and very pretty."

And Scott said "Sounds good to me."

Then KoryAnn said, "Do you have any single friends?"

"Yeah, I guess I could bring my boy CJ." And this was the mistake for which his family would later hate him. As I already told you, CJ was a junkie and KoryAnn was an accident waiting to happen. Scott never thought in a million years that Kory would be attracted to CJ. They were from different worlds. When they fell in love it was a first class disaster. Maybe, their relationship wasn't as bad as say Kurt and Courtney's, or Sid and Nancy's, but it certainly was every bit as destructive as Scott and Kelly's.

And yes, KoryAnn had seen her brother shoot dope before. But it was CJ who put her on the needle. Scott maybe should have been angry with his friend, but he knew why Kory came around, what really attracted her to this place, the same thing that attracted him here. Kory wanted to get high and she had been waiting for the syringe for a long time. If it wasn't CJ, it would have been somebody else just as easy. Scott should have thanked CJ really because there was no doubt that eventually he would have shot his sister up for the first time. That's just how this thing rolls. Addiction grows like cancer goes, and it's out of control. Scott should have been glad that CJ busted her heroin cherry, at least this way Scott didn't have to have that on his conscience.

After she was sufficiently addicted, Scott and KoryAnn were able to fix each other relatively guilt free. They'd inject the serum into each other in that unholy communion and fuck yeah they shared needles. If one of them got sick, (called being on E, for empty. Or as in, if you take the junk away from a junkie all you have left is ie.) then the other would help them out if they could. This usually meant giving up a bag or a ten shot, which was fine early on, but as the money got lower, they got progressively greedier. Inevitably, it was everyman for hisself when you got right down to it.

Anyway, Scott and his sister got high together, same as Kelly and Tony did, the same as his Uncle Alan and his Aunt Audrey did.

Now I know what you're probably thinking; it's totally wrong and immoral for brothers and sisters to get high together. Maybe even, you believe, it's ok for them to get drunk together because that's socially acceptable, not to mention legal. And perhaps, you don't even have a problem with them smoking some weed, even though that is against the law because it is totally safe and there is absolutely no chance of anyone dying from it. It might be what the French call a faux pas, but it is certainly nothing as downright evil as sticking a needle in each other's arm. In fact, probably the only thing we could mention that would be socially and ethically worse would be if they had gotten into anything incestuous. Thankfully, they never got into anything sexual like that, which would have been not only naughty, but also perverted and gross.

If we want to look at things on the bright side, we could say that the only thing they did was shoot a little dope. I guess it all depends on your perspective and personal point of view which of these dirty deeds was an unforgivable sin and which one is merely taboo. I'll leave that judgment up to you.

At any rate, Scott's uncle Al and his sister Aud have been partying together since the beginning of time and right or wrong, you best believe that they will continue to get high together until one of them dies. They also had it in their blood, that overpowering, self satisfying love of drugs.

As far as I know, Alan and Audrey never did heroin together. They did, however, drink alcohol like they were Irish and smoke marijuana like they were Jamaican. Occasionally, they would pass around a plate with hard or soft cocaine. And they knew all about pills; which ones were good for taking away the pain and which ones were good for keeping away the crazies. Percocet's and Xanies.

They were an unfortunate foreshadowing of how drug addiction was inherited in Scott and Kory's family. The next generation just took it to the next level with morphine. Scott couldn't help but wonder about and be scared of the future for his children. What would be the consequences of his habits and would this horrible gene be passed on to his babies? Poor little Ethan was born with that shit in his system and no amount of praying or education could ever change the fact that his mommy and daddy were junkies.

They could not go back in time and change things. They must carry their shame forever. Even if they stayed clean all day tomorrow and somehow wound up with twenty years of recovery, the past would remain ugly.

Ariel and Ethan would be sadly and profoundly affected by their real parent's absence in their childhood years. They would be too young to understand why they felt mom and dad had neglected them. Plus they had their adoptive parents feigning to be the saviors and heroes. Claiming they were only protecting them.

And no words of repentance would ever be enough.

They would never let Scott and Kelly try to make things right. There would be no mercy, compassion, or forgiveness. They needed to be punished for their whole lives.

And Scott's brother Chuck had a bitch for a wife. She knew, like everyone else did too, that if she let those children see their real Mommy and Daddy, (and for that matter their Grammy and Poppy too) then "her" kids would love them more.

That's why they moved them away to Pittsburgh.

Ariel and Ethan should know this. And maybe, one day, the whole façade will be shattered and come cascading down. When the truth comes out; that the people who raised you, actually stole you. That's why, Ariel could just look into her eyes and know that this women was not her mother.

And that was the real travesty, that even though the kids were raised in a safe place, their home must have been very cold because there was no room in her heart for reconciliation. Ariel and Ethan were legally kidnapped, used by their adoptive parents as leverage and held without ransom.

How could Scott and Kelly have let this happen?

How could they claim that they were willing to die for their children when they could not even stop getting high for their children?

The lure of the drugs was a mysterious and unstoppable force. Once they had you, you were drawn towards them like a magnet. To not do them was so uncomfortable, it felt unnatural. The reason, I think, that they were so drawn to the chemicals was because they were separated from God and his inspiration. They were spiritually bankrupt, empty.

Satan gave them the dope and they returned day after day without hope to that reliable almost magical source.

Let me tell you another story. Another lesson of Trenton, if you will. Perhaps it will shed some light on how deep this unholy drive actually goes. Maybe, it is even the crystallized realization of the Thanatos drive.

I mentioned Scott's Aunt Audrey a couple of times. Anyway, Audrey marries this guy. She doesn't ever love him but he provides a nice home for her and her three daughters. Tommy, the guys name was. Since, Tommy was a junkie; he was never endeared enough by the family to be called Uncle Tommy. He was a hard dude to like. Like most opiate addicts, he spent most of his day uselessly nodding out in front of the TV. Perhaps, in another life, he could have gotten off the dope and had some kind of value or productivity. As it was he was a complete waste of space.

The point of this story is not to put Tommy down or even to try and explain why Audrey framed him and sent him to jail so that she and her kids, along with Uncle Alan and Aunt Kathy could have his place to themselves. No, but suffice to say, Tommy did have to kick the dope while he was locked up. No doubt that while he went through the nightmare of withdrawal, cold turkey, he counted the days until he got out and could get his next injection and how good it was going to feel. Tommy knew about depravity.

I don't know how long it was after he got out that Tommy got his first bags, but again, that's not really the point. What happened was, he picked up where he left off and he started shooting that shit again until his veins collapsed and he nodded out, too deep asleep from an overdose.

Someone called an ambulance for an unresponsive Tommy and they took him to Capital Health Systems at Mercer. The same hospital I told ya about before, the one that Scott, his Mom, and both his children were born at.

When Tommy got there, he flat lined. He stopped breathing and heart beating.

So we can see how in these corridors life and death balance each other out.

But Tommy, he wasn't done yet. The emergency team was able to save him. They got him breathing and resuscitated. I guess you could say that god in his heaven spared him and granted him this miracle, this reprieve. But Tommy, he didn't want it, you see? Now, I don't know if Tony really intended to die, or if he was only after the euphoria of that incredible high one more time, but as soon as he was able, he called his dope dealer from the hospital. The guy met him in the parking lot off Bellevue Avenue. I also can't tell you how many bags he bought, though if he was smart and had any premonition of what was coming, he would have gotten a few of them fronted. Again, I guess it really doesn't matter much either way. As the saying goes, you can't take it with you.

Maybe Tommy injected his last bags of that poison directly into an IV line still left iun his arm, or maybe he even still had his own syringe. Whatever the case, the result was fatal. When Tommy flat lined this time, they either couldn't or wouldn't bring him back. Maybe God himself had had it with Tony and his relentless habit. I wonder if anyone at all really cared about him at this point. I wonder if anyone cried for Tommy when he died.

The reason I told you about this was because I wanted to illustrate just how bad this disease can get if you let it, if you follow it all the way through its natural progression. The idjit in Tommy had eaten him alive until there was nothing left. I suspect that the depression had him feeling so joyless and empty that his soul had been gone for a long time before he actually died. When the moment of his death finally came, I bet it was a blessing.

This is the epitome of the disease, it's the same for all addicts, and this is where it inevitably will lead. That is the moral of the story.

For now though, fortunately, things hadn't gotten quite that bad for our protagonists. We were talking about Scott and KoryAnn's double date before I went off on yet another tangent.

Things started out on a positive note, early that evening. Jeanine was every bit as pretty as KoryAnn had promised and she was a fun and interesting girl. She was, maybe a little young for Scott but, like I said, attractive.

They went to the Morrisville Tavern to play pool, have a few drinks, and to listen to music. Scott and Jeanine were on one team and Kory and CJ on the other. They joked around and flirted. This was a big night for the guys, neither one of them had been on a date for quite a while. Being addicted to heroin, dating had ceased to be a priority for them. Since this was a special occasion CJ got a shower before meeting KoryAnn, remarkable since it was his first in something like thirty two days. He also put on his best clean shirt, shaved and splashed on some cologne. Scott was surprised to see how hard CJ was hitting on his sister and even more shocked to see how KoryAnn was responding to him. He never imagined that Kory would be attracted to him.

Since this was an occasion, Scott splurged and bought a big bag of cocaine for the evening. Every twenty minutes or so, their party would adjourn to the car and blow lines in the parking lot. Everything was twinkly and sparkly.

After a couple of hours however they had had enough of the bar and the two dudes invited the two ladies from Doylestown to accompany them back to CJ's room in beautiful downtown Trenton.

So Scott brought Kory to Tyler for the first time. It was starting to get late and while the coke and drinking had been fun, recreation, it would not sustain the two junkies. It was well passed time for them to fix. They needed their opiates.

The guys hurried their dates up to CJ's room on the third floor and it was here, I suspect that Scott lost any chance he may have had of banging KoryAnn's friend. It's true that she may have found him to be too old for her, as I already mentioned. Scott needed his dope so badly at this point that he no longer cared about trying to impress her. The poor girl watched wide eyed as Scott produced his set and drew up the serum. She was horrified by the sight of him and CJ taking off their belts and tying them, tourniquet, around their biceps. She was probably planning her escape route before they even blasted their injections.

After everything was made right for the fellas, they chilled for a few more minutes, but the atmosphere had definitely changed. All the warmth and friendliness was gone from Scott's female. KoryAnn was still having a good time with CJ, who was telling her stories about life in the Pine Barrens. Before calling it a night, the group went out on the front porch for a final smoke.

Jeanine kept looking over her shoulder and up and down the street. She was obviously nervous, being out of her element, being escorted by two drug addicts in the hood. The girl was terrified, scared that any minute she would be the victim of a rape, mugging, or drive-by. When some of the neighborhood boys came walking by, Jeanine stiffened and moved closer to Scott's side. You could read the fear in her eyes, like she'd never seen a black guy. Scott felt bad for her but he thought that it was funny at the same time.

He got ambivalent when he got high.

KoryAnn, on the other hand, immediately loved the tension. She found the prospect of drugs, and guns, and crime, and gangs, and fighting; exciting. From that day on, it would not be uncommon for Scott to show up at Tyler Street and find Kory's car already parked outside. She was addicted to the dope, long before she ever tried it. For the record, Scott did not turn his sister on to heroin. But he did introduce her to the guy who did.

For this, Scott and KoryAnn's father would blame him. It was a crime for which her mother would never forgive him, even though she was a Christian and Sunday school teacher. When it came to their daughter problems, KoryAnn's parents believed that they were all Scott's fault and they pointed their fingers directly at him.

Despite Scotts own addictions and sinfulness, he really had no problem with Jesus. His beef was with Christians not with Christ. In fact, it was this type of Christianity, lacking compassion and the mercy that the Lord called for, and dripping like honey with hypocrisy that sent his mind reeling and had him feeling like the antichrist reaching for another needle. Did he not believing in the same religious fiction and dogmatic fantasies necessarily make him evil?

Surely, he was intelligent enough to receive his own enlightenment. Were we not all called to seek after God in our own ways, learning him through our own interpretations, using our own understanding and experiences?

Regardless, KoryAnn's parents viewed Scott as rotten and they equated him with Satan and held him accountable for all his sisters' transgressions. This, of course, was pure bullshit but at least one part of their accusations was true. Scott had introduced Kory to CJ and to Tyler Street, even though he knew firsthand what this city could do. How Trenton can rape you.

Anyway, that's how Kory and CJ became a couple.

As for Jeanine and Scott, I guess it's safe to say that it was not a love match. They went their separate ways, never to speak to each other again. That was ok too because Scott was still in love with Kelly in his heart. She was constantly in his thoughts. Always.

And speaking of Kelly, Scott remembered the last time she called him from jail. It was December 23, 2008. The sound of the ringing telephone made him nervous because he knew it was her calling before he even picked up the phone. He fully expected her to be upset because today was the day of her sentencing. She was calling to tell him how she made out in court and when she was moving from Mercer County Corrections to the prison in Clinton. Scott anticipated her sadness and he hated hearing her cry.

But this time he would be miraculously, pleasantly surprised.

"Hey, Baby." He greeted her ready to comfort and console.

"Hey, honey. Guess what?" and she held the silence for a moment, trying to draw out the suspense. "I'm coming home!" They were the sweetest words he had ever heard. A genuine Christmas miracle.

When Scott answered the phone, he was bracing himself for the worst. He knew it was sentencing day and he was preparing to hear his angel cry. At this point, her sentencing had already been postponed three times. Every time it got rescheduled, Kelly was disappointed. She had been locked up at Mercer County Corrections Center (M.C.C.C., not to be confused with M.C.C.C. Mercer County Community College.) for a little over thirteen months. By now she was actually looking forward to moving over to Clinton and starting her time.

They never knew why the prosecutor and the judge had a change of mind and heart. Scott had written letters to her lawyer and the judge begging them for mercy. He explained her bi polar condition, threw in some sentimental sentences about how much she missed and was loved by her kids, and blamed her actions on her addiction. He then said that nothing like this would ever happen again. A promise he had no way of keeping.

It probably wasn't his letters that helped her.

It's true too, that Kelly had a warm and winning personality and it would not be surprising to find that the guards (C.O's) along with the other girl inmates loved her. Perhaps one of them put in a good word for her to the judge. I doubt that was what did it either.

Maybe the fact that her mother had recently passed away moved them and played on their heartstrings. Or maybe it was the spirit of the Christmas season that caused them to grant her clemency and essentially gave her, her life back.

It is also possible that God heard and answered Scott's prayers for her. He had actually dropped down to his knees, bowed his head, and pressed his hands together. Humbly, and with tears in his eyes, he said a prayer for Kelly. Kelly would later tell him that she believed the reason for their leniency was because her mother was looking out for her from heaven.

Whatever it was that did the trick, the judge dropped her charges down from Armed Robbery to unlawful theft. She eagerly accepted this and was free to leave that night with time served.

"That's so great, baby. When are you getting out?"

"I guess you can come and pick me up tonight."

Scott could not wait to make love to her. He called his parents because at the time he was staying with them on their couch. He asked them if Kel could come and stay with them for a couple of days. Fortunately, they loved Kelly; she was the mother of their beloved grandchildren. She was their family. They were always optimistic and forgiving. They put their skepticism aside and decided to give her another chance. So they had a place to stay. They could be together.

It was nighttime, dark outside already, even though it was only a little after five o'clock, when Scott pulled up to those oppressive gates for the last time. The guard booth by these oppressive gates always reminded Scott of the story of St. Peter with his checklist, waiting to see who made the cut and was cool enough to be on heavens guest list, Scott didn't know if there was a guy who has a similar job at Hell's gates, or if anyone can just walk right in. He had heard of people getting cast into the pit or abyss, like they were dropped there from above, but he also heard there were gates to hell too. So which is it? I guess it doesn't matter. He didn't know.

It was cold with winter on that December 23rd, 2008 and a frigid wind blew outside his car as Scott sat outside the guard booth for his final

C.S.W.

mandatory half hour/ forty-five minute wait. When the gate rolled back and Kelly arrived, she was ear to ear with her smile. She held everything she owned in two big garbage bags and for the first time in over a year, she wasn't wearing orange. Scott hugged and kissed the girl formerly known as prisoner #529171 in front of his car's engine, which was running to keep the heat blasting in the compartment. They threw her bags in the backseat, jumped in, and drove down the hill to route 29, leaving that God forsaken place behind.

It was at this time that Kelly's nasty idjit stretched and opened its eyes. She already wanted to get high.

Now, this all happened around the time that Scott was seeing his psychiatrist. The shrink had told him that he was mentally healthy except, of course, for his heroin addiction. For which, he prescribed him Suboxone.

Suboxone was like a wonder drug for junkies. The main ingredient in it is a drug called bupremorphine, which is an opiate agonist. It mimics the chemicals naturally found in the brain and like heroin, binds to the opioid receptors and takes away sickness and cravings. The stuff really works too. For the first couple of weeks, Scott took it as directed and didn't feel the need to do any dope. Even if you did shoot some junk while taking it, you would not feel it. The bupremorphine blocked those receptors so the opiates could not tickle them. So, if you wanted to get high, you needed to stop taking the Suboxone for a day or two before you resumed.

Unfortunately, other addicts on the street were also hearing about this marvelous invention and junkies were always looking for an easy way to stop getting high. None of them looks forward to the nightmare of kicking cold turkey and the unrelenting, maddening sickness. Rehabs have even begun administering Suboxone to patients who come in for detox. It seems to be replacing methadone.

Scott soon found out, the prospect of taking a few pills to quit their dope habits appealed very much to the junkies. The medicine his doctor was giving him was a hot commodity. He found that he could easily trade his bright orange tablets for the little wax paper baggies with stamps on them. The stamps read things like "Knock out", "Bulls eye", "Pink Pussy", or "Body Bag." Scott also discovered that he preferred the rush of shooting the scag to the level, legal, normalcy of the Suboxone.

Suboxone also has another ingredient; Naloxone, which is an opiate antagonist. This is added to prevent desperate addicts from attempting to shoot the stuff. When taken as recommended, subcutaneously, dissolved under the tongue, very little of the Naloxone makes it into the bloodstream.

However, if you inject it directly into your veins it will send you into a living hell. The worst nightmare; sudden acute withdrawal. No, it is unwise to try and boot Suboxone. Believe me, some fools have tried it.

Anyway, since he was back on the smack, as Scott drove Kelly home, he happened to have a Suboxone left in his pocket. Kel had been hearing about this miracle cure from Scott over the phone for over a year and even though at the time she didn't have an active heroin habit, she really wanted to try it.

So Scott gave it to her and she ate it as they pulled into Ewing. They made a left off route 29 and turned up West Upper Ferry Rd. Again, the chemicals in the new drug upset the delicate balance of her bi polar disorder and agitated the shit out of her idjit. Once the monster got a little taste, it was ravenously hungry. Kelly would be back on heroin by Christmas. If you thought a year in jail might have taught her a lesson about the dangers and consequences of drugs, then you'd be wrong.

Now, I may or may not have told you about Scott's plan. He figured his Bella was going to be locked up for another five years. In that time, he was going to get himself clean. He figured this would happen somewhere around her third year in. then he was going to look for a nice place for them both to live. Maybe if he was lucky, by then his brother Chuck would let them see their kids. Kelly's early release, while certainly joyful, shattered that utopia like a sledgehammer through a window. The only thing he had to offer her at this point was a resumption of her heroin habit.

On top of everything else, as God would have it, because of her mother passing away, Kelly was about to inherit some money. After everything was calculated, with the life insurance policies, bonds, sale of the house, and savings, ect., Kelly and her brother Tony would receive $140,000. They would split that in half.

Scott and Kelly had planned on using that money wisely. Sure, they were going to buy a nice car because they needed one. And yes, let's be honest, there was some talk of having a little party in the beginning. Maybe they would partake in a night or two of debauchery in a sleazy motel room.

What really concerned them both though was Tony. When he found out that he was set to inherit that money, he started getting a lot of drugs fronted to him. Since the dealers knew that the cash was coming, they were willing to take the risk and advance him. Because they had to wait to get paid, they inflated the prices and exaggerated how much he owed them astronomically.

Tony in need (he was already in the middle of a somewhat suicidal drug binge), emphatically agreed. He must have owed over six thousand

C.S.W.

dollars before he ever saw a penny of his money. Scott said to Kelly "Babe, I'm really worried about your brother. We have to try and help him. He can't be trusted to have $70,000." Not like him and Kelly, who were the models of maturity and good, sound, financial planning.

Scott's friend Kenny, the one I told you about earlier, the one who would eventually become a lawyer for the Trenton prosecutor's office, once told him, while they were speaking about their mutual friend Chris (the Chris that left Scott on Hoffman Avenue to have his ass kicked.) "I ran into him the other day, man, and he looks bad. His brain is shot out. You tell him a joke and it takes him like ten seconds to get it and start laughing. I'm really surprised he's still alive. Then it occurred to me that he doesn't have enough money to buy enough drugs to kill him. The only thing keeping him alive is his poverty."

The only thing keeping him alive is his poverty. In Trenton there's a lot of that going around. Unfortunately for Chris, his poverty would run out one day. He must have come into some money because he scored enough of the poison to overdose on it at his parent's house.

So, anyway, Kelly got her money. The first check she got came in the first week of January; it was for around $30,000. They added this to the six dollars and seventy five cents that they already had saved. Now you're not supposed to use the term "niger rich" but Scott and Kelly were definitely the very definition of that ugly and offensive term.

The first thing they did to celebrate was to buy a lot of drugs. They went into a car dealership on Spruce lane in Ewing and took a green BMW for a test drive. They took it straight to Tyler Street to cop and to show off. After they had fixed and smoked some crack, they took the car back, and paid for it in cash. It was a used, green, 328i, they paid seven thousand dollars for it.

Now, in addition to Kelly having given him two of the most beautiful children the world has ever seen, plus a really awesome little dude named Dylan as a stepson, she also bought him a car. Scott always wanted a BMW. So she was pretty cool.

Next, they decided it would be fun to spend the night in a motel. Someplace nice, with a Jacuzzi, hot tub. A place where they could have a little privacy to fuck, I mean make love, and where they could do some really serious drugs. Unfortunately, Scott got way too high and ended up passing out in the hot tub so they never did have sex. While he was out, Kelly drained the water so he wouldn't slide down into the water and drown. When he awoke, he was naked and freezing. The original plan was to spend a night or two at the motel partying, but that turned into about four weeks.

The second night, after they bought the Beemer, they took it to the projects to cop more drugs. It was about 2:30 in the morning when this happened. They picked up the dealer, who was black, and bought close to six hundred dollars in product. Half heroin, half cocaine. As they came to the intersection to make a right, Five-OH. made a left in their direction. The cops eyed them suspiciously as there could only be one reason for two white people to be driving around with a brother in the hood at this time of night.

The three of them waited nervously for the red and blue lights.

The dealer jumped out of the car and disappeared as soon as the pigs were out of sight. Scott's heartbeat thumped loudly in his throat as he and Kelly waited at the next stoplight. They hid the stuff as best as they could and Scott yelled at Kel for bringing him down here and how he was sure that they were about to be arrested. He looked in his rearview mirror for Five-OH and an eternity passed before the light turned green. They gunned it across the highway and made good on their escape into Ewing. The police must have gotten caught up on one of the one way streets. That's how Scott almost lost his car after only having had it for two days. There would have been no explaining that. As it was, the BMW was short lived anyway. But we'll get to that later.

Rapper 50 Cent says in his song "Back Down" that "You can buy cars, but you can't buy respect in the hood." This proved to be very true. Even though Kelly was spending $1,200 every single day on narcotics, still the dealers wouldn't always answer their calls, made them wait for hours for delivery, and were generally rude and discourteous to them. In short, the service sucked.

I can't say for certain if the money to time spent ratio was the greatest drug binge in the history of Trenton, but I can tell you without a doubt that at that time no one in the East ward was spending as much cash as fast as they were. The stupidity was spectacular.

Every couple of days, Scott would get worried and say "Babe, we really need to put the brakes on the spending. At this rate, we'll be broke in a couple of months and we won't have anything to show for it."

And his Bella would say "Yeah, honey, you're right. We will." And they would make plans and promises to stop getting high when the money got down to $20,000. Then it was 15.Then it was 10. When they had spent everything except for a measly five thousand dollars, they admitted defeat and said "fuck it; we wasted mostly all of it, we might as well keep going with the rest."

Rehab was looming.

There was another issue too.

Do you know what pediculosis capitis are? How about sarcoptes scabiei? They are head lice and scabies mites, respectively. It seems that Kelly brought a case of the nasty little nits home with her from jail. No matter how much shampoo or lice treatment she tried, she could not seem to kill the tenacious bastards. She scratched her scalp like a crazy person. She bought special combs and lotions. She even got this machine that would electrically zap individual louse. She could not seem, no matter what she tried, to get rid of the bugs that were feeding on her scalp. She cried hysterically as she showed Scott the scabs under her hair. They say that Lice are not contracted through poor personal hygiene and that anyone can catch them, but that doesn't make the person suffering from them feel any less icky and gross. It is a creepy feeling having parasites feeding on you. Scott felt bad for her, but he would soon have problems of his own when he caught the scabies. Presumably, he got them from the dirty sheets and blankets at the Mount Motel. Housekeeping was not doing a bang up job at this establishment. He invested in a pair of tweezers and attempted to catch these insects and pull them off of him. On his left inner forearm, Scott had gotten his daughter Ariel's name tattooed. One of the gluttonous bugs chewed away some of the ink and left a scar when he tweezed it away. So our young lovers and heroin addicts were driving around in a beautiful green Beemer scratching and picking at themselves. It was not a condition you would expect from BMW owners.

Nothing they bought at the pharmacy worked and one day the heebie jeebies reached their pinnacle, when two of the critters had the audacity to begin crawling up his neck and towards his face.

They moved under the surface of his skin and they looked like two drops of perspiration, except that instead of beading down like sweat, they moved up alongside Scott's Adam's apple. He was freaking out as they made the vertical trek towards his chin. He watched them in the mirror horrified and he grabbed one of them with his only weapon; the tweezers. He caught one of the little suckers and it pulled out in a thin wormlike string. It was the color of acne puss. It twisted in agony in the open air and, sweet Jesus; there was no doubt that the thing was alive.

He imagined that he heard it screaming. It was like he was having a nightmare, but nope, he was awake and not dreaming. Again, he drove a BMW for Christ's sake.

Dope or no dope, medical attention could no longer be avoided. As he looked closer in the mirror, he noticed that several of the disgusting creatures had made it up to and burrowed in his left ear. Oh God No. If he started hearing them move around in there, he would surely go insane.

Scott fixed outside in the parking lot of the hospital. He didn't want to start getting sick while he was in the waiting room. His condition was totally embarrassing, but it didn't really warrant an emergency. Plus, he had no insurance and so he knew that he was going to have to wait. He walked up to the counter and filled out the form that asked him his name, the time and the date. There was a blank line where you were supposed to write down your medical complaint.

Scott simply wrote "bugs."

When the doctor finally came to assess him, he already knew about Scott's history of substance abuse. He said, "Mr. Westcott, it says here that you've got bugs."

To which Scott replied "Yup."

The doctor suspected that maybe Scott was hallucinating from having taking too many drugs. And he asked him as much. "Sir, are you on any drugs now?"

Again, Scott just replied "Yup."

"When was the last time you used?" The doctor did not add "because I am very important and you are wasting my time."

But Scott could read his mind. He said "I shot up in your parking lot right before I came inside." His blatant admission shocked the doctor, but Scott shrugged because he really couldn't give a fuck about this guys opinion of him. "But that doesn't change the fact that I've got bugs crawling on me. Look at my freakin' ear; I look like a fucking Ferengi from Star Trek."

The doctor was in a hurry, I think, and not greatly concerned or interested in this particular patient. He said that Scott had Scabies, but this might have been a misdiagnosis, as the creatures he had crawling on him were wormlike, almost like really thin maggots, and not like the mites that he would later see pictures of on the internet. As gross as either of these prospects were; either maggots or mites, this news came as somewhat of a relief to him, because he had half convinced himself that he was infected with some sort of extraterrestrial infestation.

The doctor prescribed him a lotion called Permethrin, pronounced (Pur MEE Thrin) which he coated his entire body with. Then he got high again and fell asleep. When he woke up the next day, all the bugs were dead. Eradicated, like army napalm on a small defenseless North Vietnamese village. The Permethrin killed them all.

So that was one less thing to worry about.

But there were other issues remaining.

Back at the Mount Motel on route 1 in Lawrence Township, the drug consumption had really begun taking its toll on Scott's body and mind. Mostly, he was living on nicotine, heroin, and cocaine, but since they had plenty of cash he was also eating whatever he felt like as well. It occurred to him after about a week that he had not taken a shit in about that long. Finally, one morning/ afternoon, he got up and found that it was time. He was ready to move his bowels. He positioned himself on the toilet, figuring he was in for a truly monumental event. That's when the labor pains hit him. Beads of sweat popped from his pours and ran down his face like he was in a sauna. He began having phantom chest pains and he started breathing like he had seen women do when they gave birth. Lamas, I think it's called. He grabbed onto the sink with one hand and a towel rack with the other. It was a small wonder that he did not rip it off the wall.

But the turd, which was roughly the consistency of a brick, was stuck. It would not come out. It refused to be laid. Scott had a problem. He was convinced that he was about to have a heart attack. He did not want to die like this, on the commode; he would be horribly embarrassed for his girlfriend to find him this way. He needed to find a way to relax.

Reluctantly and defeated, he got up off the bowl. He pulled his pants back up and went back into the bedroom. Kelly was still sleeping. Scott went into his nightstand and grabbed his cigarettes and the two bags of heroin that he was saving for his wake up shot. He took these items with him back into the bathroom. He was shaking like a man about to be strapped into the electric chair. He really had to focus so as to not spill the dope and ruin the shot. With surprising difficulty he finally got it. It was warm and soothing in his arm.

Scott dropped his jeans and boxers again and reassumed the position, ready to get back to business. Now he was in a better frame of mind. He concentrated on his breathing exercises and he pushed. At first, there was nothing, but then, slowly and not without pain, the clog finally gave way.

He had himself a complete and glorious evacuation.

And he survived.

He smoked a cigarette to celebrate. Then he tried to flush the monster down. But of course, in all the confusion, he had forgotten to courtesy flush half way through the procedure, and so the poo which had been lodged up inside him was now caught in the toilet trap. It stubbornly refused to go down. The last thing he needed was for the bowl to fill up and overflow. He could not allow it to escape.

As he waited for the water to recede in the toilet, he looked around for a plunger, but of course, there was none. He went into the other room where Kelly was now waking up. "Good morning honey, the shitters broke." He said romantically. "And there's no plunger. If you value your life, don't go in there."

But his princess knew exactly what to do. Perhaps, she had been in a similar revolting situation before. She says "take a plastic bag and reach in there and squeeze it."

Scott would have never thought of doing that, but since the Mount Motel provided them with no plunger, he was really out of options. The last thing he wanted was to go to the front desk and confess to them what had happened and to ask them for some assistance. Least of all, he didn't want anyone to see what he had created. So he reached in there with a plastic bag they had gotten at CVS and he squose the thing. It was like pottery clay. The color was the color of all the colors of play dough mixed together, with a reddish brown hue. When he squished it, two things happened. First, the clog was broken and he was able to flush it. Second, a new smell was released into the air. It was like infection, gang green, and decaying flesh. The scent of death in the summertime. Fortunately, there was a can of lilac spring air freshener. He fumigated the room for a good three minutes.

And another crisis was averted.

Anyway, I started telling you how the drugs were having some very negative effects on Scott's body. To sum it up without going into any more horrid and gory details, let's just look at the time he blacked out.

Do you know what nihilism is?

If you look the term up, you'll probably discover a whole bunch of philosopher's theories on what it means. Their ideas on how life is meaningless and how this somehow justifies hedonism and destruction, hence the tern annihilate. You're also bound to find out about Fredrich Nietzche and his wonderful views on the subject. The so called prophet of nihilism was an extreme pessimist who suffered from radical skepticism. His world became bleak and empty. He lost control of his mental faculties and went completely insane before he died in 1900.

Scott, for his part, was slowly coming to terms with the notion that there may not be anything waiting for him after he dies. No heaven or afterlife, just oblivion. This idea used to scare and depress him, but as he grew older he came to believe that maybe it's just as well. Whatever is waiting for us, as far as he was concerned, didn't have a whole lot to do with the here and now.

Anyway, nihilism comes from the Latin and it means nothing, nonexistence.

The reason I mention this is because this is the state into which I believe Scott slipped when he went into his blackout. For him, life had always been one constant stream of awareness. Even when he was sleeping, he always knew who he was, where he was, and what he was. His spirit, or soul if you will, was always with him.

This consistency of being was broken because of the narcotics one night at the Mount Motel. (Route 1, Lawrenceville, N.J.) Scott could not tell you how long he was out for. It might have been ten minutes; it might have been three hours. In that time, he may have been laughing and telling stories or committing a savage murder. There was no way to tell. He simply couldn't remember. He wasn't in there.

When he finally did start to come back, he was standing in a completely dark room. He was on his feet swaying with dizziness and the room was spinning. He was trying to not lose his balance.

Kelly was asleep in the bed.

Then Scott's equilibrium tilted and he no longer cared about life or death or balance. He collapsed face forward into the dresser. His right shoulder smashed into the television set and sent it sliding across the bureau. The TV didn't fall to the floor like Scott did, but it knocked over all of Kelly's girl products. Makeup, perfume, candles, and lice killing shampoo all mixed together, scattered in a pile on the floor. The crashing noise was deafening in the quiet of the night.

It did not disturb Kelly in her opiate dreams.

Something wet landed on Scott's chest and so when he reached for his aching clavicle he thought he was bleeding. He was scared shitless and he could not remember where he was. As everything came flooding back into his polluted brain, he crawled on all fours to the bed where his girl was sleeping. He was crying and what he really wanted was his mommy, but Kelly was the only one there and so she would have to do. He climbed in bed and shook her awake. Like a pathetic five year old he wailed "Baby? Baby, I hurt myself."

And his girl, his angel had enough maternal in her to put her arms around him and hold him. She said soothingly, "It's ok honey, you're alright. It's gonna be ok." As if he was a little kid who had just had a nightmare. He was thirty seven at the time.

The impact from Scott passing out totally destroyed the television. It never worked again.

Shortly after that, the money had dwindled to the point where the lovebirds were forced to move out of the motel. They went to stay at 277

Tyler Street. They were going there several times a day to buy their drugs anyway, so this would make things easier. They rented a room on the third floor across the hall from his friend CJ and his sister KoryAnn. Those two were an item by now and they were as hooked on the shit as were Scott and Kelly.

The situation was deteriorating rapidly.

Now, every house has its own story and history. I think everyone could tell the tale of what goes on behind closed doors of their domicile and that story would be interesting. And every house has its secrets and its mysteries. Ever since Scott was a child, when he would go on drives passed places that were unfamiliar to him, he would wonder about the people that lived in all these strange buildings. Ghetto abandos and luxurious mansions. The poor people and the wealthy. Sometimes, on these drives, he would start to daydream and make believe what went on in these dwellings. How the people would act and dress and what were their problems or how were they so successful.

He was always awed by the vastness of civilization. How many people lived in all these suburbs and all these different cities? He found it all so overwhelming. And he knew that he hadn't even seen a fraction of the world. All these people eating. Where did all the food come from? How could the world possibly sustain them all? Surely, the supply would eventually run out. And then there was the matter of all the refuse, the garbage that a million people produced daily from the food they consumed and the products that they used. Where could it all possibly go? He knew about the landfills and the dumps, but still. everyday more debris. The shit had to be piling up. Surely, there must be mountains of the stuff.

And Scott couldn't help but believe in God when he thought about the never ending supply and demand, on a grand scale and the perfect symbiotic nature of man and the land. Like, he pondered, how we breathe the air that comes off the plants and trees and they in turn take in the carbon dioxide we exhale. Only a God, he reasoned could sustain a planet so vast. Only a God could create all these beautiful people and give them what they need to continue living and having all these tragic and wonderful stories. All of them educational and all of them entertaining.

The one that we are focusing on now, happens to be in a dirty little house in Trenton New Jersey. 277 Tyler across the street from the deli. Ours is the story of Scott and Kelly.

The house they moved into was the cop spot. It was rented out to a couple of junkies named Caroline and Eddie. They were both true to the game. In the years that Scott had known them, they had never went to any rehabs or tried in any way to achieve sobriety. Their mission was simple; to stay high every day. If Scott went away for a year, there was no doubt in his mind that he could come back to Trenton and find Caroline and Eddie and they would know where to find good dope.

When Kelly got her money, she was very generous with all the junkies; Caroline and Eddie, KoryAnn and CJ, and especially with her boyfriend, Scott. In addition to the three couples who lived on Tyler, there was also a constant stream of hookers and dealers and druggies.

If you needed dope or coke, you could always find it here. Also, the girls could get you Xanex, Percocet, Valium, Klynopin, or Oxy's on most occasions. It was like a fucking pharmacy on Tyler Street, if you had money. Which of course, Scott and Kelly still did, even though the shit was evaporating rapidly. When they moved in, their resources had dwindled down to around eight grand. Two months ago, they had seventy.

It was quite a long party.

The thing about having money like that, Scott and Kelly soon found out, was that with it comes a lot of friends that you never knew you had. Best friends even, some of whom you may have never even met before.

Teddy was a black crack dealer who they met during this period of partying. He was with them every day after he found out about the cash. Teddy laughed at all their jokes, like they were two of the funniest mother fuckers who ever lived. He acted like he was Scott's brother, if Scott's Mom had had a child with a black man. Teddy was a great guy and you could just tell it was about more than the money. He would be with them through thick and thin. He was the kind of guy who you felt lucky to have as your boy, he was so loyal. When the money was nearly depleted he borrowed eighty dollars off of Kelly and they never saw him again.

Likewise, there was a hooker who called herself BJ. No joke, that's what she called herself, BJ the hooker. BJ met Kelly a couple of times on the streets years ago. The first time Scott met her, he and Kelly had been together for about 6 years. He found it a little odd that this girl, who claimed to be one of Kelly's closest friends, didn't start coming around until Kel got her inheritance.

"Baby" Scott would later say "It's so obvious what this girl is trying to do. She's trying to get in between me and you because she knows that you have money." BJ was so greedy that she couldn't even be bothered with playing the game properly. She made up some stupid lies about Scott making her feel uncomfortable and she started Scott and Kelly fighting.

Scott got rid of the stinking, nasty, conniving, bitch, but the turbulence she started lingered on after she was gone.

With so many people using her for her money, Kelly started to be suspicious of everyone. She even turned a mistrustful eye on her boyfriend. Was he milking her too? Would he be gone like all the rest of them after the money was spent?

The drugs had the both of them completely paranoid and it had been a while since either of their brains had been thinking clearly. And, for all their romantic talk and phone sex while Kelly was in jail, since she had gotten out, they had made love exactly twice. They slept together but the cocaine and heroin was what they truly lived for. It had become their God. They were partners in crime and drug buddies and they claimed love for each other, but at the time, they were not lovers. Maybe by now, neither of them was really capable of love; not in its truest sense. They were killing each other and watching one another die.

Such was the nature and make up of all the relationships that spring in Trenton, on Tyler. Scott and Kelly and dope. Caroline and Eddie and dope. CJ and KoryAnn and dope. Any true concern that they may have had for one another got twisted and withered as their addiction got fed. And fed and fed and fed.

And finally the inevitable nightmare had arrived and all the money was spent.

The withdrawal and sickness that came on them was like nothing any of them could have foreseen. And they all turned on each other. Everyone once again was looking out for themselves. It didn't matter who owed who what or how much Kelly had spent yesterday.

The nasty idjit is really only interested in today.

Debts would have to wait.

Everything of any value now needed to be pawned, for needle in arm.

It was tragic; blackness.

So, in Trenton you can rent your car out to drug dealers, if you want to. The going rate is about a bag an hour. Scott and Kelly would let their current dealer, S. take the BMW for four hour shifts for enough diesel to get them off E. For the last week, they may have had the car in their possession for a total of six hours. Having gotten used to not having any transportation and since they had this gigantic monkey on their backs, they took the next logical step in the ugly downward spiral that is addiction. They decided to sell the Beemer outright to S. for heroin. All they had to do was to sign the title over to him. In exchange, he would give them five bricks of dope. In case you're not familiar with what a brick is, it breaks down like this. There are ten bags in a bundle and five bundles in a brick. So, Scott and Kelly traded a $7,000 automobile for two hundred and fifty bags of mid grade Trenton Skag. That golden girl. That hero of the underworld. The street value of the stuff was around a thousand dollars. Scott didn't care, his sole mission and purpose was to stave off the sickness by any means necessary. He agreed to the ludicrous deal enthusiastically. It wasn't his finest hour.

The disease, which had already cost him his children, was bent on taking everything from him. It wanted him to be left with nothing. Actually, after he lost his kids, who he loved more than anyone, throwing away a car to his addiction was relatively easy. The party continued for three days after the car was gone and the channel swimmers (ones who use heroin) shared the proceeds with all their housemates. For that time everybody in the house was high, though curiously, never really happy. The laughter was forced and hallow. The thing about the poppy is that is all illusion; illusion and confusion. What little gratitude there was for Kelly's magnanimous generosity with the stuff was contrived, made up and fading. There was no real appreciation. You cannot buy the genuine affection of a junkie. And then, after it was all gone, one word reverberated through their brains, permeating all their disbelief and shock. Like the fried and frazzled survivors of a bloody and explosive war, with post traumatic stress syndrome, one word echoed in their minds like an open bass note in four-four time. Five little letters put together offered no explanation of what had happened or where it all went. The word, of course, was spent. The word was as heartless and final as death. There was nothing left. The moment had arrived, the dreaded event. Now was the time for remorse and to cry. And all around people who were once jealous of their wealth would point at them and snicker. They laughed at them behind their backs. They gossiped clichés like how a fool and his money are soon parted. And Jesus Christ, weren't they retarded. Memories of being able to have whatever they wanted taunted them, and haunted them, and scarred them as they sat in their room on the third floor at Tyler with their stomachs empty. They had no money for food. Perhaps, they even deserved to starve to death for being so wasteful, frivolous, and stupid. Truth be told, anyway, if they had twenty bucks left for some groceries, no doubt they would spend that money on drugs. That's just how it was. Now that sickness was coming. In spite of the fact that Scott and Kelly's relationship was a total train wreck, still Scott could not get enough of her. He always wanted to be with her. Because of the mess they had made of things, financially and narcoticly, them staying together was no longer possible. There was a pattern to their lives. They would burn brightly for a while and then, eventually, they would have to part and go their separate ways. This always brought Scott great sadness. Unfortunately, he had reached this point again. He would have to leave her to seek some sort of recovery and just like always, he would think about her obsessively. He would miss her terribly. He would worry about her constantly. Even though in actuality their relationship was a disaster, what he really wanted was to help her, to love her, and to protect her. He wanted to be her shelter. For some reason Scott's mind was prone to making a lot of inaccurate and irrelevant comparisons. He was doing that right now as he likened the thing he had with Kelly to an Atlantic City Slot Machine. There were nice hits that lifted them up and got them high for a time, but it was always temporal and fading. The machines mission was simple, just like the idjits, delude the poor fools and take everything from them. Again, came another comparison; this time of dirty toilet water spiraling downward as it circled the bowl. This might have symbolized Kelly's inheritance, their love affair, or just life in general. Everything was sinking. Addicts talk about hitting rock bottom and Scott had crashed into this depth of despair more times than he cared to count or think about. Every time he relapsed it seemed his bottom was lower and the impact more painful. When it seemed to him that he could not possibly feel any worse, KoryAnn and CJ pulled him aside to tell him that they had heard that Kelly was trickin' again for drugs. She did it, they said, in the back room on Tyler, while he was upstairs sleeping. The fact that Scott understood why she did it and the fact that this wasn't the first time he ever had to deal with this, didn't change the fact that he felt like someone had just punched him in the stomach. This would not change how he felt about her however, he would always love her. He was depressed, saddened passed the point of being capable of anger. As he realized that the time had once again come for he and his angel to say goodbye, a couple of tears picked that moment to run from his eyes. This was purely coincidence though, he wasn't really crying. Withdrawal from love and drugs can be an emotional roller coaster ride. So Scott left his children's mother there on Tyler Street in Trenton, broke and alone, to fend for herself. He couldn't stop thinking about how she would probably end up trickin' again to get her fixes. He came back to his parent's house in Ewing. His Mom and Dad were always there to help him. They were a safety net of love and encouragement. A support system that Kelly no longer had. He could not remember ever feeling so guilty, so ashamed, so dope sick, or so just plain bad. And now he cried for real, the seemingly endless rapidly flowing tears that came with busting a really serious jag. He hyperventilated in his misery as he confessed his sins to his mother, Nancy. Again, like he was still a toddler he cried to his mommy. It must have been heartbreaking for her to watch. What a pathetic and sickening sight. And nothing could comfort him and make things right.

Had you seen this scene, you might have even been moved to have compassion and mercy on Scott. You might have offered to buy him a couple of bags. He wailed, "I can't believe what I did, Mom. I feel like I wanna die. I say I love her but . . . but . . . but . . ." And he had to stop talking for a minute to recompose himself. "I just went along with it. I helped her spent all that money and now she's broke and I just left her. I didn't want it to be like this. Jesus, how could I have let this happen?!"

His mother's voice was soft and reassuring, there was no condemnation. "You are both sick. You're both addicts, Chip. You can't help each other. Kelly would have spent that money anyway; it just would have taken her a little longer without you. Remember how long you took care of her when she was in jail or not working?"

"But I love her so much. I want to help her. How can I live with myself after taking so much from her and then just leaving her out there to die? My God, Mom, what if she dies?!" More shameless tears spilt down and again he had to fight for his composure. "How could I ever face Ariel and Ethan if something happens to her? I have to save her."

"You can't save her, honey. She has to want to save herself. You have to pull yourself together. That's the only way you'll ever be able to help her. Look at you! You have to help yourself, so that when you see those kids again, you'll be able to look them in the eyes. Someday, they are gonna need you and they're gonna come looking for their daddy. You have to move on with your life and make yourself strong, so they can be proud of you. And Kelly needs to do the same thing for herself."

And Scott's Mom was right. A couple of days later he went back into rehab. I wish I could tell you that this twelfth or thirteenth rehab was the charm for Scott and that he would stay clean for the rest of his life, but that would be a lie. People were beginning to think that he and Kelly were a lost cause and that they would continue getting high until they died. In other words, they would never learn. One thing that Scott did discover was that the junkie's theory that you can kick dope in three to five days was bullshit; a total fallacy. For Scott, the detox lasted a hell of a lot longer than that. The two and a half bundles he had been doing everyday for the last couple of weeks had a terrible hold on his body. The councilors and doctors put him back on the Suboxone for five days and he felt alright for that time, but when they took him back off the stuff, he began getting sick again.

He could remember feeling miserable and achy, cold and sweaty and shaky, well into his tenth day. And come day eleven, he was still crispy in his thinking. A veritable mental vegetable. His thoughts were incoherent for the most part and he dreamed about needles and he spent most of his waking hours worried about Kel. But as it turned out, there was no need. Because there is a God in heaven and he looked down on the junkies and had mercy. He led Scott's babies' momma into her own facility. God called Kelly into recovery. Her journey into sobriety was a long and painful one and Scott was proud of her because she stuck it out. As you read this, Kelly has been clean for almost a year. She has a job, a sponsor, her own place, and a new life away from Trenton. She is a totally different person from the one I told you about throughout this story. But like I said, it hasn't been easy. Kelly has had to deal with adversity and tragedy. When she first came into detox, they put her on methadone to help her kick the heroin. She was high on that stuff for a while. They also gave her electric shock therapy to help her bi-polar disorder and constant cravings for drugs. (This actually made Scott nervous when he heard about it. He was afraid what else they might be frying in her brain.) Whatever. They knew what they were doing. And Kelly came through it all transformed. Dare I say reborn? Scott, of course, got out of his treatment center after 19 days and relapsed within 72 hours. He could not blame his girl for his disease. She was doing the right thing, one day at a time, and he made a choice to go back to shooting that poison alone. Without her. Why? Kelly would later say to him that it was because "their thinkers are broke." I suppose that explanation works. Anyway, Kelly was in her recovery house living life on life's terms and Scott was in the world getting mangled when she called him one day. She called to tell him that her brother, his friend, had died from a heroin overdose. Scott shot eight bags of dope himself the day Tony died.

He was too numb to feel anything as he listened into the phone and heard the woman he loved crying. He registered his pain in a sedated sort of way and he knew that he would eventually mourn Tony's passing. He would, like Kelly, miss him forever. There would be emptiness because he had been more than just a friend, Anthony Cambell was his family. So yeah, Scott knew that there was pain coming, but that was for later.

He tried to console Kelly as best he could, though he, in this condition, probably did a rotten job of it. She told him through tears that Tony had overdosed, presumably from fentanyl and heroin. Rumor had it that they found a Durigesic patch in his mouth. Scott and Kelly, who knew what it was like to live at the mercy of this disease, could agree that at least Tony was finally at peace. She said that someone had found him in some dingy crackhouse basement. I will not give the address of that unholy place. It doesn't really matter anyway, suffice to say, that in Trenton, all roads lead to Tyler Street. Anthony Cambell died on September 22, 2009. He was 34 years old. May he rest in peace forever. Idjit mother fucking ijati.

"Just when I thought maybe everything would be ok, the one fear always seems to appear. And I never thought this day would come so soon. My brother, my friend, is gone, never to return again. The only thing left is memories. Sometimes, I wish that there was something I could have done, but the disease of addiction, I also suffer from. I prayed that you would get a taste of recovery, and then you could have seen that life doesn't have to be so lonely. If you only learned to love yourself. I can certainly relate, and most definitely dictate, but it's too late, you're already gone and I can't bring you back, so it's time for me to pick up the slack. Live a life, joyous and free. And be all that I can be. I will miss you so dearly. And hold your smile so near to me. 'Til the day that we see each other again, in my heart is where I keep you, my brother, my friend . . ."

—Kelly Cambell

Chapter 12

Confusing Conclusions

SCOTT SAT AT the pinnacle of clarity after having been off drugs for a whooping 19 days. This may not be a lot of clean time, by say, Narcotics Anonymous standards but still he felt just about as alert and focused as he ever got. 19 Days for him was somewhat of an achievement, even if it was forced upon him, as he had spent those days in a rehabilitation facility.

His seat was located in the exact center of the universe. The room was set up like a classroom and he was stationed behind a desk, where the teacher would sit, with all the students facing him.

Scott scanned a sea of eyes and he noticed for the first time that everyone was staring at him. They were all listening and interested and bordering on captivated. Well, that's not quite right. Not everyone. There were a few dazed over or closed eyes in the back of the room that were not paying any attention to him. These belonged to the people lounged out in the back on the comfy couches. They were the chicks and dudes who were still in detox and they were forced to come to these life stories meetings. They were required to attend the meetings but they were not really there. Only detox patients were permitted to sit on the couches, everyone else, who had been there for more than five days was required to sit in uncomfortable plastic chairs for all the meetings. Christ, there were a lot of meetings.

Scott held no resentment or animosity towards the zombies in the back of the room sleeping or still dazed over with the drugs and oblivious to his story or message. He was one of them. He remembered lying on those couches a mere two weeks ago. Before he came through the fog, or the smoke cleared, or the haze lifted, or however you prefer to metaphor Scott coming out of the funk that the drugs had left on his brain. The drugs that had twisted his focus and shittied his thinking. Yeah, it had only been 19 days since last he'd injected that Trenton poison into his arm, but now here he was at the pinnacle of clarity.

Scott had just finished speaking for almost forty five minutes straight. The story he told them, this room full of drug addicts was pretty much the same story I just told you.

It amazed Scott how different his experiences had been from the other dudes (and chicks) who had shared about theirs. By comparison, Scott was probably better off than most of them. Some of them had done long stints in prison and some of them were headed there. Some had been dealers who moved more product in a week than Scott had done in his whole life. Some of them had been shot, brought back from the dead, and some had even killed people. Others came from privilege and had more money than Scott would ever likely see. They were black and they were white. The thing that Scott found fascinating was that despite all this diversity, the all had the same affliction, the dreaded disease of addiction. In this respect, they were all the same.

As he scanned the sea of eyes after telling his life story, Scott was surprised to see that he had mostly everyone's attention and no one seemed to be judging him. In fact, after he had finished speaking, they actually clapped. No standing ovation or anything, but a pleasant enough response. Equally intriguing was the fact that two guys actually had their hands raised in the air. They wanted to ask him some questions. He saw a black guy in the front row first. Scott called on him. "Yeah, Ralph?"

He stuttered a little bit. "Y-Y-You said, Y-Y-You got jumped on H-H-Hoffman Avenue in M-M-Miller H-H-Homes?"

"Yeah, that's right. I guess they don't like white people down there." A few nervous chuckles from the audience.

"They, they, they don't like black pe—pe-people much either. I was h-h-held h-h-ostage there for three, three, three days." Laughter now, from the crowed.

Anyway, I guess that now would be a good time to clear up a little misconception. If you are familiar with Trenton streets, than you know that Miller Homes are not located on Hoffman and Oakland. Scott had been misinformed about the name of the projects he had gotten jumped in that night. For years he had told people that he was in Miller Homes. Apparently, Ralph was either a liar, or he didn't know any better either.

As it turns out, Miller Homes are located off Monmouth Street, not far from the train station. They are two ten story towers that, if you looked down on from space, are shaped like the inside of the Mercedes Benz emblem. Though technically they are referred to as a public housing complex and not "projects", still the buildings were vacated in 1994 due to crime, drugs, and violence. They sit vacated to this day, like so many other vestiges left behind in this worn and tired city. When the people left Miller Homes in 94, renovations were begun and the people were supposed to move back after the construction was done. That hope was soon abandoned, like the buildings themselves. The city is waiting for federal funds to demolish and replace the sister towers. Between me and you, it's never going to happen.

As for the true name of the apartment complex where Scott had gotten himself fucked up, that beautiful section of city is called the Roger Homes. Somehow, that doesn't sound as tough and ghetto as Miller Homes, though I am not entirely sure why. Suffice to say you would not want to bring the family down there to picnic either.

Now that we've cleared that up, I'd say it's safe for us to move on.

Another hand was raised in the air, back in rehab. This one was white. Scott kind of knew the guy from bumming smokes from him at break time, "Yeah, go ahead Brian."

And here it came. "Chip, no offense and don't take this the wrong way because I've been in the same position myself. One of the things I'm learning in here is that love is an action and not a feeling. I heard you say in your story that you love your kids, but what have you ever done to show them that you love them?"

Brian's question landed like a punch in the stomach and it knocked the wind out of him. In front of all these people, this audience, he was speechless. But Brian wasn't done.

"I'm the same way. I want to play with my kids and have them love me and call me daddy, but I don't stick around to change their diapers or feed them. When I think of all the money I wasted on drugs . . . money that should have been saved for my children's future, I feel sick."

And Scott had no answers for this room full of drug addicted strangers. More so, as he thought about it, he would never be able to make up for his mistakes to his kids. How would he one day answer this same question when it was asked of him by his own daughter, Ariel. When she says "Daddy, why didn't you live with me?" or "I thought you loved me." Or his son Ethan when he wants to know why his father never taught him to catch, or took him fishing, or to the movies, or a baseball game.

What in God's name, could he say?

Would they understand that it was like a prison sentence to him, the day they were taken away? And that every day since had been tainted with loss and regret and pain?

"I don't know, Brian." Was all he could say. "I guess I never really did anything for either of them. I want to. I want to change. I wish I could go back in time and make things right, but unfortunately, it's too late." Scott was taken by surprise when he noticed that in this room full of dudes, he actually had tears in his eyes.

He hated Brian for his question and he used his anger as a way to suppress his urge to cry. That kind of emotional blockage always made him want to get high. Now was no exception. Plus Scott was totally aware of the cold and calloused fact that fifty years of sobriety wasn't going to get him his children back.

Anyway, this line of thinking always eventually leads him to contemplate and make comparisons between his own fatherhood and the relationship he had with his biological father. History is a whiny bitch that repeats herself. He was left to grow up without his old man around and now his children would have to do the same. In spite of all the promises to himself, and Ariel, and Ethan his kids were methodically taken from him and their mother, when Chuck went against his family.

Scott had gotten lucky though and he was raised by two of the greatest people on earth, his parents. A warm hearted woman and a loyal, decent and selfless man.

Wes's son Chuck had the same blood in his veins as their mutual father. Chuck who adopted his kids. With that bitch. Would Chuck turn out to be a blessing on those two children like Wes had been to him? Scott always hoped so. And Scott still loves his brother. Would Chuck be like a savior to his progeny? Time will tell. The jury is still out on that one.

Unfortunately, the children would probably never be given a chance to meet and get to know their real mother. A tragedy because Kelly really had grown into a very beautiful woman in recovery. As Scott writes this to you, she is coming up on one year clean. Clean and sober. For some maybe that doesn't sound like a long time but for the addict it can seem like eternity. It is unfair that there can be no forgiveness for Kelly. For the record she asks about her children all the time and she misses them.

Ariel and Ethan should know that. Chucks wife is cold, and closed, and says "No" There can be no compassion and mercy on Kelly. Obviously Chuck's wife was threatened by the blood bond that connects those kids to their mommy and daddy.

So it will be a long time before Ariel and Ethan will be given a chance to reunite with their parents, Scott and Kelly. That same time, that now haunts Scott and Kel, also stalks Chuck's wife as the kids are getting older

C.S.W.

and the truth of the situation will become known. When it comes into focus. Scott sat at the pinnacle of clarity. The day would one day come when She no longer has control over them. Then the truth will come to light. Even if some shit can never be made right.

Maybe by then Scott will even be cured of his sickness, and found a way to defeat that nasty idjit. To tell the truth, Scott was very ashamed and even a little afraid of what he was going to say when he looked into his kids eyes again on that glorious day.

Until then, he waits.

As he waits he ponders the similarities between his own situations with his father. Down deep at the core of the thing there is an undeniable love, it is at the level of blood. Would his relationship with his children suffer the same strain? Would it be peppered with animosity and destined to be labored? Forced feelings, if you will. And is there even some level of resentment that goes beyond a harmless dislike? On any level will his kids grow up to hate him? These questions I cannot answer so I will leave them to you as a point for speculation.

And there are others.

Will Chuck be fortunate enough to be blessed with some of the good and decent genes of his birthfather? Will he inherit at least some of the admirable qualities of Scott's Dad Wes? Will he earn the love of Scott's children through his giving nature, his warm heart, and his actions?

And Love is an action, or so they tell me.

Again, time will tell and we can only don a wait and see attitude on this inquisition as well.

What we do know however, about the plight of Scott's children is that they were not blessed with a mother like Scott had. There are no similarities between Chuck's wife and Nancy. Bluntly, Chuck selected his bride poorly. Unfortunately. If that comes out sounding harsh, Scott makes no apologies.

Anyway, speaking of Wes, he had a concern that I'd like to address. In speaking of the destructiveness of this disease, a comparison was made between Scott and Kelly's brother Tony. It speaks of the overwhelming power and control that addiction wields over its victims.

Wes was afraid that it might have sounded like Scott stole medicine from his grandmothers IV bag while she lay on her deathbed. The way Tony had done to his mother. This was not the case. The medicine that Scott stole from her was from her pill bottles at home. Wes felt that this was an important distinction to make. Out of respect, we can concede that there is a slight difference.

This is not said to condemn his friend Tony, may he rest in peace forever. And Scott makes this distinction reluctantly, as he knows that their crimes are virtually the same. Scott deserves no absolution. Junkies are all moved by the same obsession.

Anyway, since we're talking once again about Kelly's mother and Scott's sweet MomMom, maybe we can use this as a final example to illustrate how love and honor get compromised and how our virtue ends up getting traded.

Scott promised himself before his kids were born that he would stop using, clean up his act, and be a good father. Surely his daughter would be motivation enough, he had wanted to quit the drugs for a while now, he just never seemed to be able to. He always wanted his children. He swore before God that this baby would be just what he needed to save him.

Only instead of redemption, things went from bad to worse. He met heroin and his promise to the divine was easily discarded. Thrown away, shattered, and broken.

Things went pretty much the same before and after Ethan was born. Scott living his life with a constant need for more. His weakness was his vanity. He always felt spoiled and princely. Like he was entitled to and deserved whatever he wanted. But he was always thirsty. As much as he loved his Ariel angel, his baby cakes, he also wanted a son. He was determined to pass his bloodline to a male heir, no matter how bad a shape his life was in. No matter how many people told him it was a bad idea. "You can't take care of the kid you have." They would correctly say.

But like the recovering addicts in NA always say "We want what we want when we want it." Scott was no exception. And though the pride and love for his son ran through him very deep, this was just another promise that Scott couldn't keep.

The idjit was so embedded in him that it had seized total control of his mind, body, and soul. Now for some twisted reason, the idjit loved the city of Trenton. Whether it was in spite of the fact that it was ugly or because of the fact that it was ugly, Scott just didn't know. But he felt like he needed to be on Trenton streets, streets like Tyler and Division. Maybe they were somehow beautiful to him because they reflected how he felt about himself back at him. Like looking in a mirror. They reflected discontentment, and ruin.

Furthermore, when his precious MomMom had her time and she died, Scott promised to honor her memory by never using drugs again. He was not strong enough to keep this commitment.

Regretfully the needle always slid back into his arm.

And Scott failed everyone he loved. And God above.

C.S.W.

And now we get to the end of our little story about me and my girl, and my city and it turns out that maybe the ending is going to turn out a little darker than expected. And where does that leave us anyway? Who is to be forgiven for what? Who is good and who is evil? Who gets acquitted by law? Maybe we were even sort of hoping for a happy ending, like some sort of redemption or absolution.

Unfortunately, these are legends of Trenton and there are few happy endings around here anymore. Words of legends are formed in reality and truth. This tale has never been about fantasy, it's just a fucking commentary.

Like I said, we are talking about Trenton N.J. and not some sort of Utopia, or Garden of Eden. And yes, I guess this raises a few more questions. Like what will become of this city, now that it's sinking? More to the crack cocaine and heroin. Morally deplorable. There is always anger in the atmosphere, down here, where we get to sinning.

And what about our characters, the ones that are caught up in all of it? You probably want to know the answers to some questions before I reach the ending. "What about Scott and Kelly?" "Did they ever get back together?" "Are they still getting high?" "And if not, will they?"

I have decided to leave these questions unanswered for you. I don't know the answers, if you must know the truth. Besides, who really knows what the future holds? So you've got questions and I have questions too.

What I can tell you definitively is that Kelly moved away from this place and found a way to recover. Scott loves her enough to pray to God that she never comes back. The streets that she took out of the city are two way and they can also lead back into relapse. She has found a new home and she seems to be free of her disease, one that she believes can never be cured, only arrested. And Kelly knows all about being arrested.

Maybe even, that nasty idjit, that monkey on her back is just waiting for her here in Trenton, if she ever comes back.

I guess every once in a great while, a sinner and junkie can find a way to break free from the devil. Kelly had to come to the sad realization that she needed to leave this place and the man that she loved to go find that freedom. They were both so corrosive.

Maybe Kelly never really was the devil, as some people liked to blame. Maybe it was Scott the whole time. If she has truly found a way to permanently beat it, again only time will tell.

Let us, you and I, wish her well.

Anyway, if you'll allow me, I'd like to leave you with one final scene before we say goodbye and go our separate ways.

It was gray outside and rainy, when Scott the poet and junkie hopped on the bus. The bus he rode was the 609. 609 is also the area code for the city of Trenton and the great Mercer County. Now Scott wasn't feeling very well. Drug abuse is violence committed against one's own body and 24 years of constant mistreatment inevitable lead him to sickness. He was coughing, sweaty and achy when he got on the 609. He rode the bus alone and the route it traveled was familiar and ugly.

As he rode, he looked out the dirty, scratched up Plexiglas window. Fear and loneliness pressed in on him like the lover that he longed for, it knew him so personally, it wanted to crush him. Sometimes, his isolation threatened to suffocate him. He had lost his angels and Kelly was now on a different path from his.

So here he was in a state of near sobriety, clean except for the Suboxones that his psychiatrist Dr. Jim had given him. They saved him from the overwhelming sadness that he was susceptible to. The rain lost some of its power to depress him.

Puddles resonated in the drizzle on West State Street as the bus tires splashed through them and sprayed an occasional unlucky pedestrian. Then, they drove by the museum where Scott had taken field trips with his class, when he was still a kid in school. When he was still a child with hope in his eyes. Nostalgia brought with it a mournful smile. Those were happier times. He could vaguely remember what it had been like to be that young, what it had been like to have all those dreams. That was many tattoos and a billion cigarettes ago.

Sometime after that Scott snapped out of his trance, his daydream, and everything he had pondered, only to discover that he was the only white man riding the bus. This was not unusual and he was used to it. Still, he let his eyes roam up and down the aisle, trying to meet anyone's glare. In Trenton, it's best to be aware of any openly hostile stares. But no one was noticing him. It was like he wasn't even there. This too, was nothing new. He was alone. He was the invisible man.

He returned to his thoughts as he rode the 609 down State Street towards North Clinton. He didn't really want to be going where he was going, the heroin house on Division. It was as if those days, that part of his life was over, but he just didn't know what else to do or where else to go. He was just acting on habit.

His ponderings bled from one to another as they always did until he found himself once again thinking about his children and their mother. For the first time he began to wonder if they would ever end up together.

C.S.W.

Doubt had finally cracked his certainty of a joyous reunion and it began to seem to him that theirs would not be a happy ending. Perhaps, they had drifted too far apart. Scott smiled as he cried a little and he wished the best for her. He still loved her, always would, she was his Bella.

He looked out the window again as the rain fell down. There wasn't enough water in all of heaven to wash this town. Scott and Trenton were both polluted and dirty. Corrupted. In fact, if you're not from around here, you'd probably be better off to just stay clear.

The spirit of the idjit lives here.

Scott wondered if he would ever get away. His mind flooded with flashbacks of faces of strangers and horrible places that he had been. His fear was that maybe he wasn't strong enough or smart enough to escape.

His boy CJ had moved away. He had found what it takes. He moved all the way to Nebraska, fleeing the garden state. CJ became a cowboy (as ridiculous as that sounds) fell in love with a cowgirl and found happiness. Scott would have never thought that CJ had what it took to leave these streets. Somehow, he broke the hold that the dope and the city had on him.

Most were not so fortunate.

Caroline and Eddie still haunt Trenton, playing the same game every day, looking for their next fix. It's a shame to say, but they will never change. They enable and destroy each other, much like Scott and Kelly used to do. They will probably die that way.

Then again, who knows?, Scott would have said the same thing about CJ.

And don't get me wrong, there is some recovery in this town too. Scott had an NA sponsor, a guy named Rob, who lived on Genesee Street, who has been clean and sober for almost four years. Four years of living there among the hookers and dealers and crime.

So people do recover from time to time. They meet at the church on the corner of Hamilton Avenue and Chestnut. They have their meetings there and they read their literature, and they drink their coffee, and they smoke their cigarettes. They try to follow twelve simple steps to improve their lives. And they celebrate clean time, which they accumulate one day at a time. Scott had nothing but respect and admiration for them. Even though he knew he could never be one of them. They had saved a girl he loved, his children's mother. How could he ever be anything but grateful to them?

Anyway as Scott got off the 609 cattycorner, a crossed the street from the train station, he threw his hoodie over his head. It was still raining and he hated the feeling of cold water hitting him in the back of his neck. He zipped up his jacket against the weather and he headed up North Clinton Avenue. He looked to his left and saw the ridiculous piece of art on the corner. The train station had bought it in hopes of beautifying the city as they revitalized. The monstrosity was twenty feet tall and its metal form was painted every color of the rainbow. It stood bright and cheery in the cold, gray Trenton day. The monument completely missed capturing the spirit of this sickened city.

He looked on his left at the train station. Christ, he had shotten a lot of drugs in there. Shooting with toilet water is gross, yes, but shooting Heroin is already pretty gross, so maybe the two nastiness's cancel each other out. He had done it in there more times than he could count. He wondered if he would ever actually work up the nerve to jump on one of those trains and ride it away.

Scott crossed the bridge and dissected Greenwood Avenue, with all its loveliness. As he proceeded he walked past the aptly named High Street on his right. Then he crossed Tyler Street, where all that shit had happened with Kelly and her addiction.

As he made the left on Hamilton he once again started thinking about his kids.

And he looked around at all the ugliness that he had put himself in.

He felt a moment of gratitude towards his brother that the children didn't have to grow up here. And he thought about what he would say if he was allowed to talk to his children. If he could explain honestly to them what had happened to their mommy and dad. He would probably tell them how both were eternally sorry that things had turned out so bad. He would remind them that life is not about where you come from, it is about who you become. Be proud, you come from good blood. And he would tell them to stop, look around and enjoy the beauty. Take time to be grateful to the Creator. Love and wonder and discover.

Scott walked over Chestnut Avenue, passed the church where the anonymous junkies have their meetings.

Scott thought of where he was going and why. Was this disease fatal? and if so would this be the time that he died?

When he was in rehab, the one I just told you about, the one where Scott had told his life story, he had read a medical report on addictions and neuropath ways in the brain. They conducted these experiments on rats. They got them hooked on some really good cocaine. After a couple of days, they let the rats choose between food and water or Coke. Right until they died they choose the cocaine. This was, the doctor said, because of these pathways in their brains. Scott, they said, had an addiction and it worked the same way. They never called it an idjit, or likened it to a bug being drawn to the zapper.

Anyway, Scott came to the corner by Columbus Park and made a right. As he turned to walk down Division Street, memories of the past came back and haunted him. He imagined he could see Anthony and Colleen Cambell's faces watching him from the porches of the row homes. Their ghosts would remain on this street, even if only in his own mind, for a long time. He would think about them often as he went on with his life. Them and a girl that he once loved that used to live around here.

After words.

THANKS FOR READING my book, I hope you enjoyed it and were moved in some way by it.

I finished "Legends of Trent'n" in 2010 and was excited to get it out to you. I believed from the beginning that writing this story was God's will for me and (crazy as it may sound) that it was my destiny to tell you this twisted story. When I felt like giving up, there was something unseeable pushing me towards completion. And yeah, this story was written so my children will one day know the dubious nature of their births and of their parent's addictions and their struggles with authority and others judgments. Above all I would hope they would understand that they were loved, are loved, and are always in my heart and mind.

May they understand that for whatever reasons they were told, they were ripped from my life and not given away.

When I finished the last words of "Legends of Trent'n" I expected easy publication, fame, and money. My vindication at last! But instead, (again, I believe God had a hand in this) my reward for obedience was that I met a beautiful young woman who showed me love like I've never known. This was a gift beyond any I could have imagined. Lauren is my best friend, my lover, my companion. She is my person.

But me, as you could tell from the story, I always want more. And I refused to let the book die. I had invested too much energy, too much thought, too much time. And I refused to let those in positions of authority over me win.

So I took my manuscript online and what do you know? the first company that read it recognized its greatness. Now surely fame and fortune would come.

But no, alas, PublishAmerica was a scam that tried to steal my story. As it does to hundreds of other poor authors. They turned "Legends of Trent'n" into a book only to try and sell it back to me and my friends and family.

PublishAmerica are scum and if you are interested in the saga between me and them, you can check out my facebook links.

The thing I find most ironic about this is that PublishAmerica never lets authors out of their contracts. The only reason I was released was because the woman who stole my kids from me, read the book and issued PublishAmerica a threat of legal action because she didn't want the kids to grow up and one day learn the truth. (That she calls herself their mommy but she is not their mother and that she may want to portray herself as a savior to them but that quite frankly is delusional bullshit.) Only because of this woman's vindictiveness and hurtful intentions were the douchebags at PublishAmerica so moved as to cancel my contract.

They never called to tell me and I assumed the book was available online for you to buy until I received reports that copies were not available. I called PublishAmerica and was told by the secretary that my book was discontinued. PublishAmerica decided to steal my royalties on the books that I did sell. So this woman has my children and PublishAmerica was going to steal my dream.

And fuck them both very much.

So if this woman had not written her letter to silence me, "Legends of Trent'n" would have, most likely, died in a closet somewhere down at PublishAmerica. Her letter freed me from those bastards and that is how God was able to bring the book from certain obscurity and into your hands.

Again, thank you for reading. And for thinking.

C.S.W..

In loving memory of:

Elizabeth P Wyckoff

(Rest in peace, MomMom)

Joseph F. Correia Jr.

Kathleen Correia

CPSIA information can be obtained at www.ICGtesting.com
Printed in the USA
BVOW03s1843170315

392106BV00001B/101/P